THE FIFTH ACE

"Peach of a town," he repeated with added conviction

THE FIFTH ACE

BY
DOUGLAS GRANT

Frontispiece by
GEORGE W. GAGE

NEW YORK
W. J. WATT & COMPANY
PUBLISHERS

PRESS OF
BRAUNWORTH & CO.
BOOK MANUFACTURERS
BROOKLYN, N. Y.

CONTENTS

THE FIFTH ACE

CHAPTER I

GENTLEMAN GEOFF'S BILLIE

KEARN THODE mounted his pinto and rode out of the courtyard of the Baggott Hotel and down the Calle Rivera under a seething tropic sun. Limasito's principal street was well-nigh deserted in the lethargy of the noon-day siesta, but the flower-market was a riotous blaze of color in the glistening white plaza, from which radiated broad vistas of fantastically painted adobe and soberer concrete, ending in a soft green blur.

The young petroleum engineer had pictured a ten-year-old boom town in the Mexican oil belt as a wilderness of rough shacks and board sidewalks, with possibly a dance-hall or two and an open-air movie as the only attractions, and the thriving little city had proved a welcome surprise.

"Limasito," he mused. "That means 'Little Lemon.' Wonder who tacked that name to this burg? Peach of a town, I call it."

A long, low adobe house, tinted a screaming blue which rivaled the skies, faced the southern end of the plaza, covering nearly an entire block. As Thode jogged past, a door in the side wall opened, and a girl appeared. She was tall with a lithe slenderness that betokened well-poised strength rather than fragility. Masses of sloe-black hair waved beneath the broad brim of her sombrero, but her skin was unbelievably fair and the eyes she lifted to his in frank scrutiny were the deep blue of a wood violet.

The young man caught his breath as she turned and started across the plaza, walking with long, free, swinging strides.

"Peach of a town," he repeated, with added conviction. "All to the good!"

The Calle Rivera dwindled into a dusty, white, winding road, straggling, flower-choked gardens replaced the city blocks and gave way in turn to haciendas whose flat fertile acres teemed with the luscious harvest. The pinto covered the ground at an easy lope which ate up the miles, and Thode sat his high Mexican saddle, as easy as a rocking-chair, scanning each turn of the road for landmarks.

The sun was well upon its western course when he reined in at a low stout gateway. A peon, lazily hoeing in the ditch, straightened his bent back and eyed the stranger in mild curiosity.

"This Hallock's ranch?" Thode asked, laconically.

The peon nodded and waved a brown hand toward the house half hidden among the trees.

"Señor Hallo', si, Señor."

The engineer wheeled and cantered up the winding driveway, with the serried rows of grapefruit trees spreading out endlessly on either side of the little rising where the square white ranch-house squatted, its broad wings outstretched like those of a brooding hen.

In the shade of a mahogany tree, an excessively fat, excessively bald person sprawled in a low chair by a rustic table, alternately sipping from the tall glass at his elbow and mopping his ruddy glabrous brow with a vivid bandanna.

He rose to his short legs as Thode swung himself from the saddle and advanced.

"Mr. Hallock?"

"That's me, Stranger. Howdy!" He held out a pudgy hand, and noting the fresh coat of sunburn on his visitor, he added: "Just come over the border?"

"Further than that, Sir; from New York. I'm Kearn Thode. Perhaps Mr. Larkin mentioned me to you; Perry Larkin, of the Mexamer Oil Company."

"To be sho'! I'm right glad to see you, Thode."

Benjamin Hallock pumped his hand vigorously. "Been kinder expectin' you down in these parts. We'll set a spell out here, it's hotter'n blazes inside. Hey, Luis! Juan!"

Two mozos scurried from the veranda in response to the bull-throated roar, and Thode found himself seated opposite his host with another tall glass before him and a slender black cigar between his fingers.

"Great country for you folks, down here," Hallock remarked. "We've got the largest producing oil wells in the world right in this leetle strip of land along the Gulf and, at that, the undeveloped resources are a damn' sight greater'n you can judge from what's been brought to light. Yes, Sir, I shouldn't be surprised any day to strike a gusher right here on my ranch! Rufe Terwilliger, twelve miles yonder at the Dos Zapotes, spudded in only six months ago on a hunch, and now with the valve-gate only part-way open, he's bringing in a thousand barrels a day!"

"I know that the development which has taken place here is, speaking relatively to the possibilities, only a beginning," Thode assured the heated enthusiast. "I'm down here to look after Mr. Larkin's interests, and those of the Mexamer Company with a view to extending their holdings if I can pick up anything promising. By the way, Mr. Hallock, that was a curious yarn you told Mr. Larkin, about some mysterious lost pool in a swamp with surface oil indications. He happened to mention it one day. The Pool of the Lost Souls, wasn't it?"

Hallock nodded, grinning expansively.

"You've got it right," he chuckled. "So Larkin bit, did he? It's nothing but pure bunk, one of those old Mex' legends that run back to the beginning of time. We pass it on to every green operator from over the border, but I reckoned Larkin was too wise a bird to take any stock in it."

"He didn't," Thode returned carelessly. "Up in Oklahoma where I've been locating some sections for the company there are any amount of Indian myths and queer old traditions handed down from the first settlers, and I made a collection of them. It's rather a hobby of mine. I was discussing them with Mr. Larkin when he recalled this odd tale. He had forgotten the particulars, but he said you would be able to supply them. The pool was supposed to be located somewhere around here, wasn't it?"

"Anywhere within a radius of two hundred miles." His host drained his glass and settled back comfortably. "I judge it about that, for I've been pretty much over this whole country and it's only around these parts that you hear of the Lost Souls' Pool. I got the tale from a hunchbacked half-breed and he got it from his grandmother.

"It seems that away back in the times when the Spaniards were scrapping with the Indians for a foothold, an old grandee named Del Reyes had staked out a claim hereabout. Mighty poor judgment he showed, too, for he wouldn't have known what to do with oil if he'd found it in those days and by all accounts the land couldn't have been much good for anything else; swampy and low-lying, without even timber. He had a beautiful daughter, Dolores, of course. Funny how that gal Dolores manages to get herself mixed up in every yarn below the border, ain't it? There was a kid brother, José, too, but he don't figure much.

"Dolores must have been some Jane for all the male population, what there was of it, went plumb loco about her, among 'em a young Spanish explorer and the son of the chief of the tribe, whose claims Del Reyes and the rest had jumped. Dolores favored the explorer, but the young chief had seen her first, and being a simple-hearted child of nature, he decided that the way to get what he wanted was to go right out after it.

"Accordingly, he showed up unexpected at the Del Reyes hacienda with his outfit one moonlight night and laid hands on the gal. Dolores was packing a knife, though, and she let him have it, full to the hilt. His outfit vamoosed, taking the corpse with them, and the settlement got ready for trouble.

"Nothing happened, howsomever, until the night of the fiesta for Dolores' marriage to the explorer. Then, the old chief dropped in, informal like, and wiped out the whole wedding party. He macheted all but the bride, throwing the bodies into a shallow pool on the claim. Her he roped up, tied heavy weights to and stood up in the pool; the water came about to her shoulders. Then he held the knife before her eyes, the knife she'd stuck his son with, and waited for the weights to drag her down. I reckon he waited some time, for Dolores must have been a right-strong young woman, but she went under finally. The only one that escaped the pool was the kid brother, José, and him the old chief carried off.

"According to the yarn, Dolores still breathes in the pool, the bubbles rise to the surface and there's a murmuring from the other souls that went down unshriven. What's more, the water is never ruffled but smooth and glassy, with streaks that gleam in the moonlight. Of course, that's oil, all right, or would be if the pool ever existed, but nobody's found it yet."

"It's got the punch to it, as a story." Thode paused to relight his cigar. "Did your hunchbacked friend give you any further description of the pool itself or its location?"

"Nothing to work on, Son. This flat part of the country don't run much to scenery. He did say something about a mahogany tree close by, that grew up with two outstretched branches like a cross and then turned to stone, but I'm not letting my peons loaf on the job while I go moseying around looking for it."

"It's a great little ranch you have here." Thode turned in his chair to survey the close-packed avenues of low-hanging trees. "Any oil on your land, Mr. Hallock?"

"Not here. Got two gushers over near Tuxpam, next

to some property that I reckon you'll want to look into for the Mexamer people. Larkin told me himself that he thought of taking it over."

The talk drifted into a discussion of relative values and prospects, and when Thode cantered down the driveway an hour or so later he had secured a good working knowledge of the surrounding country with which to commence his labors. He had parted with some little difficulty from his host, who insisted on sending in to Limasito for the young engineer's baggage and wholeheartedly desired that he make the Hacienda de Rosa his headquarters.

Kearn Thode, however, had other intentions. He must be free to go and come as he pleased on his mission and he determined to make the town itself the center of his activities. Moreover, Hallock's hacienda was a bachelor establishment and in Limasito there were girls; girls with blue eyes and black hair and incredibly white skin, who looked a man straight in the eyes and made him feel as if maybe he'd found a friend.

That blue adobe house on the southern end of the square began to loom large in the architecture of Limasito. Thode had caught a glimpse of the patio as he swung past; it had looked cool and green and inviting, with a fountain playing and little tables scattered about. What was it, anyway, and how could one meet a girl who lived there?

The curious old tale of the Lost Souls' Pool was temporarily forgotten in speculations of a more warmly personal nature. Was she an Americano? She seemed of too fair a type for a native daughter, in spite of her dark hair, and that, together with her violet-blue eyes, gave more than a hint of Irish ancestry. What could bring a girl of her sort to a boom town below the border?

So absorbed was the young engineer in his cogitations that he had reached the outskirts of Limasito before he awoke from his reverie. The swiftly falling curtain of twilight had wrapped the spreading orchards and haciendas in fragrant gloom and a myriad of mysterious chirpings and rustlings forecasted the coming night, when the harsh, grating screech of a horn blared upon their monotone and a low roadster appeared suddenly around a turn in the road, careening sharply on two wheels, and bore down recklessly upon the lone rider.

Thode's pony was quicker than he and leaped aside barely in time to avoid disaster as the car shot past and hurtled on into the dusk. He turned in his saddle and watched its unlighted shape swerve drunkenly from side to side of the road, until a further turn hid it from view. With a muttered imprecation, he gave the sure-footed pinto its head, and as it floundered out of the ditch the white, jeering face of the man at the wheel, as he had seen it in that flashing glimpse, rose again before his consciousness. It seemed for a startling instant to be grimly, portentously familiar, then the fancy faded before the fact of its obvious absurdity, and he laughed contemptuously. The danger of the moment had played tricks with his nerves.

A long-drawn, tremulous moan from the roadside broke in upon his thoughts and he halted the pinto abruptly. A small crumpled figure lay face downward in the ditch, twisting and quivering like a shot rabbit, and, bending over it, Thode saw a slender feminine form which made his pulse miss a beat or two and then race

on with unaccountable acceleration. He flung himself
from the saddle and reached the edge of the ditch, hat
in hand, just as a pair of soft violet eyes were raised to
his. It was the girl of the adobe house on the plaza.

"There has been an accident?" he stammered.

She nodded briefly.

"Put on your hat and help me tote him. He lives in
that shack just over yonder."

Her voice was low and musically clear, but it bore a
ring of authority as well as of impatience at the obvious-
ness of his question, and Thode meekly obeyed.

The prostrate figure was that of a boy, dark-skinned
and thin to the point of emaciation. He was clad only
in a ragged shirt and trousers, with a battered straw hat
lying torn and crushed beside him.

"Stand aside, please. I can carry him," Thode directed, and as he slung the inert form gently over his
shoulder he saw that the boy's shoulders were pathetically
humped.

In spite of his assertion, he found it no easy matter to
struggle up from the steep ditch, cumbered by his helpless
burden, but the girl steadied it with a capable hand and
leaped lightly up beside him.

"Put him across your galapago. I'll walk on the other
side and hold him up. It's only to that shack there,
where the light is."

Again Thode obeyed, but he could not forbear a further query.

"You are not hurt yourself, are you? It was that
maniac in the car who ran him down?"

"I came on him just now, lying that-a-way in the ditch.

Poor little José! I know who did it, though; he passed me a minute before, going like hell. It was Wiley."

Thode started as the forceful comparison fell artlessly from her lips, but at the final word a hot wave as of rage swept through his veins and receded, leaving him tense and cold. So his vision had not tricked him, after all. The man in the car had been no stranger.

"I know. He almost ran me down, too." Thode set his jaw firmly. "Is this where we turn off?"

"This" was a narrow rutted lane, half-obliterated in the encroaching underbrush, at the end of which a weather-beaten shack squatted in a clump of zapote trees. As they drew up in the little cleared space before it the door opened and a shriveled, white-haired woman peered out, a light held high in her trembling hand.

"Madre de Dios!" she cried. "José!"

The girl turned to her with a rapid flow of soft liquid Spanish and the old crone, weeping and muttering, stood aside to let them enter. Thode was forced to stoop under the low, sagging doorway and he stumbled as he made his way to a rickety bed in the corner and laid his burden down.

The girl took the light from the old shaking hands and together they bent above the injured lad.

"I don't think there are any bones broken," Thode announced at last. "But he's had a pretty bad shaking up for a cripple and that is rather a nasty cut on his head. Can you find anything clean to tie it up with?"

Without reply the girl stooped, turned back her short khaki skirt and tore a wide strip from a snowy petticoat. Then with a basin of water dipped from the bucket upon a bench beside them she bathed and bandaged the wound deftly. The old crone had lighted a flaring oil lamp and by its leaping glow Thode saw to his surprise that the shack although old and ramshackle was scrupulously, incredibly clean, and its châtelaine bore herself not without a certain dignity, despite her agitation.

She was tall and stiffly angular with piercing black eyes deep-set in her wrinkled face, and there was a peculiar wild grace in the rapid gestures of her withered claw-like hands. She hovered anxiously about as between them Thode and the girl ministered to the stricken lad, and dropped to her knees as his eyes opened at length.

For a moment his startled gaze roved over them and then settled upon the face of the girl.

"Señorita!" His voice was a mere convulsive whisper. "Señorita! It was the Americano, Señor Wiley! He cursed me and laughed! I heard him when he struck me!"

"Never mind, José. You must rest and get well quickly and then we will attend to Señor Wiley. I will come to you to-morrow. Tia Juana—" she laid her hand gently on the old woman's bowed shoulder—"I will send Margarita—"

The rest was lost in a rapid patter of Spanish, but its purport was unmistakable, for the woman seized her hand and kissed it, and even the boy flashed a worshiping smile.

As they turned to the door, Thode jingled some coins in his pocket tentatively, but the girl stopped him with a decisive gesture, and when the door closed behind them and they stood out in the starlit darkness, she gave a little, soft, low gurgle of laughter.

"Reckon you're new to these parts!" she exclaimed.

"Let her see one wink o' gold, and you'd have been knifed good and proper. Tia Juana's no beggar, to be insulted with alms. She's proud; some of the half-breeds are, when the strain is strong enough."

"I didn't know," Thode responded humbly. "I'd like to do something for the kid. Shall I send a doctor out, if I can find one?"

The girl shook her head.

"He'll do, all right. It was a wicked thing to run him down like that, but Wiley hasn't got the decency of a coyote, and he had it in for José." She broke off suddenly, and held her hand out to the young engineer. "Adios, stranger, and thanks for your help."

"But won't you let me take you home, or wherever you are going?" Thode asked.

"No, thanks. I left my basket down in the ditch—"

"I'll get it for you," he urged. "It isn't safe for a girl like you to go about alone after nightfall in a place like this."

The girl's eyes sought his wonderingly in the darkness.

"Me?" she ejaculated. "Stranger, I came to this town when it was nothing but four shacks and a gusher, and I know everyone in it, white, yellow and Mex. Not safe? Why every dog knows Gentleman Geoff's Billie!"

"You?" he stammered.

"That's me. My Dad is Gentleman Geoff," she explained proudly. "He owns the Blue Chip, and it's the squarest gambling-house from Chihuahua to Campeche. It's kind of you to offer to go with me, but I don't need any protection. I sort of belong to Limasito, I reckon. Adios!"

CHAPTER II

A Superfluous Knight-Errant

KEARN THODE rode back to his hotel with his
brain in a whirl. That girl with the sweet, steady
eyes and naïve, fearless manner, the product of
a gambling-house and associate of its habitués? The
thought filled him with repugnance akin to horror. He
was in no sense a prig, but although this was his first
venture below the Rio Grande, he had spent three years
in the roughest corners of the West and he knew the
type of women who infested the dance-halls and gambling-
joints; unclean camp-followers of the army of Chance.

How had she grown to budding womanhood without
contamination in such an atmosphere? Self-reliant she
had shown herself to be, but tender in her pitying care of
the injured boy and innocently free from coquetry or
cynical suspicion in her frank acceptance of the stranger.
There had been open amusement in her tone at his suggestion of danger to her from any in Limasito, and genuine love and pride when she spoke of her father and his
calling. How was it possible that the mire of her surroundings had left her untouched?

The huge, squat adobe house was ablaze with light as
he urged his jaded pony into a gallop to pass it quickly.
Lights gleamed also in the patio and Chinese servants
flitted here and there among the crowded tables. He felt
a hot surge of resentment as the subdued murmur of

masculine voices and jarring laughter floated after him. What an environment for such a girl!

After a hasty wash-up and a meal he sought further enlightenment from his landlord. It was promptly and enthusiastically forthcoming.

"The Blue Chip?" Jim Baggot tilted his chair back restfully against the wall. "Finest place in the country; square as a die and the sky's the limit to a regular hombre. Gentleman Geoff's just about one hundred per cent. man, and don't you forget it. Everything's on the level at his place."

"Got a daughter, hasn't he?" Thode asked, proffering a cigar.

"You're on. Fine gal, too. Ain't afraid of nothing, Billie ain't. When the Yellow Jack hit us, two years ago, and not another woman in town—and damn' few o' the men, fur that matter—but cleared out, Billie went right in under the flag with the old Doc, and stayed till the fever was stamped out. Thin as a wisp o' cotton she was, when it was all over; face no wider'n this——" he measured with a burly thumb and forefinger—— "and eyes clean gone into the back of her head, but she only grinned and said it had been fun while it lasted, to fight the thing. First day she was out o' quarantine, she rode thirty miles to Dan Willoughby's 'cienda 'cause she heard he was on a tear and mistreating his kids and she brought him to terms, too. There ain't an hombre in town that don't worship her and even the women like her."

"I saw her to-day," remarked Thode. "She's a remarkably pretty girl."

Jim bit the end off his cigar and spat it forth with emphasis.

"Wal, we 'uns that've watched her grow up from a rangy, long-legged, stringy-haired leetle colt think more o' what she *is* than what she looks like, but now that you mention it, I'll lay there ain't a Jane this side o' the border and mighty few above it that can give her odds on looks. And there ain't a man in these parts but has his trigger set for the guy that'd look cross-eyed at her."

There was a friendly but unmistakable hint in the concluding words and the young engineer went to bed in a curious reversal of sentiment. Gentleman Geoff had evidently earned his title; and from the tawdry, fevered atmosphere of the Blue Chip his daughter, miraculously enough, seemed to have drawn only strength and a warm-hearted abiding faith in human nature.

The still heat of mid-afternoon lay like a stifling veil upon the little weather-beaten shack among the zapote trees, when Gentleman Geoff's Billie lifted the latch next day. The single room was empty save for the boy who tossed restlessly upon his pallet, but the movement ceased and the sunken eyes glowed in the thin brown face, as she bent over him.

"The pain is better, comment?" she asked gently. "See, José! I have brought you broth and wine."

He stammered his gratitude with weak but fervent voice, then the elfin face darkened.

"The Señor Wiley!" he muttered. "It was because I would not tell him of the Pool! He is great and strong and he would crush me for that I keep silencioso, but when I am cured of this hurt——"

"We will pay back the score to the Señor Wiley." The girl spoke quietly, but a swift ominous light gleamed for a fleeting moment in her eyes, turning their blue to steel.

We'll teach him what fair play means in Limasito! But where is thy grandmother, José?"

The lad shivered in spite of the heat.

"She stirs her cauldron," he whispered. "She crept in at the dawn and since she has muttered of strange things. There must have been a warning, Señorita."

With a stifled exclamation, Billie straightened and crossed to the door. A thin spiral of smoke rose like a gray wisp above the zapote trees and a low-crooned, rhythmic chant was borne to her on the stirless air. Without hesitation she followed the narrow, scarcely discernible path toward the opening in the clump of trees.

A battered pot was slung above a blaze of dried wood and before it Tia Juana sat upon her heels, swaying from side to side with half-closed eyes and outstretched tremulous hands.

For a moment the girl paused, and then stepped forward.

"What is it, Tia Juana?" she asked softly in Spanish. "Would you brew a cure for José or a curse for the evil which has befallen him?"

The swaying ceased and the arms dropped as the old woman turned swiftly.

"Neither, Señorita, but I would learn the truth," she responded solemnly. "Last night I beheld a thing which passed my understanding, but of it only evil can come, and I would know it now."

"What did you see?" asked Billie, seating herself on a moss-grown log. "What was this evil thing, Tia Juana?"

"I went to the hacienda of the Señor Wiley." The old woman announced simply. "He had harmed my José, child of my blood, and I would have taken revenge upon him."

"Tia Juana, that was wrong!" Billie cried. "I have told my father and he will see that justice is done. You —you found him?"

Tia Juana nodded and her thin lips compressed.

"Behind the casito where the carro is stored I came upon him in the shadow. Beside him was a figure I could not see, to whom he talked low and quickly, with many gestures. Me he did not see, and I waited. Then in a moment, Señorita, the figure moved so that the moonlight fell upon him. It was that messenger of the Evil One, De Soria."

"John Sawyer?" the girl repeated in a hushed tone.

"So you know him, Señorita." The old woman's lip curled. "Before your coming, or ever a rooftree was raised in Limasito, he was Juan De Soria, son of thieves and black of heart as his master's skin."

The girl shivered.

"El Negrito!" she whispered. "You think he came from Alvarez? But what dealings does the Americano Wiley have with El Negrito?"

The old woman muttered and her withered, clenched hand struck her breast.

"It is that which I would see in the cauldron," she hissed. "Before El Negrito, comes always his creature, De Soria, and with him come fire and looting and death! The Señor Wiley turns all things to his purpose and if he has sold himself to the Evil One and traffics with El Negrito, I would be warned. I have seen one of his raids, Señorita; it was as if the sky rained destruction and slaughter!"

Her head sank on her breast and a brief, tense silence ensued.

"I do not believe such evil of the Señor Wiley," Billie remarked at last. "Cruel he is and like a madman in his anger, but between him and El Negrito there could be no covenant. It may be that he came upon Sawyer skulking about and was warning him off the hacienda. Sawyer has been in Limasito for many days, and he plays high at my father's casa."

"With what gold?" the old woman retorted. "He who has been beggar and thief since the hour of his birth. Much gold he could not steal for he has not the wit. For what evil compact has he been paid in riches?"

The girl shrugged.

"Luck turns," she said laconically. "Once a man came to the Blue Chip with pesos ciento and broke the faro bank. Fortune—buena suerte—has smiled on as worthless ones as Sawyer. But you, Tia Juana; what did you do last night when you saw?"

"I crept away, silently, so that none knew of my presence and returned to José." Tia Juana chuckled mirthlessly. "My vengeance can wait. The Señor Wiley is a fool, and the son of fools! It was not to the boy he should have gone for knowledge of the Pool; José knows no more than the idle words he repeated one evil day to the Señor Hallock, for which I beat him soundly! It is I who have seen the Pool of the Lost Souls, only I who knows where Dolores and her lover sleep."

Her voice died in an unintelligible murmur, and the rhythmic swaying recommenced. The legend of the Lost Souls' Pool was no new one to Billie; she had heard it often from the lips of the old crone, who could never be persuaded to divulge its supposed location and the myth had become an old settlers' joke around Limasito.

She stole away presently, leaving Tia Juana to her incantations, and returned to the shack, but José had fallen into uneasy slumber, and after moistening the bandage about his head, she started for home.

The old woman's account of her nocturnal adventure would not be exorcised from Billie's thoughts. The Señor Wiley was a young Eastern capitalist, who held vast oil and fruit-growing properties in the surrounding countryside. It was incredible that he could hold any communication with the rebel bandit and murderer, Alvarez, the "Little Negro," whose name was enough to strike terror to native hearts.

El Negrito had pillaged and burned, raped and killed unhindered until he was glutted with blood and loot, but that was in the old days, only a few years ago before the newest government was in power and the white men came in force. Of late he had retired to the hills, the memory of his atrocities had faded and only when news came of a burning village far away, or the murder of a lone prospector was the sporadic attempt to capture him renewed, and then in a half-hearted manner.

It was rumored that the nomadic, down-at-heel half-breed, John Sawyer, was an agent of the killer, but no proof could be brought to bear upon him and he was allowed to go his cringing way unmolested. Billie wondered now, with a cold, unaccustomed sense of dread, if rumor spoke truly. What if Sawyer were indeed the forerunner of a visitation from the bandit of the hills?

The girl had turned mechanically into a side road, shadier than the highway and leading by a short cut to the plaza and the heart of the town. She was still in the open country, with orchards stretching out interminably on either side and not even a peon within hailing distance, when the chug and snort of a motor reached her reluctant ears. Billie knew that irregular rattling hum, and insensibly quickened her pace.

Then as the car drew close behind her she slowed, a peculiar light glinting in her eyes.

"Buenas tardes, Señorita Billie!" A merry, mocking voice called, and she wheeled about.

A sallow, sandy-haired young man, with pale protruding blue eyes and thin curling lips, sprawled low behind the wheel of his roadster, leering familiarly at her.

"Good-afternoon," she responded formally. "You must be in a hurry, Mr. Wiley, to have taken this short cut instead of keeping to the highway. It was good of you not to run me down, but the way is clear now."

She stepped aside into a mass of flowering low-grown bushes, but with a light laugh the young man sprang from the car, hat in hand.

"I am never in a hurry to go when you are about, Billie! But you always run away; you never will play with me. Why aren't you kind?"

Involuntarily she stepped back still farther as he advanced upon her.

"Are you in need of kindness?" she asked.

"I should think I was." He paused before her, still laughing, but his pale eyes glittered. "You're the only girl in this God-forsaken town that I want to be friends with, and you won't play. Be a good sport and come for a little ride now; I'll show you some speed."

"Thanks," she drawled, her hand moving to rest lightly

on her hip. "Have you a few more old scores to settle to-day, with that tin Juggernaut of yours?"

A shadow had fallen across the dazzling white of the road, but neither noted it. The girl stood straight as a sapling, smiling up fearlessly into the twisted, sardonic face thrust close to hers.

"You mean that yellow dog I ran over yesterday?" The semblance of mirth was gone from his voice. "The fool wouldn't move quick enough, and if anyone stands in my way I get them, sooner or later. You're a little queen, Billie, and you've been lording it over the roughnecks around here so long that you think you can set your heel on the neck of the universe. A little cave-man stuff would be good for you, my dear."

"You being the cave-man?" Her clear laughter rang out scornfully. "You aren't very well acquainted with us around here, Mr. Wiley, or you'd realize that it isn't right healthy to appoint yourself to office in these parts. The road is still clear, but you might find it barred with something you couldn't run down if you don't move quick."

"You little she-cat!" He sprang forward and seized the wrist which swung at her side. "You'll take a ride with me, do you hear? And you'll come now, or I'll pick you up and carry——"

He got no farther. Something caught him sidewise and whirled him headlong into the bushes, and a very calm, very resolute voice sounded in almost forgotten tones.

"You'll pick yourself up first, Starr Wiley, and come back for more if you want it. You know what's coming to you!"

Billie started in sheer amazement. There before her, sprung from nowhere, was her companion of yesterday, the smug young man who had wanted to play the chaperon, and who had seemed surprised and shocked when she revealed her identity. Her eyes blazed.

"How come you to butt in on this little argument?" There was an ominous note in her slow drawl. "No one asked you to sit in, Señor Duenna, I'm playing my own hand. You durn fool, don't you see I had the coyote covered all the time?"

Her hand moved from the hip pocket of her khaki skirt and he saw the glint of the sun upon a small but business-like, blunt-nosed revolver.

Kearn Thode stepped back, his face crimson at the name she had dubbed him as well as at the unexpectedness of her attack, and at that moment Starr Wiley leaped, snarling, from the undergrowth.

The girl stood fascinated. She had seen many rough-and-tumble fights in the history of Limasito, but the clean-cut scientific way the two lean, lithe, well-matched figures sprang to combat thrilled her.

Wiley was the heavier of the two, but indolence and dissipation had softened him and Thode was in the pink of condition. After the first blind onslaught he steadied himself and parried, waiting for the opening his opponent's uncontrolled rage would give him. It was soon forthcoming; a side-stepped lunge left Wiley's pallid face exposed and Thode caught him fairly on the point of the jaw. He shot across the road, crumpled into the ditch and lay quivering and still, as his victim of the day before.

Panting, Thode turned to the girl.

"I am sorry," he said stiffly. "I didn't mean to butt in on your game, but, having started, I had to finish."

She seemed not to have heard. Her eyes were shining and a little spot of clear rose showed in her cheeks as she held out her hand.

"A good, clean knock-out!" she cried. "I wish Dad could have seen it. You're some fighter, Mr. ——?"

"Duenna," he supplied grimly. "Do you wish me to leave you here with him now, or shall I wait until he comes to, and see if he wants a fresh deal?"

She laughed merrily.

"Wiley won't be looking for anything but home and a stiff drink of hooch when he gets back to the world," she remarked. "I reckon he's in for quite a siesta."

"We can't very well leave him there." Thode spoke reflectively. "Last time, he had a buckboard and I dumped him back into it. The team took him home, all right, but you can't very well expect that of a motor."

Billie eyed him curiously.

"But you've only just come, and he hasn't driven any team around here."

"We've met before." Thode's face had darkened and his tone was terse. "His car's drawn well up on the side of the road. I'll just put him in it and he can find his way when he wakes."

The girl watched as he hauled the limp body out of the ditch and thrust it unceremoniously into the seat behind the wheel. Wiley stirred, grunted and then slumped forward, his head resting upon his arms.

"He'll do." Billie gave the unconscious figure a last contemptuous glance. "I like the way you play when you do get into a little game, and unless you want the whole town to be calling you 'Mr. Duenna' inside of three days, you'd better tell me your name."

He complied, and quite naturally they swung off down the road together.

Thode stole a glance at her in utter bewilderment. A girl who could watch a fight without timidity or squeamishness but in impartial, impersonal joy of the conflict was unique in his experience. She had been angry, contemptuous of them both; would she as heartily have congratulated his adversary, had the tables been turned?

"You are still angry with me for my interference, Miss ——?" he began, but she stopped him with a gesture.

"I've been just 'Billie' to all Limasito since the first well was spudded in; you don't want the boys to think you're putting notions into my head, do you?" She smiled, frankly. "I hated you because I'd bragged to you that I could take care of myself and nobody would molest me in these parts, and then you had to come along just when it looked as though I was a maiden in distress. You see, I hadn't reckoned on Wiley showing yellow; we don't have many like him in Limasito; at least not long."

"If I thought you a maiden in distress, I proved to be a very superfluous knight-errant," he retorted. "You were well able to take care of yourself, so your boast was no idle one."

"Dad taught me that," she responded simply. "He runs the Blue Chip on the square, but there are times when an extra ace appears in the show-down, and then it isn't a question of who produced it, but which one is quickest on the draw. Five aces never grew in a straight deck, and I sometimes think I can see the fifth ace in an hombre's eye. I saw it in Señor Wiley's."

"I'm going to look in at the Blue Chip, if I may." Thode sheered the topic away from his late antagonist, and Billie followed his lead.

"Of course you must," she said cordially. "You'll find the whole works going; monte, Fairbank, stud and black-jack. There's roulette and craps, too, but it's mostly the women who go after them."

"And you—do you play?" He could not forebear the question.

"Dad says there never was a good bartender yet who drank." Billie grimaced. "He even stopped me being mascot; it always raised a riot. It isn't the winning hand or the stakes themselves that I care for, it's the fun of the game, but Dad says gambling is a poor game for women. They never count the odds they stack up against, and when they over-play, they're bad losers. You'll like Dad, Mr. Thode; he's the whitest hombre that ever crossed the Rio."

Secretly, Thode was beginning to think that he should. The girl was an anomaly and he was curious to see what manner of man her idol was and learn how he had kept her so singularly free from the dross of his world and managed to hold so unswervingly before her the real stakes of the game, truth and honor and a high heart.

When he left her at the side door of the Blue Chip, the young engineer held her hand for an appreciable moment longer than the occasion demanded.

"I'm coming to-night," he announced. "Will you—will I see you?"

"In the patio," she dimpled swiftly. "Buena suerte!"

"Good luck!"   The phrase echoed in his brain, but oddly enough his thoughts did not go forward to the hot, crowded, smoke-hung card-room, or the girl waiting in the cool, fragrant darkness of the inner court, but instead there arose before his mental eyes the vision of a petrified wooden cross beside a glassy pool, and mingled incongruously with it, the face of Starr Wiley, distorted as he had last seen it, with the bruised lips twisted into a mocking leer.   Would the lightly expressed wish of Gentleman Geoff's Billie prove a presage of victory in the great game they two were playing?

CHAPTER III

The Coming of El Negrito

WHEN he entered the Blue Chip that night, Thode
found play already in full blast. The tables
were crowded, smoke hung in low-banked
clouds below the flaring oil lamps, and the glittering bar
at the far end of the room was phalanxed three deep by
a jostling, good-natured throng. Soft-footed, wooden-
faced Chinese mozos glided about, and the whining
monotone of the croupier came from a distant corner.

The scene was not an unfamiliar one to the young
engineer, but he glanced about him with quickened interest. The walls of the huge room, like the exterior, were
painted a garish blue, the floor bare but scrubbed clean,
and the chairs and tables had been obviously selected with
a view to utility and strength rather than ornamentation.
No attempt had been made to render the place attractive
and in this Gentleman Geoff's psychology was sound;
Limasito wanted its play, like its liquor, without frills.

Leisurely, Thode approached the roulette-table and
stood looking over the shoulder of a burly drill-shirted
tool-dresser as the little ball spun in the whirling wheel
and dropped into seventeen. The tool-dresser grunted
with satisfaction and raked in the heap of silver pushed
toward him by the croupier, but one or two of the watchers turned away. The play was evidently not yet high

enough to hold their interest, and Thode was on the point of following when a hand clapped his arm.

Turning, he found a tall, lean figure beside him clad in immaculate white duck from top to toe, with a drooping gray mustache beneath a high, thin nose, keen, twinkling eyes and a mass of grizzled, waving hair. He might have been anywhere between forty-five and sixty, and in a flash his identity was disclosed to the young engineer.

"Howdy!" The hand which had rested on his arm clasped his in a hearty grip. "Glad to see you here, Sir. My daughter told me to expect you."

"You're Gentleman Geoff?" the younger man asked quickly, smiling in return. "My name is Thode. I met your daughter yesterday——"

"So she told me." The twinkle brightened in the genial eyes. "I'm glad of a chance to thank you for helping her with that poor little cuss, José. He's a special favorite of hers. Were you thinking of sitting in right now, Mr. Thode?"

"Not just yet. I was having a look around——"

"Then come out where it's cool, and have a man-sized drink."

His surprising host led the way to the patio where they found a little table close by the plashing fountain and a hovering mozo attended to their needs. When the servant had departed, Gentleman Geoff folded his arms on the table and leaned forward.

"You're a newcomer, Mr. Thode, and down here we don't ask a man where he came from or the nature of his business, as long as he attends to it strictly and doesn't interfere with others. There is no objection to his playing a tight game providing he is on the level, but when he makes a crooked move, it's time for the rest of us to take a hand. My Billie tells me you are an old acquaintance of this man Wiley and I am going to ask you one question straight, Sir. Do you know anything good of him?"

"Well," Thode temporized, "he's rated a millionaire in New York and his father was one of the pioneer Pennsylvania oil men. He is a partner of Harrington Chase, and together they hold some of the best leases in this part of the country, I understand."

"They do. But I was speaking of the man himself." Gentleman Geoff's eyes smiled a perfect understanding. "I was wondering if there could be some point in his favor that I'd overlooked."

"In that case, we've been mutually blind," said Thode, frankly. "I met him first out in Oklahoma two years ago, and I've run across him more than once since, and I don't mind telling you candidly that each meeting has given me less pleasure. I didn't expect to encounter him down here, and I guess Limasito is big enough to hold us both, but if he wants to see me after to-day he knows where to find me."

The older man nodded, slowly.

"I reckoned as much. He hasn't been any favorite since he blew in here, to draw it mild, but he's getting just a little bit too offensive for the good of the community. I know his breed, but I didn't think even he would snap at my Billie's heels. I would have looked you up at the hotel to-night to shake hands with you for what you did this afternoon, Mr. Thode, but Billie told me you intended to pay us a little visit."

"It was a pleasure," the other responded with sincerity.

"It has been coming to Wiley for a long time. But your daughter had the situation well in hand. She is a remarkable young woman."

"She is an honest one, honest with herself and the world. There wasn't much else I could teach her and it hasn't been possible for her to have regular schooling and the influence of women. I've always reckoned fair play was about the biggest thing in life, and woman-like she's gone further than my teachings and worked out an eye-for-an-eye creed of justice for herself that would shame a vigilance committee, but she's wholesome and sound in mind and limb."

"I've learned a little of what they think of her in this town." Thode hesitated, and then went on earnestly. "I know the strict code of even the roughest mining camps up over the border, where good women are concerned, but I'll own that it gave me a jolt to see how freely and fearlessly she goes about down here. You may think, Sir, that I'm exhibiting a lot of nerve, and it may be that I have a distorted picture in my mind of the life in this part of the country for a young girl like your daughter, but is she safe with all these low-caste half-breeds about?"

"As safe as in a convent." Gentleman Geoff's eyes had narrowed. "I appreciate your interest, Mr. Thode, but let me remind you that it was a man from the States, a New York swell, who molested her this afternoon. There isn't a low-caste Mex' who would take a chance, for he'd know that every gun from here to the Sierra Madre would be cocked for him, and even the hills couldn't give him a hiding-place! But as to Wiley. I had a reason apart from his little attentions to Billie, for asking about him. Whatever lies between you two is your own game, but I know you better than you think, Mr. Thode. Your chief, Perry Larkin, told me he was sending you down, and what manner of hombre you were. If Larkin can trust you, I'm going to take a chance. I thought I had Wiley's number, but I learned something to-day, aside from that little fracas, that makes me doubt I've given him credit for his limit of crookedness. Mr. Thode, do you figure that Starr Wiley is enough of a man to be a very big rascal?"

Thode hesitated again.

"I think," he began at last, "that it would depend wholly on the size of the stakes. He's a coward when it comes to a show-down, but money and place and power are his gods. If it was a tremendous piece of villainy with a big incentive he mightn't have the courage to see it through himself, but he is quite capable of aiding and abetting it, or hiring others to do it for him."

Gentleman Geoff's fists clenched and he drew a deep breath.

"That's it!" he cried. "You've struck it, Mr. Thode! Unless I'm mistaken, he's dealing the biggest, crookedest hand of his life right now, but we'll get him, Sir. We'll show him what fair play is below the border—"

He broke off and for a minute the two men sat in silence, straining their ears.

Above the click of glasses and sound of many voices in the gambling-rooms had come the sharp, staccato clatter of a horse's hoofs upon the hard-packed road. It was not unusual in a land where hooch was cheap and stimulating and every drunken roysterer celebrated in the saddle, but there was an ominous, tragic suggestion

in the irregularity of the hoof-beats as of an exhausted,
failing beast urged on by grim and vital need.

The young engineer leaped to his feet as the clatter
ceased in a harsh scraping thud, and with Gentleman
Geoff beside him, he crossed the patio and re-entered the
gambling-room. The voices had hushed as if by magic,
and every motionless figure was turned toward the entrance door.

It was flung open and a man staggered blindly over
the sill, reeling and clutching at his breast with both
gnarled, sinewy hands.

"El Negrito!" his voice rose in a smothered sob. "He's
hit the trail and coming fast. Look out for your——"

The stranger choked, caught at his throat and crumpled
slowly to the floor, a thin scarlet stream pouring from his
lips. The silence held for one tense moment and then
pandemonium broke loose.

"A raid! A raid!"

Hoarse cries filled the room and a mad stampede ensued, but somehow through the rampant throng, Kearn
Thode found himself before that fallen figure. Gentleman Goeff was still at his side, but another had been
quicker than they. Soft hands raised the dying man's
head and Billie knelt beside him, her pallor intensified
but her eyes steady and calm.

"Sam! can you speak to me? Where are the babies,
and Mamie?"

"Gone!" The breath whistled through the tortured
lips. "Macheted—thank God, I saw them die. Tell
Geoff—save you——"

The whisper died in a rattle and the head slumped
inert against her knee.

"It's over, Billie. Get on down to the cellar, quick——"
Gentleman Geoff's tones rang with command, but the girl
shook her head.

"Where the liquor is stored?" she smiled. "Alvarez's
men won't leave a cask unturned. No, Dad, I'd rather
take a chance with you, here. If it comes to a show-
down, they won't get me."

She made a significant gesture, and the lethargy of consternation fell from Thode as he saw for the second time
that day the glint of her revolver.

"Good God!" he exclaimed. "Isn't there something
to be done? We're only a handful! Are we going to
wait here for that black devil to come and slaughter us?"

"No, Son," Gentleman Geoff drawled. "We're going
to put up the stiffest fight we know how, but there's no
help nearer than the barracks at the oil refinery ten miles
north, and El Negrito is on the way."

As if in corroboration of his words a new sound broke
all at once upon their ears, distant at first but drawing
rapidly close, a fusillade of shots, and the pounding of a
multitude of hoofs.

Gentleman Geoff drew one slim hand across his reeking
forehead.

"It's come, Boys! Steady now, to the finish!"

"Look here, Sir! I'm going to try for it." Thode
caught his host by the arm. "I can slip out before they
have the house surrounded and find a horse somewhere.
If they down me, one man more or less here won't make
any difference, and it's a chance!"

"Look!" Gentleman Geoff waved the young engineer
to a narrow window beside the entrance door.

Down the straight level expanse of the Calle Rivera

clattered an unending stream of horsemen, their accoutrements jingling a sinister diapason as they poured helter-skelter across the plaza in the waning moonlight. Tatterdemalion as they were, the ragged army were well-organized as Thode saw at a glance; no haphazard, leaderless crew was this, for at their head rode a diminutive, jockey-like figure, his face glistening and ebony in the eerie radiance, his teeth flashing white as he turned in the saddle. The Little Nigger had come!

His company halted in an irregular line against the eastern end of the plaza, flung themselves from their horses and came on in a rushing, yelling horde. A weak scattered volley rattled from the dwellings about the square, but the raiders made unswervingly for what was obviously their main objective, the Blue Chip, where most of the male population, unlimited alcohol and a fabulous ransom in gold were theirs for the taking.

They had reached the center of the Calle, when Gentleman Geoff barked a brief command and a withering blast of shots rang forth from the besieged garrison. The advancing line crumpled, wavered, then at a cat-like yowl from its dusky leader, closed in and came forward with an answering roar.

Kearn Thode sprang from his point of vantage and faced the other man once more with undiminished determination in his eyes.

"I've got to get to the barracks—it means death to us all if I stay here! Isn't there a door on the other side of the house somewhere back of the patio?"

"Yes. It opens on a little alley that leads to the plaza." It was the girl's eager voice which replied.

"And the Carranzistas, the government troops, are ten

miles away to the north. I'm going to ride for it, Sir, it's the only chance. I can slip out of that alley and around the edge of the plaza to where their horses are picketed. There'll be interference there, and I may have a running fight for it, but I'll take the odds."

"Come then. You're a brave man, Mr. Thode!" Gentleman Geoff led the way swiftly across the patio to a little door half hidden in the creeping vines. But even as he laid his hand upon the rusty bolts, there was a storm of feet in the alley and a rain of shot pattered against the outer wall.

Gentleman Geoff stepped back with a gesture of defeat, but Thode cried desperately:

"I can cut my way through them. I must, Man! Open the door!"

Instead, his companion shot the hasp of a small oblong look-out on a level with their eyes, and Thode beheld the alley choked with figures, their carbines bristling and maniacal, distorted faces pressed close.

"No use." Gentleman Geoff snapped the slide in place as a stray bullet whistled past their ears. "It's too late. Even had you gone when Sam first came, they would have cut you down in the plaza. You can only lend a hand here."

Wordlessly, Thode stumbled back beside him to the gambling-room. That which but a moment before had seemed like a wild, purposeless stampede had resolved itself into an unorganized but determined defensive. Few of the men had departed, those few who had ridden in from nearby haciendas where unwarned families waited in ignorance of the menace sweeping down upon them from the hills.

Thode worked with heaving chest and straining muscles, but his brain was singularly clear and his observation acute. Gentleman Geoff seemed to be everywhere at once, urging, exhorting, commanding. The mozos, their yellow faces gray, were huddled in a corner, clucking like dismayed fowl at the approach of a storm, but a word from Billie sent them scurrying for the store of guns and ammunition.

She, too, it was who opened the door of an inner room where a group of disheveled women, their faces ghastly beneath the cheap paint, cowered about a roulette-table, and ranged them behind the shelter of the stout mahogany bar, seeing to it that each was armed.

Her calm face in the tumult and smoke and dust seemed etherialized, glorified to the wondering eyes of the young engineer; the marvel of her strength and courage shone forth like a radiance, imbuing even the panic-stricken Celestials with a spirit of defense.

Thode's eyes were smarting, his veins on fire and in his nostrils the reek of powder mingled with a strange, new, sweetish odor. The table-top on which he stood was slippery where Rufe Terwilliger had doubled up beside him and rolled to the floor. Others were falling, too, stumbling and clutching vainly for support, but Billie's slim white figure still stood unwavering beside her father and Thode turned grimly to his task.

Twice more the bandits charged, and twice they were beaten back, leaving augmented blotches of huddled bodies in the road, but the toll had been heavy within. Groans and curses filled the air as men pitched headlong from their loophole posts to writhe upon the floor and once a woman's shrill scream rang out as a tawdrily clothed shape dropped across the bar.

Thode's shoulder burned and a warm stream raced down his arm; his forehead, too, was seared as if by a white-hot brand, but he dashed the blood impatiently from his eyes that he might see what this sudden lull in the hostilities portended. He was not long in doubt for a thin skirmish line leaped across the road, yelling like demons and firing as they ran, and close behind their protecting curtain of shot appeared a double row of half-crouched forms, bearing a huge battering-ram.

Heroically the little garrison sought to stem the tide of destruction, but as quickly as a gap appeared in the on-coming wave it was filled and the flood swept irresistibly on. More than one narrow window now was unmanned against the attack and as the bullets pattered like hail through the unobstructed apertures, Thode heard a sharp little cry which turned his heart to lead within him.

Wheeling, he saw through the murky reek that Gentleman Geoff was down at last, his head cradled in Billie's arms, a spreading stain upon the soft white silk of his shirt. Thrusting his rifle into the hands of a neighbor, Thode leaped from the table, and as he reached the girl's side a thunderous crash smote the heavy door.

"He isn't —— ?"

Billie shook her head and at the unfinished sentence Gentleman Geoff's eyelids lifted and he gazed full and understandingly into the face of the young engineer.

"Not yet, but I'm done for. See that—Billie—cashes in before ——"

"Listen, Sir! Can you hear me? I'm going to make a

break for it, do you understand?" Thode's voice rang
out clear above the strife. "How long will that door
hold?"

"An hour, maybe. It's as solid as a rock, and the bolts
are steel, but nothing could withstand that ramming for
long." Gentleman Geoff had rallied his waning strength
to meet that new note of quickened impulse.

"It's the one chance left! They've found by this time
that they couldn't batter down that iron door at the back,
set as it is in the solid masonry, and it may be that they've
concentrated all their efforts here on this side. At least
I'll have to try my luck and cut through. We've got to
have the troops! Ten level miles, and the dawn is coming; I ought to make it and back in an hour, before the
door gives way."

Gentleman Geoff raised himself on one elbow and
extended his hand.

"You're right! It's the last chance, and maybe your
luck will hold. Go to it, Thode, I know you'll play—to
win!"

The girl was staring at him with shining eyes, and he
paused only long enough to lay his hand upon her arm.

"You have your revolver—if they break through before
I get back——?"

"Don't be afraid for us." Her voice rang out steadily
and clearly above the roar of conflict. "I'll take care of
myself and Dad until you come! Hasta la vista!"

Thode drew a deep breath, and, turning, made for the
door and across the patio, miraculously cool and calm
beneath the dimming stars. The little door at the farther
end of the house wall was guarded now by a dark-skinned
youth whose teeth chattered in his head, and Thode, with

a hasty explanation, shot the bolts and slipped through into the rubbish-heaped alley.

Not a living thing was in sight but a yellow cur crouching under a cask, and Thode reached the mouth of the narrow passage to see only the backs of the mob clustered about the corner.

The moonlight was gone, and slipping into the darker shadows of the wall, he sped off in the opposite direction around the square to where the moving bulk of the line of picketed horses showed at the end of an intersecting street.

Unnoted, he reached them and laid his hand upon the bridle of the nearest. The beast plunged nervously and a dark figure sprang up with a hoarse cry, which died in his throat as Thode brought his clubbed rifle down upon his head.

Other shouts arose above the distant crash of the battering-ram; other figures advanced, and in the patter of stray shots a horse screamed and fell kicking among his terrorized fellows, but Thode had twitched free the knot which haltered his mount and was off and away up the narrow street, in a thunder of hoof-beats which outran the fusillade and pounded steadily on into the silence of the coming dawn.

CHAPTER IV

GENTLEMAN GEOFF PASSES THE DEAL

WITH the departure of Kearn Thode on his mission Gentleman Geoff sank into a stupor from which all Billie's efforts failed to arouse him. She glanced at the little watch on her wrist. Twenty minutes past four! One hour for the massive door to hold against those crashing blows which seemed beating upon her brain. One hour for the young engineer to ride ten miles on an already jaded horse, provided he had succeeded in making his perilous start, and bring the Carranzistas to the rescue!

The din of the volley which had greeted him from the pickets could not reach her ears above the roar of conflict surrounding her, much less the receding hoof-beats of his mount. From the moment of his passing into the darkness of the patio the girl could only wait, but her spirit was staunch and unflagging. He would win through! He would return in time!

At her order, two mozos had dragged a couch from an inner room and the insensible body of Gentleman Geoff was placed upon it. Billie bound the hideous gaping wound and forced a few drops of brandy between the set lips, but he only moaned faintly and drifted into a deeper oblivion.

Twenty-five minutes of five! Unless he were lying

stark and still in the plaza, Thode must be well upon his way.

But Billie had no time to nurse her suspense; she could not even linger by her father's side, for there was grim and urgent work for her hands, and one by one the women crept out from behind the comparative safety of the bar and joined her. Barely a man of all those who had thronged the gambling-rooms remained unscathed, and the cries of the wounded rang in her ears with piteous insistence.

As she passed from one fallen man to another, heedless of her own exposure to stray bullets, administering brandy and water, improvising rude bandages and comforting as best she might, one thought echoed like a chant through her brain, solemn with its intensity. He would come. Her head seemed bursting with each reverberating crash of the battering-ram and her heart pulsed time to the slow march of the interminable hour, but the thought remained. He would come.

Ten minutes to five. Thode must have reached the barracks at the refinery by now, unless—— She set her small teeth firmly. Half of the hour had passed, but already the door was sagging with each renewed assault and the bolts were snapping beneath the strain. She dared not look again toward that last failing defense, dared not consult the little watch lest her self-control, her very reason give way. He would come, of course, but would he be in time?

All at once the hammering strokes ceased and the rattle of rifle fire died out in a desultory spatter as stray bullets impinged against the stout adobe wall.

Jim Baggott from his perch upon a heap of chairs before the window called out in amazement:

"They've drawn back clear across the road! Reckon they've given it up as a bad job at last! The dawn's almost here."

"Don't fool yourself!" A burly gang foreman rested his rifle against the wall and seized avidly upon the dipper of water held out to him by one of the women. "Thanks, ma'am.—Maybe they're just taking a breathing spell, but it's my opinion they're planning some new devilment. Alvarez knows that once that door's down——"

He glanced toward the woman and the sentence ended in a shrug.

"What's the matter with Geoff?" Baggot for the first time had noted the inert form stretched upon the couch.

"Dad's hit," Billie responded simply.

"Is he bad?" The foreman's tone was hushed.

"I'm afraid so. He's dreadfully cold; he's—he's bleeding internally, I think. Perhaps, if a surgeon comes in time——"

"A what?" Baggott exploded. "Gosh almighty, where's a surgeon coming from?"

"From the barracks," explained Billie, naïvely. "Mr. Thode's gone for the troops."

"When? How? What do you think of that young—— Hurrah!"

The eager questions from a dozen throats ended in a husky cheer, but it died as swiftly as it was born. From across the road a huge dark blur had detached itself and was moving forward stealthily to the attack. The fusillade of shots recommenced, but a groan had started and spread among the watchers at the windows.

"What is it?" Billie's tone was still steady, but a chill had crept into her veins.

"They've got a new battering-ram; looks like a telegraph pole! No door could hold against it," Baggot muttered. "It's all up with us now!"

The rifles popped valiantly, but a thunderous impact fairly rocked the house, and, fascinated, Billie watched the door bulge toward her, then spring back into place as the topmost bolt snapped like a knife-blade. One more onslaught, perhaps two——

Billie's hand closed on her revolver and she moved instinctively closer to her father's couch. Then all at once she threw up her head, and her voice rang out

"Hark! What is that? Don't you hear it?"

None heeded as she stood with every muscle and nerve tense, straining her ears. The night was no longer dark and a faint rosy light seeping in at an easterly window reddened the glow of the swinging oil lamps and transfigured her drawn blanched face. What sound, distant and far away, had been borne to her on the wind of the dawn?

Again the giant battering-ram stove at the door and the middle bolt crashed. The flimsy impromptu barricade toppled, then swayed back into place and a shuddering sigh went up from the handful of white-faced men. One more drive, and the end would come.

The other women had huddled again behind the bar, but Billie still stood with uplifted face. And now she was smiling! Swift and sure the rhythmic echo of galloping hoofs reached her consciousness and even as the third shock came and the door crashed inward carrying the barricade with it, a ringing shout burst upon the air and the staccato rattle of a machine-gun sounded the final note in the symphony of battle.

The ragged, wild-eyed horde, sweeping in at the shattered doorway, brought up standing, then turned madly and scattered like chaff. In their stead, through the aperture leaped a tall, unrecognizable figure caked with dust and clotted blood which reeled to the couch and collapsed beside it, labored breath hissing from tortured lungs and blood-shot eyes filmed with exhaustion.

Outside, the tide of conflict raged up and down the street and swept out over the plaza, but neither the girl nor the man at her feet could hear it.

"You made it! Dad said you would play to win!" There was a new note of which she was herself unconscious in Billie's tones, and she added softly, "You were just bound and determined to take care of me right from the start! Weren't you, Mr. Duenna?"

The new day dawned and quiet was once more restored to Limasito. Those of the bandits who escaped swift justice had fled toward the distant hills with the troops in full pursuit and the plaza was a humming hive of survivors, augmented, as the tidings spread, by all the countryside.

The dismantled Blue Chip had been turned into a temporary hospital and the wounded lay in rows upon the tables and hastily improvised cots, but Gentleman Geoff was not among them.

He had been moved by his own wish out to a shady corner of the patio where he lay with a quiet, whimsical smile lifting the drooped ends of his mustache and his genial eyes, with a curious questioning look in their depths, stared straight before him.

Billie, huddled on the ground, her head pillowed against the side of his cot, slumbered deeply, and Gentleman Geoff's slim, delicate fingers touched her hair in a wistful caress. On a nearby bench Thode, bathed and freshly bandaged, slept also. Jim Baggott had tried in vain to drag him back to the hotel, for the young engineer had read a mute desire in the dying man's glance and refused to leave his side.

The army surgeon had done his best, but the end was near and only the superb vitality of the old gambler glowed still, like a living spark. Now and then the surgeon paused in his busy round within to glance speculatively from the doorway and each time Gentleman Geoff nodded reassuringly to him. Not yet!

The blaze of noon subsided, and as the shadows lengthened in the patio, Billie stirred, and Thode stretched and opened his eyes.

"Oh, Dad, I must have fallen asleep!" The girl's tones were filled with contrition. "Do you want anything? Is the pain very bad?"

It seemed to her that a shadow had crept into her father's eyes, but his faint voice was steady.

"No. Billie. No pain—just tired. Has young Thode gone home?"

"No, Sir, I'm here." He came eagerly forward. "Is there anything you want me to do?"

"Only shake hands with me. You rode well, last night. I reckoned Perry Larkin knew a man when he saw one, but he didn't know all that was in you. Billie, girl, go ask the Doc if I can have a drink or a little shot to pull me together." As the girl flew to do his bidding, Gentleman Geoff's thin fingers tightened their grip. "Thode,

the boys will all stand by her and play square, but I'm
leaving her alone. She isn't their kind; she doesn't know
it, nobody does, but my little girl's of different blood.
There's no one around here in her class, except you. Kind
of—look out for her, will you?"

"I will, Sir." Thode's voice shook with the fervor of
his vow. "You want her away from Limasito, from this
environment? I have a sister up North——"

"That's what I mean." A spasm of pain contorted the
pallid face and he went on hurriedly as if fearful of the
inevitable interruption. "I couldn't take her myself and
couldn't part from her, but the life hasn't been right for
her, though I did all I could. She's a lady and she must
go back to her own. I'd like to myself, for an hour,
now. That's a Harvard seal on your cigarette-case, if
I'm not mistaken, Mr. Thode."

Thode leaned forward, a sudden exclamation half
halted on his lips.

Gentleman Geoff nodded slowly.

"Name Rendell," he said. "Class of '84. I haven't
mentioned it this quarter of a century and I'm going to
ask you to forget it now, but—you'll do what you can for
my girl?"

"On my honor, Sir," Thode reaffirmed solemnly. "It
is a sacred charge."

"Jim Baggott will sell out the Blue Chip and give her
the proceeds. It ought to bring her a comfortable sum
and the bank deposits are in her name already. I'm not
afraid she will throw it away; she has a level head on
her young shoulders, but I want to be sure she will have
the best of everything; all that she has missed. You'll
see to it?"

The reappearance of the doctor precluded other answer on Thode's part than a long hearty handclasp, but Gentleman Geoff understood.

Later his vigilant mind wandered and the watchers averted their faces.

"Best I could for her, Vi! Kept her like you—clean and true and God-Almighty sweet! Never knew—not my own. . . ."

Still later, when the sun like a glowing ball of fire had sunk beneath the wall of the patio, his lips moved again.

"Tell the boys I'm not cashing in—just passing this deal. I'm in on the next one. . . . Billie . . . square, always——"

"I'm here, Dad!" The girl's voice choked with sobs breathed close to his ear, but Gentleman Geoff did not hear. He had slipped into the silence.

In the days that followed, Kearn Thode pondered long and deeply upon his trust. The arrangement with his sister would be an easy matter to adjust, he knew, but the immediate task confronting him was more difficult of solution. The suggestion of a guardian thrust upon her would meet with scant complacency in the girl's independent spirit and secretly he quailed before the thought of her displeasure. Her comrades of a lifetime, the rough, staunch men of Limasito, might well resent the intrusion of a stranger, an alien, into what was evidently to them a family affair; still less would they be able to understand and appreciate the fact that Billie belonged to another world than theirs.

He decided at length to lay the matter before her frankly in detail, eliminating only the admission of Gentleman Geoff's identity. He respected the dead man's confidence, but it only precipitated him into a fresh quandary.

Billie's naïve surprise when the question of her surname arose brought the matter to a crisis in his mind.

"Why, I'm just 'Billie,' I suppose," she had stammered. "I—I never heard any other name. Do I have to have one?"

Jim Baggott settled the matter, for the moment at least.

"You do not!" he announced, with emphasis. "Not around here, anyway. You were Gentleman Geoff's Billie and that's name enough for us. When you do need a handle to it, I reckon there ain't any law 'gainst you pickin' out one to suit yourself."

Baggott was the chief executor of the late gambler and mightily puffed up with the pride and dignity of his office. Gentleman Geoff's private papers were few and carefully indited, their instructions unmistakably clear. Under them, Baggott sold the Blue Chip scrupulously to the highest bidder, although it broke his heart to see Limasito's proudest institution pass into the hands of a Tampico syndicate. He placed the two hundred thousand, American, which the establishment brought, unreservedly to Billie's account.

"If you ain't of age, nobody knows the difference," he announced. "Gentleman Geoff left word it was to go 'to my daughter, known as Billie,' and there you are. The money's your'n, and it's up to you to do what you like with it."

Bewildered and numb in her first contact with poignant grief, the girl had taken up her temporary abode at Henry Bailey's fruit ranch, a mile or two out on the

Calle Rivera, where his buxom wife, Sallie, mothered her to her heart's content.

Thode rode out each day to see her, but a new inexplicable shyness in Billie's attitude toward him made his task still more difficult and he deferred the question of her future in sheer funk. The magnitude of her fortune, too, was a stumbling-block. The girl knew nothing of him save what intuition had taught her. What if she assumed that his object were to gain control of her estate? The thought maddened him into action at length and one day as they cantered slowly back from a visit to the little José, he forced the issue.

"Billie, have you thought of the future, of what you will do?" he asked.

"Oh, yes." The reply was prompt and decisive. "I can't tell you, Mr. Thode, or anyone, but I've got something to do, something big, and I've made up my mind to see it through. It's just as much an inheritance from Dad as the money and I mean to let nothing stand in my way."

There was a grim earnestness in her tone which made him glance curiously at her.

"You are sure you can't tell me, and let me help, whatever it is?" he asked gently.

Billie shook her head.

"It's my job. I'll have my work cut out for me, I expect, but nobody else can share it. I've got to play a lone hand, but when it's over, I—I don't know. I haven't made any plans beyond that."

"But surely you don't intend to remain here in Limasito all your life?"

"Why not?" She shot a swift glance at him. "It was good enough for Dad."

"But not for you. That's the point. I—I had a talk with your father just before he died, and he wants you to go away; to travel and study and mingle with people of your own kind."

"Aren't these my kind?" Hot loyalty blazed in her tone. "They're all the friends I have in the world, the folks right here in Limasito, and all I want! What would I do among a lot of city people; stuck-up snobs who don't know I'm alive? I wouldn't even know how to talk to them, or what fork to eat with, and what's more, I wouldn't care. Why, I haven't even got a second name! 'Gentleman Geoff's Billie' would look well in the society papers, wouldn't it? No, thanks! I'll stick to the folks I know and—and care for!"

"But they're not all snobs, Billie, just because some of their ways are different from yours. I have a sister who can play a stiff game of poker and ride as well as you. Edna spends most of her time out in the open, and nothing feazes her. You would get on beautifully with her and I thought perhaps you would let me take you to her, sometime."

Billie was silent. She was staring straight ahead of her, into the vista above her pinto's ears, and had Thode looked at her he would have seen a quick flush mantle her face, but he was occupied by his own problem.

"You are different, you know, from the people about here; or anywhere else for that matter, Billie. I—I've never met a girl like you, so brave and true and wonderful! I want to take you away from all this and show you how different the world can be. What does it matter

about your name? You are *you,* and that's all that
counts. Everyone will love you, they couldn't help
it!——" He rushed on heedlessly, oblivious to any ulterior construction which might be put upon his words,
intent only on assuring her of her welcome in the place
which her father had said was her rightful one, and in
convincing her of his disinterested friendship.

"I told your father that if you were willing I would
gladly take you to my sister, and we would all do our
best to make you happy." He reddened, in his turn.
"Please, don't misunderstand; no one will ever attempt to
advise or suggest anything concerning the disposal of
your fortune, it is only that you must have, as your
father said, the best of everything; all that you have
missed."

"Oh, don't talk of the money, please!" She stopped
him with a swift gesture. "I do understand, but I—I
don't want to say anything now. Maybe you'll change
your mind. You were shocked, you remember, when I
told you Dad ran the Blue Chip, and you might be sorry
you—you tried to make your sister friends with a
gambler's daughter, without a family name. Besides, I've
got a trust to perform, don't forget that. When it's finished, perhaps—but let's wait until then."

He was well content to acquiesce, relieved that she had
taken his suggestion in good faith without impugning his
motive. Had he dreamed of the meaning she had read
into his offer, his awakening would have been illuminating.

On the following day Billie put her newly acquired
wealth to its first use. She cantered away from the Casa
de Limas on her pinto without taking the Baileys into her

confidence, and at sundown careened in at the gate in a battered touring car, the bewildered pony following on a rope behind.

"Land alive!" Sallie ran out in the yard with Chevalita, the criada, at her heels. "I didn't know you could run an automobile, Billie!"

"I couldn't this morning," Billie responded through set lips as she grazed the hitching-post and came to a stop with a grinding jerk which all but precipitated her through the cracked wind shield. "I've got to get the hang of this in a couple of days or die trying. I'm going on a little trip."

"Where to?" Sallie circled slowly around the dilapidated vehicle. "Don't look as if this would carry you very far. Where on earth did you get it?"

"It was poor Rufe Terwilliger's." The girl answered the last question first. "I bought it from Mrs. Terwilliger for three hundred dollars. Ben Hallock has got some tires to fit it that he'll let me have and if the engine will only last for about four hundred miles I don't care what happens to it after that."

" 'Four hundred miles!' " repeated Sallie. "What have you taken into your head now? There's nothing within four hundred miles o' Limasito!"

Billie regarded her with an enigmatic smile.

"There's a dream to bring true!" she said slowly. "That is Tia Juana's; she's going with me. And there's a start to be made on something I've set out to do, and this journey is the first step of the way. No one must go with me but Tia Juana, no one must even know where I have gone. Someone owes me a debt, Sallie, and they're going to pay!"

There was a grim note in her quiet tones which boded ill for the debtor, and Sallie hastily changed the subject.

"And Mr. Thode? What'll I tell him? Does he know?"

"Not where I'm going, but you can say that I've made the first move in the game I'm playing; I've started on what I've got to do. He'll know what I mean. I can't tell you or anyone, Sallie, because I want to see it through alone."

When next Thode rode up to the Casa de Limas, Sallie met him with strange news.

"She's gone. Went off this morning in a car she bought from Rufe Terwilliger's widow, and she bundled old Tia Juana along with her. She said to tell you she'd made a start on what she had to do, and you would understand."

But Kearn Thode didn't. What was this trust, this unknown inheritance from Gentleman Geoff? There had been an ominous note in her voice when she spoke of it, and he remembered what the gambler had told him of her eye-for-an-eye creed of retributive justice. In her splendid, reckless courage could she have pitted herself against El Negrito, the bandit of the hills?

CHAPTER V

A GRINGO CINDERELLA

"WHETHER you're here for health, pleasure, or business there ain't a more up-and-comin' town this side o' the Rio than Limasito," Jim Baggott remarked with the air of publicity-promoter as he "set 'em up" for a plump, white-mustached stranger, who had drawn up to the hotel an hour before in an impressive car, and whose equally impressive array of luggage was even then distributed about the best suite the establishment afforded.

"I'm here on business, Mr. Baggott," the stranger replied promptly to his host's tactfully implied question. "Did you ever hear of a gambler known as 'Gentleman Geoff'? I understand he located somewhere about here ten years ago."

"Hear of him?" Jim repeated gruffly, and turned his head away. "He was one of our most prom'nent citizens; ran the Blue Chip over yonder."

"Indeed?" The stranger tasted his liquor and replaced the glass with a fastidious shudder upon the bar. "He is not here now?"

Baggott shook his head.

"You may have heard that Alvarez—El Negrito, they call him—paid us a little visit a few days ago." He added a profane and heartfelt abjuration of the bandit. "Most of us were corraled in the Blue Chip, and Geoff, he was shot down along with a lot of others."

"Dead! How unfortunate! Can you tell me if he left any family; a daughter, for instance?"

"Sa-ay!" Jim folded his arms on the bar and gazed levelly at his guest. "What's it to you if he did? I happen to be Geoff's executor——"

"Ah, that simplifies matters." The stranger drew a card-case from his pocket. "I am Mason North, of the firm of North, Manning and Gilchrist, attorneys. We are looking for a young woman known as the daughter of this Gentleman Geoff, to notify her of something to her advantage. Can you tell me where she may be found?"

"Known as his daughter?" Jim stammered. "Billie *is* his daughter, damn it! There ain't no other young woman——"

" 'Billie'?" repeated North sharply. "A derivative, no doubt. That is significant. I should like very much to see this Miss 'Billie'——"

"Then you've only got to turn your head!" A clear young voice sounded from the doorway, and the attorney wheeled to confront the object of his quest.

"Lord, Billie, where'd you vamoose to? The whole town's been askin' for you for the last three days!" Jim remembered his manners. "This is Mr. North. He's a lawyer and he says he's got some news for you."

Billie shook hands gravely.

"Pleased to meet you, Mr. North."

"And I to meet you, my dear young lady. I have had a long search for you."

"Do you mean——" her eyes were wide—"that you've come all the way down here just to see me?"

He smiled.

"I have been searching for you for more than two years. There are some questions I must ask you. Can we talk here privately without interruption, Mr. Baggott? —No, don't go!" as Jim started for the door. "As the chief executor of—ah, Gentleman Geoff, you are presumably this young lady's de-facto guardian and your presence is imperative."

Considerably impressed, Jim turned a chair around and seated himself astride it, folding his arms across the back.

"Fire away. I'm listening," he said briefly.

"Has this news anything to do with Dad?" asked Billie.

"Partly, my dear. It concerns you, principally; you, and your antecedents." North took a sheaf of papers from his pocket, and produced a fountain pen. "Did you ever hear of a place called Topaz Gulch?"

"Yes. Dad and I were there when I was a little girl. There was a big fire; I can just remember seeing it. We left soon after, I think."

"And then where did you go?" The lawyer made rapid notes as he quizzed her, and Billie stared in growing wonder.

"Oh, we just traveled. I can recall a lot of places, but not their names; mining camps, and cattle towns and farming centers. Then we came here, when the boom first started, and Dad built the Blue Chip——"

The lawyer nodded as she faltered.

"That will do, I think. We can go into the details more exhaustively later, but I am convinced that you are indeed the young woman in the case. But first, can you tell me anything of your mother?"

"Dad said she died a long time ago." Billie's voice was very low. "I don't remember her at all, unless——"

"Unless what?" North urged her, not unkindly. "Think, please."

"It seems to me there was someone, when I was very little, who sang always. There was one song; I should know it again if I heard it, but it won't come to me now."

"Aha!" The lawyer cleared his throat. "That confirms it. I am going to tell you, and your good friend here, a story. It goes rather far back, but I shall ask you to be patient for it concerns you vitally. Some twenty years ago there lived in New York City a noted financier, Giles Murdaugh. You do not recall having heard the name?"

Billie shook her head mutely and North went on:

"Giles Murdaugh was a very wealthy man, a power in the world of finance. He was a widower and his only living relatives were his son, Ralph, and a niece. At the time I mention, Ralph was a young man, just out of college. He fell in love with a—a young person who was not his equal socially; in fact, she earned her living by singing and dancing upon the stage of a music-hall. She was a most respectable, most exemplary young woman," he added hastily, "but Giles Murdaugh was violently opposed to the union. Her name was Violet Ashton."

He paused, but the girl before him made no sign.

"Young Ralph Murdaugh married her, and his father disowned him. The boy had no income of his own, no profession, and his father's influence prevented his obtaining any remunerative position. He was very bitter, and hoped to starve his son into submission and force an annulment of what he considered a disgraceful marriage, but Ralph was as determined as his father.

"The young couple left New York finally and went out West to make their way, but it was a most disheartening experience. Giles Murdaugh's influence was far-reaching and all doors were closed to them. They changed their name and went on, but Ralph had been a student rather than an athlete; he was not strong enough to attempt the rough work which was all that presented itself, and their resources were gone.

"They drifted at last into Topaz Gulch, Nevada, where Ralph obtained a position as time-keeper at the Yellow Streak gold mine, and where a little daughter was born to them, whom they named 'Willa'."

Billie started, and her lips opened, but no words came. Jim Baggott, too, was silent, his jaw agape and honest eyes almost popping from their sockets.

"When the baby was two years old, Ralph Murdaugh died, after a long illness which ate up the little they had been able to save. His wife, destitute and unable to support the child in any other fashion, turned to her old profession; she became what was known as a song-and-dance artiste at a hall named for its owner, 'Jake's'.

"Two years later, the dance-hall burned and Violet Ashton, as she called herself once more, was lost in the holocaust. As a thoroughly good woman, she had always been held in the utmost esteem by the community, rough as it was, and the child, Willa, had become a great favorite, but on her mother's death the problem of caring for her arose. There were no women in the town of the proper character to be trusted with her future, and the camp was in a quandary.

"Among what might be called the shifting population, was a peripatetic—ah, gambler, who traveled under the sobriquet of 'Gentleman Geoff'. He had set up a shack where he operated a roulette-wheel and faro-bank, and was very much attached to the child. Can you not surmise the rest? He adopted her, without legal form, and took her with him on his wanderings."

"Then I—I——" Billie stammered, aghast. "I am not——"

"You are Willa Murdaugh."

"Holy Christopher!" Jim Baggott passed his hand across his dazed forehead, and then all three were silent for a space.

The girl sat as if in a dream, her face flushed, her eyes vacant and fixed, and North forebore to intrude upon her reverie. At length she roused herself and turned to him with quick decision.

"If I am what you say, you must know my age. How old am I?"

"Nineteen. You will be twenty on the sixth of January, next."

"And now," she drew a deep breath, "will you tell me, please, why you have taken the trouble to find me?"

"I was about to explain. Your grandfather, Giles Murdaugh, nursed his resentment for a long time, but at last, finding himself in failing health and alone, remorse came to him, and the desire for a reconciliation with his son and daughter-in-law. This change in his sentiments took place about five years ago. We had been Mr. Murdaugh's attorneys for ten years or more and he instructed us to institute the search.

"It was a very difficult one, after the lapse of so long a period of time. In three years, however, we were able to establish the fact of Ralph Murdaugh's death, the supposition of his wife's and the fact that the child had been taken away by the gambler known only as Gentleman Geoff.

"We were inaugurating a new investigation, when Mr. Murdaugh died very suddenly. His will, which we had drawn up, directed that a large reward be offered for trace of his granddaughter, but not through the medium of the press. The entire search was conducted in a most discreet manner, I can assure you, and none of your future associates save the immediate family need know the details of this later episode, my dear young lady. I refer, of course, to the—ah, adoption.

"In the event of your being found, your late grandfather has made you his chief beneficiary, but with an absolutely irrevocable condition; that you make your home with your father's cousin—the niece whom I mentioned previously—Mrs. Ripley Halstead, and submit to being educated and trained befitting your station. A generous bequest is made also to Mrs. Halstead, providing that she agrees to undertake this charge. I may add that she has been most anxious for the conclusion of our search, and will welcome you with all her heart. I must congratulate you, my dear, on your great good fortune."

The erstwhile Billie eyed him steadily.

"Thank you, Mr. North. You were very kind to spend all that time searching for me, and to have come this long journey to tell me the truth about myself——"

"Not at all, my dear Miss Murdaugh!" The lawyer beamed. "It was a matter of business, you know, and I am gratified to have brought it to a successful conclusion, but aside from that I assure you that I am delighted to be of service."

"I can't just believe it yet; it seems as if it must be someone else that all this has happened to." She glanced at the still dumfounded Jim in an instinctive appeal. "Mr. North, if I really am awake and this is all true——"

"Yes?" he encouraged her, smiling.

"Then——" her little teeth snapped together, and a cold light flashed in her eyes—"I am sorry you have had your journey for nothing."

"You—I'm afraid I don't understand."

"Please go back, Mr. North, and tell them that Gentleman Geoff's Billie refuses to become Miss Willa Murdaugh. I don't want that wicked old man's money, I don't want anything to do with any of that breed! If those two poor young folks you tell me about were really my father and mother, he was as guilty of their deaths as if he'd shot them down in cold blood! Of course, he did not need to help them if they defied his wishes, but to starve them, to drive them from pillar to post and deny them the right to earn the money with which to live, to force other people to close their doors—oh, he wasn't square!"

"But, my dear young lady! All that was long ago, and he is dead. He regretted the past, he tried to make restitution. As an evidence of that he has made you his heiress——"

"Not if I refuse." Her tone was still quiet, but her breast rose and fell convulsively. "You said awhile ago that no one need know about my being adopted. You meant no one need know about Dad, didn't you? That I'd been brought up by a gambler in an oil-boom town? You thought I'd be ashamed of Dad among all those fine people? Why, I'm proud of him! Proud that I was known as his girl! He took me when nobody else cared whether I lived or died, and he's loved me and been everything to me ever since I can remember. And he was square! It's my own grandfather that I'm ashamed of for his crookedness! He stacked the cards, and that's all I need to know about him. Give that Mrs. Halstead what she was going to get for making me over into a lady, and tell her she needn't bother. I was raised Gentleman Geoff's Billie and that's good enough for me. I'm going to stay right here."

"You cannot realize what you are saying!" Mr. North betrayed symptoms of imminent apoplexy. "You can have no conception now of what this will mean to you in the future. Millions are involved, I tell you, millions!"

"I don't want them," she reiterated doggedly. "I don't want even the name. If I've got to have another, I'll take my mother's—Ashton, wasn't it?"

The rotund little lawyer bounced from his chair and strode up and down before the bar, his hands clenched behind his back and his mustache bristling. The girl watched him curiously, after a brief glance at Jim, who was sitting very straight, obviously fighting back the words which choked him.

There was a pause, and then North halted before her.

"I trust that you will not complicate matters by adhering to this hasty resolution, Miss Murdaugh. It is perhaps natural that you should resent the treatment accorded your parents, but the past is dead and I am convinced that when you will have had time for calm, sober reflection you will realize the absurdity of attempting to maintain your present attitude. Fortunately the decision does not rest with you. You cannot know your own mind, you are still a minor——"

"Yes." Billie acquiesced. "That was why I asked you, first off, just how old I am. You'll have a tough time trying to get me out of Mexico if I don't want to go, Mr. North. I've seen some law fights over oil leases down here and I know how cases can be strung out. I'll be of age in a year and four months and I reckon I can bluff you till then. I don't know why you should be so anxious to force that money on me and make me acknowledge myself the granddaughter of a man who didn't play fair!"

"It is entirely for your own benefit. Surely you can see that?" The lawyer spoke almost pleadingly. "It would be idiocy, madness to throw away such a fortune for a quixotic idea! You have never come into contact with young people of the class to which you really belong or you would realize all that circumstances have deprived you of heretofore."

"Oh, I've met one or two." The girl's lip curled. "There's a rich young New Yorker down here now, named Wiley——"

"Indeed? Starr Wiley?" Mr. North bit his mustache. "H'm! That is awkward, for you will inevitably encounter him again in the circle to which your cousins belong. I had hoped—ah, that you would not be hampered by associations or reminders of your former circumstances, but Mr. Wiley is a friend and I will see him——"

"Not here, you won't!" growled Jim. "He's gone."

The girl wheeled upon him, her face darkening.

"Gone where?" she demanded. "What do you mean, Jim?"

"How should I know where?" The hotel-keeper shrugged. "His hacienda is shut up tight, except for the caretaker. Reckon he's gone home for good. It wasn't none too healthy for him around here."

Billie rose and stumbled to the window. Across the plaza beyond the flower-market, the Blue Chip could be discerned in an unfamiliar aspect of transformation. Scaffolding had been erected against its walls and their cerulean expanse was being rapidly hidden beneath a coating of brick red. Her eyes blurred for a moment, then a swift hardness came into them and her small fists clenched at her sides.

"We will not discuss the matter of your inheritance, further, for the moment." The lawyer's voice, smooth as oil, came from just behind her. "You will listen to reason, I know, when you have had time for consideration. Mr. Baggott, here, will agree with me that you must accept the conditions of your grandfather's will——"

"Mr. Baggott will do nothing of the kind," vociferated that gentleman, suddenly. "I've listened to all you had to say, and kept my mouth shet, but since you're bringing me into this, you might as well know where I stand. Billie's going to do just what she damn' pleases about this. She don't need the old scoundrel's money—she's got plenty of her own, and she's not going to be shanghaied across the border while I'm here to prevent it!"

"Sir——!"

"Never mind, Jim." The girl wheeled quickly. "I've changed my mind. Mr. North, I'll go with you. I'll accept the conditions and whatever goes with them. When do we start?"

The lawyer gasped.

"Why—ah, as soon as you can arrange your affairs here. Allow me to say, my dear Miss Murdaugh, that I am delighted——"

"That's all right, Mr. North," she cut him short with a weary little gesture. "I—I guess I was kind of hasty. I've got a lot to learn, and a lot to do, and I may as well begin right away. If you don't mind, I'll ride back to the Casa de Limas now, and I'll be ready to start to-morrow morning. So long, Jim."

Avoiding the bewildered reproach in Jim Baggott's honest eyes, and unmindful of the lawyer's congratulatory hand, Gentleman Geoff's Billie turned and went out of the door. A moment later, the wild scramble of her pinto's hoofs echoed back to them from the hard-packed road.

"Women, my dear Baggott!" North shrugged expressively. "They are the curse of the law courts; they never know their own minds."

"Don't you believe it." Jim awoke from his stupor. "Billie knows her'n, all right. She's got something up her sleeve, you can bank on that, and its an ace card in whatever game she's playing. But what in tarnation the stakes are that she's after is more'n I know. I don't envy you, Mr. North, you and that lady that's going to make our Billie over. You'd better take off your coat and spit on your hands, for you've got the stiffest job ahead of you that you ever tackled. There's a joker wild, somewhere, and she's playing to win!"

CHAPTER VI

TIA JUANA'S CAULDRON COOLS

LIMASITO received the tidings of the amazing turn in the affairs of Gentleman Geoff's Billie with mingled emotions in which pride and respectful awe predominated, but to Kearn Thode it came as an uncomprehended disaster.

In vain he told himself that he should rejoice at her change of fortune; that he had divined from the moment of their first meeting the subtle shade of difference in caste between the young girl and those who surrounded her, and strove to exult that she had indeed come into her own.

A strange, unacknowledged depression assailed him. His proffered aid had once more proved superfluous; the young relative of the Ripley Halsteads and heiress of Giles Murdaugh would have no need of the good offices of his sister, nor in their reversed positions would his friendship be as instrumental in her future as he had hoped.

She was quick-witted and adaptable; she would be a tremendous social success with a little expert coaching, and he——? A petroleum engineer, a mere cog in the wheel of a great corporation, without prospects other than might lie in the success of his present doubtful mission, could be of no future interest to Willa Murdaugh.

Decency demanded that he congratulate her on her

good fortune, he assured himself as he rode out that evening to the Casa de Limas. But decency did not explain or defend the fact that he roweled his willing pinto all the way, and arrived in a state of mind that was the reverse of felicitation.

She received his forced greeting with the matter-of-fact directness which was characteristic of her.

"Yes. It's a pretty big thing to have come to me all of a sudden," she remarked, "but I reckon it isn't going to carry me off my feet. Dad always told me never to start anything I couldn't finish, and although this seems to have been kind of started for me before I was born, I reckon I can see it through. I never guessed I wasn't Dad's own girl and I'd just as lief never have known, but it's going to work in with what I want to do."

"Of course!" He essayed to speak lightly. "Your future is assured now, the future your—Gentleman Geoff wanted you to have. It sounds like presumption now; my offer to take you to my sister——"

"Why?" Her clear eyes turned wonderingly on him in the moonlight, and he mentally cursed his dog-in-the-manger mood. "I thought it was real kind of you, kinder than anything that anyone except Dad has ever done. I didn't even have a name, you know. I was just the daughter of—what did that lawyer call him?—a 'peripatetic gambler', but you—you——"

She broke off in sudden confusion, and he drew a swift breath.

"You were yourself, and I told you that nothing else mattered." His tone was very low.

"But I'm something else, now." There was a note of shy, wistful eagerness in her voice. "I—I'm Willa Murdaugh and that seems to mean a lot, up in New York. I'm not just Gentleman Geoff's Billie, I'm going to be a lady, like your sister——"

"You will be a much more important one, with a highly exalted social position and hosts of influential friends," he responded slowly. "You will meet her, she is an acquaintance of the Halsteads and their set, but you will find her a simple, unfashionable girl, compared to the rest. If you had gone to make your home with her, as I suggested, you would not have known the smart crowd that will flock about you now, but clever people who have done or are doing big things. I wonder how the social life will strike you?"

"All of a heap, I expect," she replied, absently. Her voice was colorless, stunned. "That was what you meant, that I should go and live with your sister? And you, would you have been there, too?"

"I?" he laughed with a trace of bitterness. "I am a rolling stone, Miss Murdaugh. My work calls me to the ends of the earth, but I would probably have looked in on you every few years to say 'hello.' However, you would scarcely have been with my sister as long as that. Some lucky fellow would have persuaded you to make him happy. You will be a great social success——"

"As if I cared!" She stopped him with her familiar little gesture. "I—I didn't just understand what you meant. I thought—but it doesn't matter anyway, does it? I've got to get in the game anyway, but you don't suppose I want to, do you? You don't suppose I want the money of that old man who stacked the cards against my poor father, or care about these Halstead people that never knew I was alive? I am doing it because I think

Dad would want me to, and because it will help me in something else I've set out to do."

"The thing you spoke of, that you could not let me or anyone in on?" he asked in surprise. "Haven't you relinquished it, whatever it was? You'll be too much taken up with your new life to remember old plans and ideas when you plunge into the society game."

" 'Relinquish'?" she repeated, and he saw her whole form grow tense and rigid. "Why, it's what I'm living for—what I'm going through with this inheritance outfit for! Dad said the Indians were right, they never forget a kindness or an injury. I'm like them, in that. I'll never forget, never, until the score is wiped clean!"

"Someone has hurt you?" he demanded. "You have another trouble, aside from your grief? The government will take care of El Negrito, it must be something else. Won't you tell me? It may be that I can help, in some way. I—I would do anything for you!"

"Nobody can help me." She shook her head gently. "I told you once, Mr. Thode, that I must play a lone hand."

"But you can trust me," he urged. "If I could only make you believe that! If I could only make you see how much it would mean to me to be of the slightest service——"

He halted abruptly, and she waited, scarcely breathing, for there was an impetuous fervent ring in his tones which made her heart leap suddenly and then almost cease to beat. But the young man did not continue.

"Thank you," she said at last, very quietly. "I am sure that I could trust you, Mr. Thode, but there is nothing you or anyone could do; it is just that I owe a debt to someone, and I mean to pay it. But don't let us talk of that any more. Shall I see you, sometime, up in New York?"

"Perhaps, when my work here is finished." He turned his head away from her. "You will have so many new friends that you will scarcely remember those you leave behind down here."

"How unjust you are!" She faced him hotly. "Do you think I could ever forget what you did when El Negrito came; how you rode to the barracks at the risk of your life?"

"I had small choice," he reminded her. "Had I stayed I would have been killed."

"So would we all. But it was not for yourself you took the chance, it was for us." She laid her hand upon his arm. "I—I don't want you to think that I will ever forget and I hope that we shall be friends."

"Always that!" He took her small hand in both of his. "It doesn't seem likely, but if there is ever anything that I can do for you, any service that I can render, I would like to feel, in spite of the little time you have known me, that you would call on me before anyone else you may meet. After all, Gentleman Geoff laid a charge upon me, you know, and I want to be worthy of it. When I return, if I may, I will come to you."

"Oh, will you?" She flushed and gently withdrew her hand. "That is, unless you will be ashamed of me. I reckon I'll be kind of a shock to city folks, the same as they'll be to me."

"Now it is you who are unjust!" he cried. "I shall always be proud of your friendship, and remember these days in Limasito as the most wonderful I have ever known——"

Thode checked himself once more.

"Good-bye, Billie. When next I see you, it will be Miss Willa Murdaugh who will greet me, but it is Gentleman Geoff's Billie who will linger in my thoughts always. Will you say once again what you said to me in the lane: 'Buena suerte'?"

"Good luck, with all my heart, but not good-bye." She hesitated. "I sha'n't see you to-morrow before we start?"

He shook his head.

"The whole town will be on hand to give you a send-off. I would not intrude on the leave-taking of all your old friends, and besides I must ride far out to-morrow," he prevaricated. "There is a lease I must look into for the company over near La Roda. So it must be good-bye, now."

"Not that, but hasta la vista!" She lifted her chin valiantly, although her smile was a trifle wan. "That means 'until we meet again', you know, and I feel somehow that it will be soon."

"I hope so, with all my heart!" With a swift, impetuous movement he bent and kissed her hand. "Hasta la vista!"

Billie watched him until he disappeared down the avenue of flowering trees, then, brushing her hand across her eyes, she turned and went into the house.

Sallie Bailey looked up with a twinkle from the shirt she was patching.

"Well, carita, did he?" she demanded with much interest.

"Did he what?" Billie paused at the foot of the stairs.

"Did he—say anything?"

"Oh, a heap. I'm going to be a hit in society and forget all my friends and everything down here and roll in that money like a pinto in the pasture. I wish to goodness that I was dead!"

"No, you don't," Sallie retorted comfortably. "You're just beginning to take notice, that's all, and so's he. He ain't saddle-broke yet and he's gun-shy, but he'll get used to the report o' that money o' yours in time. Men are a good deal like pintos; some you can coax and some you can bully, but they all of 'em buck at the first gate. Don't you worry your head about Mr. Kearn Thode, honey; wait till the next round-up, and you'll have him roped, tied, and branded before he knows where he's at."

Billie mounted three steps and halted, her head held high.

"Him?" she queried with infinite scorn. "I don't want him! Dad asked him to look out for me, you see, and he thinks I'm kind of on his hands, but I'll show him! I'm liable to make some big mistakes, and I reckon that Mrs. Halstead will earn all the money my grandfather left her to teach me the rules of the game, but I'll sit tight and learn if it breaks me and when it comes my turn to play, I'll show them all I'm not a piker, anyway!"

"You wasn't ever that, Billie," the older woman observed gently, for the girl's hurt heart was on her sleeve. "I reckon he only meant to be kind."

"I don't want kindness!" the ungrateful Billie responded savagely. "I don't want condescension and duty-friendship. I want, I want—oh, I want Dad!"

Limasito was indeed out in full force to speed her on her way the following morning. The news had traveled quickly over the countryside and every style of conveyance, from a mule-team to the latest improved jitney, lined the plaza. White, Mex', and Mongolian, from the richest oil operator to the lowliest peon, her friends had gathered to say farewell.

They stampeded her on the Calle Rivera and unceremoniously held up Mr. North's impressive car before the hotel, while Jim Baggott, in an ancient silk hat and bibulously primed for the occasion, read an ungrammatical but fervent valediction.

Billie could only throw both hands out to them, laughing and sobbing in one breath as the car moved off down a lane of solidly packed humanity and disappeared in a whirl of dust.

" 'S on the house!" Jim Baggott waved toward the bar with one hand and openly wiped his eyes with the other. "Gonna make a gosh-almighty swell of her, are they? Well, I wish'm luck, but they'll never change her heart or break her spirit. She's our'n, an' she'll come back if I have to go after her myself, so help me! What you-all have?"

True to his word, Kearn Thode had ridden out at daybreak and ridden hard, but only the pinto knew where they were going and he was too jaded to care. A sleepless night of bewilderment and self-disgust at his own surly, unaccountable mood had brought a revelation that stunned and humbled him.

He loved her! In a blinding flash of realization, he saw that from the moment of their first meeting she had possessed him, body and soul. It was that which had stirred his resentment to berserk rage when Starr Wiley had laid insolent hands upon her in the lane; it was for

her and her alone that he had run the gantlet of El
Negrito's forces and dared the desperate ride.

And she? Immeasurably removed from him now,
impenetrably walled in from his presumptuous gaze by
the newly-gained inheritance, there was yet a golden key
which he might find here in this flower-grown wilderness
which would grant him entrance to her world on an equal
footing with all men. She could not have learned to care
for him in their few hours of companionship, but at least
no one else held claim to her. There was still a chance!

It was characteristic of him that, having worked out his
problem, he wasted no thought on futile regret or selfish
repining at the fortune which had smiled on her. It
should smile on him, too, and then, and not till then, he
would go to her.

The Pool of the Lost Souls! That was the solution,
that the golden key to the future! That others had been
before him in the fruitless search of weary generations
past was of no moment in the fire of his enthusiasm.

The noontide blaze of heat found him many miles
upon an unfamiliar road, and, heedless of lurking enemies
in the undergrowth, he flung himself down in the shade
of a mighty orchid-laden tree, while the puzzled but
equable pinto grazed nearby.

Worn with the emotional conflict through which he had
passed, and the sleepless night preceding the hard-ridden
hours, his day-dream faded into deep slumber and the
shadows were slanting across the road when he awoke
with a sudden start. No living thing was in sight save
the pinto tethered close at hand; the road ran level and
white and deserted as far as the eye could see and only
the afternoon breeze rustled the dense foliage above and

about him, yet Thode could have sworn that he was under observation.

He flung the thought from him with a laugh as he picked himself up, but it persisted in spite of his efforts to exorcise it. Something unexplained but almost tangible rode at his shoulder on the homeward way, and he caught himself more than once straining his ears for a betraying sound behind him. So acute was the sensation of surveillance that he pulled up abruptly around a sharp turn in the road and listened, but no following hoof-beats broke the stillness, and mentally deriding the notion, he cantered on into town.

His mid-day reverie had carried him back over every detail of the legend Ben Hallock had related of the Pool, and one chance remark returned to him with the force of an inspiration. Hallock himself had learned the story from a hunchbacked Mexican who had it from his grandmother, and the little José, the crippled victim of Starr Wiley's heedless brutality, had been hunchbacked; the old crone in the shack by the zapote trees, his grandmother, looked as if many mysteries and legends might be hidden behind her fierce, inscrutable eyes.   .

This was slender foundation on which to build a theory, but how else had the little lad awakened the vengeful antipathy of Wiley? What was it that he refused to tell him?

Thode had more than a suspicion that Wiley's objective in Limasito was closely allied to his own. If José had indeed been Hallock's informant, and the unscrupulous promoter had traced the legend to this latest source, his anger at being unable to bully the boy into further disclosures would be easily understood.

That night, when the moon had risen, Thode crossed the plaza and started out on foot for the shack. He would not allow himself a glance in the direction of the metamorphosed Blue Chip, but resolutely held his thoughts to the immediate issue. José had accepted him not only as a benefactor but as the friend of his adored señorita; would he be induced to speak?

The shack was dark when he finally reached it and only silence greeted his knock upon the sagging door. It yielded to his touch, and after a moment's hesitation he stepped inside, and groping, found the lamp.

Touching a match to the wick, he replaced the cracked chimney and looked about him. Gone!

The little one-room dwelling was in chaos, the chest of drawers ransacked and even the two poor beds had been pulled violently apart. Everything spoke of hasty and frenzied flight. What could it mean?

As the young engineer stood bewildered at this unexpected scene, there came over his senses once more the inexplicable intuition of the afternoon. Someone, something was spying upon him!

He thrust it into the back of his mind, however, striving to recall a memory which eluded him. What had Billie told him of a witch's cauldron in the grove of zapote trees, where the old crone had wrought magic which to her, at least, was very real? Could the explanation of this amazing evanescence be found there?

Shading the lamp with his hand, he stumbled out the door and followed the weed-choked path to the little clearing. A huge battered kettle lay on its side in a heap of ashes which looked as though they had recently been alight. Thode stirred them with his foot, then bent hastily; they were still warm, and from their midst protruded a gleam of something white.

Kneeling, he set the lamp carefully upon the ground beside him and pulled the scrap of paper from its hiding-place. It was partially burned, but some freak of air-current or flame had left its destruction incomplete, and he saw that a rude plan or map had been drawn upon it.

He had only time to note that an irregular oval was traced in its center, with a crooked, wavering cross at one end. Then as he bent closer to the light a twig snapped treacherously behind him and a crushing blow upon his head blotted out consciousness.

CHAPTER VII

Alien Kin

MR. MASON NORTH'S elation at the culmination of his protracted search gave way to vague but undeniable misgiving before the end of the return journey. Miss Murdaugh was utterly unlike anything he could have preconceived. His trained legal mind, unburdened with imagination, had nevertheless presented possibilities, during the two years of his previous investigation, from which his fastidious soul shrank. What could a creature brought up by a wandering card-sharp in mining-camps and frontier towns offer for rescue and redemption?

His fears had vanished at first sight of her, however. Here was a girl, untutored and unconventional, to be sure, but singularly free from any corruption and with distinct social possibilities.

He patronized her in bland condescension at their journey's start and found her gratifyingly amenable, but they had scarcely crossed the border, before he found to his stupefaction that he was confronted by a will as serenely implacable as his own.

Willa listened to his didactic suggestions with an open mind and a direct unwavering gaze which he found mildly disconcerting, but she acted upon them only after due and independent consideration and those that did not meet with her approval she rejected in a quiet finality of manner which, while it left their surface cordiality undisturbed, nevertheless brooked no further argument.

His idea of engaging a maid or chaperon for the trip she had vetoed promptly.

"I've always looked out for myself, and I reckon I can now, so long as you're around to see that the train don't get uncoupled while you're in the smoker or I'm in the observation car," she informed him. "I have to kind of get on to myself, after all that's been happening to me, and I couldn't with some nosey Jane at my heels every minute. I suppose there will have to be someone to shine up my nails and fix my hair and cinch my clothes on me, but that can wait till Mrs. Halstead picks one out."

Mr. North shrank from such unfeminine candor, but he made no further reference to a duenna, although as the journey progressed he regretted his weakness. Willa had an inexplicable penchant for disappearing at intervals, suddenly and without warning. Where she could get to on a train or station platform, from under his very eyes, and what errand prompted her were beyond his comprehension; but she eluded him with the utmost ease and sang-froid whenever the spirit moved her, and her matter-of-fact explanations when she returned were obviously and designedly open to question.

He could feel himself aging beneath the strain and he heartily wished his charge in Mrs. Halstead's capable hands. His wife had been dead so long that the paths of feminine idiosyncrasies were an untrodden maze to him, and his condescension turned to consternation and an awed respect.

In spite of his anxiety, the girl proved a fascinating study. She showed no interest in the outside world and rarely glanced from the car window, but her naïve curiosity concerning their fellow passengers and friendly familiarity toward them kept him constantly on the qui vive.

It was only when at last their journey drew to a close that she evinced the slightest desire for information concerning the family of which she was to be a member.

"Mrs. Halstead is my father's cousin, isn't she?" she asked. "Has she any children?"

"A son and daughter." Mr. North laid aside the newspaper from behind which he had been furtively watching her. "Vernon is twenty-three, and a friend of my boy, Winthrop. Angelica is two years his junior, a most accomplished young woman and quite a leader in the more youthful set. You will be able to learn a great deal from her."

Willa pondered this in silence for a minute or two.

"What does she do?" she queried, finally.

"Why—ah, she drives her own car, and goes in for all the latest fads and diversions. I am not familiar with them myself. She sings and dances——"

"My mother did that," Willa remarked, with a quizzical glance at him.

Mr. North reddened.

"Oh, not——not in that fashion! I mean for charity; war relief and that sort of thing. Quite respectable and praiseworthy."

"I see," said Willa slowly. "It's only proper when you do it for nothing, just because you like it. If it's work, it isn't nice."

Her interlocutor writhed, but cannily forbore argument. He had learned more valuable pointers in the past

few days on the matter of rebuttal than Blackstone ever
revealed to him.

"And the boy, Vernon. What does he do?" Willa
resumed.

"He motors and plays golf and tennis." Mr. North
cast wildly about in his mind for an inspiration. What
did the young beggar do, anyway, that would meet with
the approval of this socialistic Amazon? "Cards, too.
He's an inveterate—I mean, enthusiastic, card-player."

Willa rewarded his efforts with a wriggle of interest.

"Monte, stud or blackjack?" she demanded. "What's
his limit? Good loser?"

"Very!" The family lawyer was on solid ground here.
"In fact I may say the best and most consistent loser I
have knowledge of. It has not been decided yet what—
ah, field of industry he will enter. He is just out of the
university."

"There's a Mr. Halstead, I suppose?"

"Yes, of course. He is the first vice-president of the
Vitality and Casualty Insurance Company, and director
in several banks and corporations. A very busy man and
an important, influential one."

"What does he do that he likes?" Willa persisted, unim-
pressed.

"Bless me, I haven't an idea! I've known him for a
quarter of a century, but I've never heard him discuss
anything except finance."

"And Mrs. Halstead?"

"Ah, my dear, there is a character for you!" Mr.
North beamed. "She's chairman of a dozen charity
organizations, leader in every new movement that
appears, and manages to find ample time for her social

duties, besides. A wonderful woman! You are fortunate in having her for your sponsor and mentor, and I—
ah, I trust that you will follow her directions in all
things. You must show your appreciation of her kindness in taking you into her home and making you one of
themselves by obeying her without question. Her experience and knowledge of the world will be invaluable to
you."

The swift roar of the train into the tunnel precluded
comment from his charge, and in the vast station she
vanished once more. This time she remained absent for
so long that the distracted attorney was on the point of
despatching a battalion of porters to search for her when
she reappeared, slightly flushed but serene.

"In heaven's name, where have you been?" Mr. North
demanded testily. "How many times have I instructed
you to remain close at my side when we alight!"

"I knew where you were, you see," she exclaimed
calmly. "There was something I had to attend to."

"Telegrams to your friends? Surely they might have
waited until a more suitable time! You have caused me
great anxiety——"

"I'm sorry if I worried you, Mr. North." Her tone
was chastened, but there was an undernote of warning.
"I've been free so long that I kind of forget I'm under
extradition."

A wave of contrition swept over his ill-humor as her
slim-clad figure preceded him out to the waiting motor.
She had been coolly insubordinate, of course, but she was
young and very much alone in a strange environment.
She could be led, perhaps, but she would never be driven.

Cesare, the Halsteads' chauffeur, touched the brim of

his cap smartly, and Willa bestowed upon him a dazzling smile. Only the snap of the limousine door prevented her shaking hands.

"He looks like a right-nice boy," she remarked naïvely. "Do you suppose he'll teach me how to drive a car of my own?"

"If he is told to do so," Mr. North replied with dignity, "and it is decided that you are to have a car."

She darted an appraising glance at him, but he vaguely felt a certain ambiguous quality in the silence which followed, and congratulated himself that they had reached their journey's end.

Mrs. Ripley Halstead awaited them in the drawing-room. She was a tall, commanding woman in the indefinite forties, with a high, thin nose and cold, slightly protruding eyes. Her dark hair, still untouched by gray, was arranged in a modishly severe fashion and her smile extended no farther than her straight lips.

"So this is our little cousin?" She brushed the girl's cheek with a light kiss. "My dear Willa, words cannot express our pleasure that you have been found at last, we have doubted and feared for so long. I hope that you will be very happy here with us, and I am sure that we shall all manage famously."

"Thank you," Willa murmured, through stiffened lips. "This situation has been kind of thrust on both of us, but I reckon we can make the best of it."

The lady gasped and turned to the attorney, who was watching with a gleam of speculation in his eye.

"Mason, we have much to thank you for in restoring our young relative to us, but I must defer that now. You will dine with us?"

"Thank you, no." He bowed over her hand. "To tell you the truth, I am rather fagged out from my trip, and I am anxious to get on up-town. Please, tell Ripley that I will see him to-morrow, and transfer the necessary papers to him.—Au revoir, my dear. Try to remember what I have told you."

Willa stared with dazed eyes about the pretty room to which she was ushered. The furniture was of ivory and dull gold, the walls, draperies and floor a soft French blue, and delicate rose-shaded lights glowed delicately in many brackets.

The drawing-room she had taken as a matter of course; it impressed her as being not unlike that of the big hotel at Tampico, but to be expected to live and move around and sleep in this fragile, stifling, cluttered doll's house of a room was unthinkable. It was hers, the maid had said so; therefore, she would make the best of it, in her own fashion.

A half-hour later the house-maid presented herself at Mrs. Halstead's door in a state bordering on hysteria.

"If you please, Madame, the young lady, Miss Murdaugh, has taken her room all to pieces. The draperies are down from the windows and piled in a corner with the cushions from the chaise longue, and the bed is moved over to the windows and stripped down to the blanket. All the rose shades are off the lights and the furniture is pushed back against the wall. Miss Murdaugh rang for me just now to take all the drapery and things out of the room, and I thought I had better come to you."

Mrs. Halstead stepped forward, but stopped with a slight compression of her lips.

"Very well, Katie. You may remove them, for the time being. I will see Miss Murdaugh about it later."

When the housemaid had withdrawn, her mistress dropped rather than seated herself in the nearest chair. The mechanical smile had vanished and her eyes narrowed. She foresaw friction ahead.

Willa, serenely unconscious that she had offended, slipped into the one thin black gown which she possessed, a mail-order purchase which had given her immense satisfaction, but when dinner was announced and she descended the stairs, she paused aghast at the splendor before her.

A girl stood in the drawing-room door in a marvelous creation which seemed made of diamond-tipped, rainbow-tinted mist. From it her youthful shoulders and slim neck rose creamily, surmounted by a small head banded boyishly with golden hair. Her wide eyes were china blue, her nose piquantly retroussé and she was as vacuously pretty as a wax doll.

"How do you do?" She came forward with a graceful fluttering movement. "You are Willa, aren't you? I hope we are going to be terribly good friends. I'm your cousin, Angelica."

"Named after a dessert." A languid, teasing voice came from behind her. "Welcome to our city, my dear cousin! Hope you won't find us too peaceable after Mexico."

"No fear!" The doll-like eyes snapped dangerously. "This is my brother Vernon, Willa. Mother will be down in a moment."

Willa had suffered herself to be pecked at by the other girl's perfumed lips, and now she took the hand of the dapper youth who confronted her. He was fair like his sister, but the resemblance ended there. His nose was long and sharp, his forehead slanting, his close-set eyes a greenish-gray. She wondered how anything human could look so like a fox, as she returned his quizzical stare with a direct, level one, and relinquished his hand.

"I'm pleased to meet you," she remarked simply, and noted the quick flash of amusement which passed from brother to sister. "I reckon I can stand a little peace and quiet, after what I've been through lately. I don't hardly know where I'm at, yet."

Vernon's mouth twisted suddenly as he turned away, and Angelica responded in obvious haste.

"Yes, I imagine you do feel rather upset. Mr. North must have seemed like a fairy godfather when he appeared with his astounding news for you."

"A fairy godfather? He's kind of a hefty one, isn't he?" Willa smiled, adding quickly: "He was real kind on the trip coming up; didn't seem like he could do enough for me, but I reckon he was glad to get me here at last."

"As we are to have you, my dear." A mild, genial voice sounded from the stairs' foot, and the three young people turned. "Let me welcome you to your home. We hope to make up to you for being exiled for so long from it."

A tall, iron-gray head bent, and Willa found herself gazing into keen, kindly eyes. Her own blurred as her hand rested between those of Ripley Halstead and something seemed to grip her by the throat. Gentleman Geoff's face swam for a moment before her in a mist of tears.

She essayed an unintelligible phrase, and perceiving her emotion, he tactfully covered it.

"You must be starved; I know we are. Children, where's your mother? After dinner we must have a little talk, eh? There will be so much for you to do and see that we shall have to plan out a sort of campaign.— Oh, there you are, Irene!"

Willa's secret anxiety as to forks being allayed by the discovery that service was laid for but one course at a time, she was able to give herself up during the meal to a frank study of her new-found relatives. She was going to like Ripley Halstead; already liked him, and each passing moment confirmed her first opinion. Concerning the others, she was not so sure. There was a mental reservation behind Mrs. Halstead's surface cordiality, and the bewitching Angelica seemed too seraphically sweet and gentle to ring quite true. Vernon was a type with which in a more crude stratum of humanity she had become familiar in the gaming-rooms of the Blue Chip. Weak without being absolutely vicious, crafty without initiative, he would be a mere tool in dominant unscrupulous hands or an average, decent fellow if his better instincts were aroused.

Dinner over, they repaired to the drawing-room, but the little family gathering soon disintegrated, to Willa's profound relief.

Angelica flitted away to a dance, Vernon betook himself to his club and Mr. Halstead, forgetting his expressed intention of a talk with her, shut himself in his study. When she found herself alone with her hostess, Willa mentally braced her nerves for a cross-examination, but the ordeal was deferred.

"My dear, you must be quite worn out. We have much to talk over, for we must all readjust ourselves, and become really acquainted, but you must rest first, and accustom yourself to your new surroundings." Mrs. Halstead smiled. "I am sorry you did not like your room! I had planned it very carefully for you."

"Oh!" Willa cried, in quick dismay. "I didn't know! It was awfully pretty, but I'm used to air and space and I didn't feel like I could breathe in it. I'll put them back to-morrow, and try it, all those hangings and things, if you say so."

"No, you shall have your own room arranged as you please. You will soon grow accustomed to pretty things. We must get rid of that somber mourning at once, and plan a suitable wardrobe."

"But——" Willa paused in dismay. "Maybe Mr. North didn't tell you. I—I have lost someone who was all the world to me! I feel somehow that I couldn't give up the black, not yet anyway. It would look as if I wanted folks to think I'd forgotten——"

"I understand. You refer to your former guardian? But, my dear, that life is behind you now, and you must put everything from your thoughts but the future and what we are all going to help you make of it."

Willa rose.

"You are all very kind," she said in a stifled voice. "I'm bound to be a heap of nuisance to you, I'm afraid, though I made up my mind not to buck the game strong till I'd learned the rules. But don't ask me to be a piker and forget Dad! You don't know what he was to me! I appreciate what you-all are trying to do, Mrs. Halstead, and I sympathize with you, for it's going to be a tough job all around, no matter how I try to follow your lead, but don't stack the cards on the first deal, please. All

I've got in the world now is my memory of the best friend that ever lived!"

"Your loyalty is very touching, dear child, and I would be the last to impugn it." Mrs. Halstead put two rigid dutiful arms about her. "Your clothes are a mere detail which we will take up later. You must go to bed now, and sleep."

Willa stumbled from the room with a sense of baffled defeat as if she had incontinently butted against a wall of granite. Her aching heart cried out for familiar things and faces, but she steeled herself valiantly. She must play the game!

CHAPTER VIII

WILLA SITS IN

"WELL, what do you think of her?" Mason North's eyes twinkled as he put the question to the Ripley Halsteads in solemn conference on the following evening.

"A very interesting young woman," Halstead replied emphatically. "She's refreshingly genuine and original, in this artificial, cut-and-dried age."

Mrs. Halstead shuddered.

"Aboriginal, I should say," she murmured. "And quite astonishingly impervious to the social amenities."

"I gathered that, myself," Mason North nodded. "I talked to her till I was blue in the face, but unless she could see a direct reason for doing a thing, or not doing it, she followed her own instinct."

"It wouldn't lead her far wrong," declared Halstead. "She may lack the minor hypocrisies, but she'll wall herself in with them soon enough, the Lord knows. She's willing to listen to reason, that's something.

"The life down there may have been rough, but it has not destroyed her native fineness and high principle. I don't say that I should care to have Angie go through such an experience, but it might have made a man of Vernon to buck up against it. Look at young Thode!"

"Kearn Thode?" The attorney glanced up quickly. "I thought he was out West?"

"No. Larkin tells me he sent him to Mexico a few months ago. I wonder if Willa happened to run across him? He's a splendid fellow and Larkin banks on his judgment and efficiency. That's the sort of life to bring out the best in a man, or a woman either, to judge from our small cousin. I like her independence, I don't mind telling you. It shows self-reliance and strength."

"But Willa has not the slightest idea of obligation," his wife remarked. "She seems rather to look on the situation as one for mutual commiseration. Any other poor, neglected, friendless creature from the backwoods would be transported into the seventh heaven at such great good fortune, but she accepts it as a more or less onerous duty."

"You wouldn't call her exactly friendless if you had witnessed the parting ovation she received; the whole town turned out. She's more than a popular favorite down there, she's an idol. Everyone seems to worship her, down to the lowest half-breed. If we handle her right, I shouldn't wonder if she turns out to be a mighty-fine woman."

"If we do?" Mrs. Halstead raised her eyebrows. "Perhaps you have some method to suggest. I admit that for the moment I am baffled. She refused flatly last night to go out of mourning, and I was really thankful for it after reflection; we can at least keep her in the background now, until I have succeeded in eliminating some of those frightful gambling expressions from her vocabulary. She seems to have been passionately fond of the impossible person who brought her up. I shudder to think of the impression she would make now on our circle of friends. She doesn't seem in the least ashamed of her past environment, or desirous of concealing her connection with such a character."

The attorney chuckled.

"I wouldn't advise you to tackle that subject for awhile," he said. "You ought to have heard the flaying she gave me when I suggested that no one but the immediate family need know about her foster father. Her opinion of her respected grandfather, in comparison with Gentleman Geoff, was illuminating."

He gave them the gist of it, and Mrs. Halstead listened with tightened lips.

"I shall tell Willa quite plainly that we and our friends are not interested in her past but only in what she is and may become. She appears to have at least a glimmering of sense and she must soon perceive for herself how disgraceful the whole unfortunate affair would seem to outsiders." She paused. "There is something that I do not quite understand about Willa. You are sure, Mason, that she has no vulgar, clandestine affair on her hands?"

"Good heavens, I should hope not! We've got enough to contend with as things stand without that." The attorney bounced forward in his chair. "What on earth put such an idea into your head, my dear Irene?"

"She was already in the breakfast-room when I came down this morning, and I thought she looked remarkably fresh, but with these naturally pale people you never can tell." Mrs. Halstead, too, leaned forward impressively. "Willa said nothing about having been out, and naturally such a possibility never occurred to me, but Welsh tells me she drove up in a taxi-cab at half-past nine. She must have slipped out very early, for he did not see her go."

"Surely you questioned her?" her husband asked. North was speechless.

"'She had been out to take a look about the city.'" Mrs. Halstead shrugged. "She hadn't thought it worth while mentioning; she had always gone and come as she pleased."

"Exactly the same stall she gave me!" the attorney exploded. "We'd better look into this, for she gave me the slip half a dozen times on the train and in stations and I never could get any satisfaction out of her."

"I explained that young ladies did not go about alone in that fashion, at least unless their families knew and sanctioned it, and I pointed out the danger of losing her way. She promised to be more careful another time, but her manner was ambiguous, to say the least. She may have privately intended to be careful lest her future expeditions be discovered, but I have arranged to circumvent that. Whatever we do, we must have no breath of gossip until she is firmly established."

If Willa was aware of the respectful surveillance to which she was subjected thereafter she made no sign, possibly because she eluded it whenever she felt inclined with the utmost ease, and no tales were carried back. The servants beneath Mrs. Halstead's iron rule were too fearful of losing their positions to admit a failure of duty unless they were cornered and secretly they sympathized with the strange young lady. Thus Willa came and went as her pleasure dictated in the early-morning hours.

Her first real clash came during a discussion of finances with the attorney and Ripley Halstead. The latter had insisted on showing her exactly how the fortune left her by her grandfather was being manipulated for her interests, and she listened in grave attention. When the matter was concluded, Mr. North cleared his throat with a nervous but ingratiating smile.

"Now, my dear, I think we should come to an understanding about your other inheritance; that left to you by—ah, Gentleman Geoff. Mr. Baggott, the executor, informed me that the sale of your foster father's establishment alone netted two hundred thousand dollars and there are other securities and bank deposits, besides. He very ill-advisedly turned them over to you, but you, of course, cannot think of handling such a sum on your own initiative. It must be invested under mature judgment, and you are still a minor. If you will place the necessary deeds and memoranda in our hands——"

"I am not a minor under Mexican law." Willa bent a steady gaze upon him. "Dad trusted me with absolute control and I'm going to play a lone hand as far as that money is concerned, Mr. North. You can tie as many strings as you please to the Murdaugh fortune, I'm not worrying about that; I have enough without it, and what I've got I'm going to keep."

"Little cousin, that would be impossible." Halstead shook his head. "I would not interfere in any way with your personal liberty, but this is a matter in which you must defer to your proper guardians. You are incapable of managing it alone, and it is unthinkable that you should try."

"I'm very sorry, Cousin Ripley; I seem to be saying that all the time, don't I?" She smiled faintly, but her little chin was set in determined lines. "You may not have known it, but I've banked and invested Dad's money—and speculated with it, too—for the last three

years, and he always said he would trust my judgment
before any hombre in Mexico. I know you don't like
me to speak of Dad, but I only wanted you to know
that I'm really quite capable."

"Willa, my dear—" began Halstead, but the lawyer
stopped him with a gesture.

"Do you realize that we can have the entire estate
taken out of your hands by process of law and turned
over to us as your guardians? We most certainly shall,
if you persist, in order to protect you against your own
wilful recklessness. My dear, you will not force us to
such a disagreeable and expensive step? You are not
going to disappoint us by proving ungrateful for the
interest we have taken in you?"

"I am not ungrateful!" she cried passionately. "I
know you are all trying to help me and look out for me,
and I am thankful. I—I can't give up the control of
my own money, for I may have to use it. It's really
mine, Dad gave it to me, and I'm not going to have to
ask for it when I want it, or explain what I want it
for. If you try to take it from me, I'll have to fight
for it. Everyone in Limasito will back me up, and the law
down there is on their side and mine, remember. Everything else is in your hands and I am grateful to you
for taking care of it, but Dad's money isn't part of the
Murdaugh outfit, and I mean to keep it for myself."

No further argument could avail to move her an iota
from her position and the matter perforce rested, but
when the two men were alone together, Ripley Halstead
looked at his attorney with a troubled question in his
eyes.

North nodded solemnly.

"It's blackmail!" he announced. "She's paying hush-money to someone and planning flight if the truth, what-ever it may be, is discovered. Why else would she insist on retaining control of the money she considers peculiarly her own? I thought I had learned every detail of the past, and that her life was an open book, but you never can tell. There may have been some foolish romance or entanglement—"

"No." Halsted shook his head. "You're on the wrong track there, I'm sure of it. Willa is too high-minded to compromise herself, and level-headed enough to be safe from sentimental folly under any circumstances. If she had become involved in any difficulty, you can bank on it that she would come out with the truth, straight from the shoulder; she would be the last person in the world to allow herself to be intimidated. She may be being bled through pity or a mistaken sense of loyalty, but I don't see what we can do now to stop it."

"The first step will be to discover what her game is." The attorney chuckled ruefully. "To use her own par-lance, Ripley, that young woman called my bluff, and her cards are high. Litigation would be a wearisome business and we couldn't buck her crowd down there. She'd have the executor, Baggott, appointed as trustee of the old gambler's estate, and he would be wax in her hands. We can only watch her, and try to prevent her doing anything foolishly quixotic."

The next day Willa paid her first visit to a famous modiste in Mrs. Halstead's company, and returned ex-hausted but impressed. The latent feminine instinct for adornment had taken possession of her and through the long evening she dreamed in a hazy rapture. The motive

which had so far actuated her on her course was temporarily laid aside and in its stead came vague scenes of
the future, when she should have learned how to carry
those marvelous creations with the trained ease and
elegance of Angelica, and was wholly transformed from
the plain, awkward creature of the Limasito days. Perhaps, when Kern Thode came to New York—

A sudden sound, subdued but unmistakably familiar,
roused her from her reverie. What could it mean? She
sprang from her chair and stood listening intently. The
family were supposed to have gone to a dinner-party,
yet from somewhere above had come a chorus of male
laughter, and down the stairs to her opened door echoed
the rattle and clink of poker chips.

Willa crept out to the hall wistfully, drawn by the
well-remembered sound as by a magnet, and step by
step ascended the stairs. A door at the left was ajar
and through it came a warm ray of light and the odor
of cigarettes.

"If that wasn't a hunch, I'll eat my shirt!" A buoyant
voice exulted. "Stuck two raises before the draw and
then filled an inside straight! What do you call it?"

"Lunacy, even if it did break for you," Vernon
drawled. "You ought to be shot at sunrise. No more
post-mortems. Ante up there, Cal."

Willa tiptoed to the door and peered within. Vernon
and four strange young men were seated about a table
in the center of the room, which was evidently a den or
study.

Vernon was dealing, and his neighbor at the left sat
with his back squarely to the door. Over his shoulder,
Willa could see his cards as he picked them up; an ace,

king, ten, jack, and another king. He refused to open, but the downy-mustached boy on his left, whose voice Willa had first heard, performed that service. The other two strangers stayed out, Vernon trailed and Willa eyed the slim, dark youth whose hand she could see in fascinated suspense.

"Mine are punk." He yawned indifferently, and threw his cards down upon the table.

The eavesdropper gasped, but watched with narrowed eyes as his tapering fingers lingered, gathering up and sorting the discards with studied listlessness.

The opener checked, the boy next raised him two and Vernon dropped.

"Brace of manicurists!" The first boy showed his openers ruefully. "Couldn't better 'em. It's all yours, Art."

The dark youth shuffled the cards twice dexterously and dealt. This time he held four kings and a seven.

"Go to it, Winnie," he said lazily.

"No, thanks." Winnie shook his head. "The tall grass for mine."

His neighbor refused likewise, but the lad with the tortoise-rimmed glasses next Vernon straightened involuntarily.

"I'll open it." His voice trembled.

"Good-night!" Vernon dropped his cards as if they burned him. "Sure you're looking at 'em straight, Pete?"

"Come again." The dealer shoved two blues out on the board.

"Back to you." The opener's fingers twitched as he dropped four.

"Once more."

"And two."

"That's enough for me." The dealer shrugged, and pushed forward two chips more.

The others sat in wordless enthrallment as Pete stood pat and the dealer, with a smile, laid down the pack untouched. The betting proceeded cautiously at first, then by leaps and bounds as Pete lost his head and plunged wildly.

A small mountain of blue chips lay in the center of the table, and the dark, smiling youth seemed prepared to raise it indefinitely, when Pete sighed and drew his hand before his blurred eye-glasses.

"Call you!" he squeaked. "What you got, Cal?"

The dealer spread his hand out upon the board and his opponent emitted a moan of anguish as the four kings were exposed.

"And I opened—*opened* mind you, with four messenger boys, pat!"

Willa did not wait for the buzz of excited comment. Instead she turned and sped noiselessly down the stair to her room. When she reappeared a few moments later she wore a corsage bunch of violets which stuck out oddly from her black gown, and carried a jingling purse.

Ascending once more, she tapped at the door and then slipped shyly in.

"Excuse me!" she said to the open-mouthed group who rose as one man. "I heard the game going on and I thought maybe you'd let me sit in for a round or two. It isn't just regular, I know, but if you won't tell, *I* won't."

"Willa!" Vernon's face was crimson. "I—I'm quite sure mother wouldn't approve of——"

"Of the game?" she smiled. "Who's going to carry

tales, if I don't? I reckon you've forgotten to introduce your friends."

"Forgive me." Vernon gathered his wits together with an obvious effort, and complied. The loser of the last phenomenal hand, she learned, was Peter Follinsbee, his right-hand neighbor Arthur Judson, and "Winnie" proved to be the son whom Mason North had mentioned. His was the voice she had first heard, and she shook hands cordially with him, but merely bowed to the slim, dark youth, whose name was Calvert Shirley.

"My—my cousin, Miss Murdaugh." Vernon finished, adding desperately: "Really, Willa, I'm sorry, but it's out of the question——"

"Vernie, have a heart! We'd all be delighted if Miss Murdaugh will join us!" Winnie's eyes twinkled with mischief. "We're only playing a ten-cent limit, Miss Murdaugh, if you're familiar with the game——"

"I'm on speaking terms with it," Willa nodded. "Ten-*dollar* limit you mean, don't you, Mr. North? I'm right here with you."

"Oh, I say!" Follinsbee blinked deprecatingly. "We couldn't allow a lady to play such a stiff game with all of us——"

"Son," Willa admonished him, "I've bucked a game that hit the skies more than once, so don't you worry about me. Who's banking?"

"Oh, all right, if you really want to," Vernon capitulated, in deadly fear of further revelations. "Only keep mum about it or there'll be the very deuce to pay."

Willa seated herself between "Pete" Follinsbee and "Art" Judson, directly across the table from "Cal" Shirley, and the game recommenced.

Winnie Mason looked upon her advent as a huge joke, but the others were plainly ill at ease, until a hand or two showed them that they were in the presence of a sure and expert player.

If she realized their stupefaction at the unexpected materialization in their midst of the mysterious and much heralded Miss Murdaugh she gave no sign, but played conservatively, her eyes always upon the slim, agile fingers of her vis-à-vis.

His deal came and passed without incident, but when the round of the table had been made once more, and Vernon dealt, Cal Shirley again refused to open and dropped out.

Willa, with a pair of aces, did likewise, and watched him gather up her hand with his own and the other discards.

Vernon crowed triumphantly as he raked in the pot, but Willa scarcely heard. One hand had flown to the violets at her belt, and she waited, tense and motionless, until Shirley had shuffled and lifted the top card to deal.

Then there came a sinuous, silken rustle; fingers like steel wires tore the pack from his grasp and he found himself looking into the mouth of a small but eminently practical revolver.

"Hands up, you yellow son of a Greaser!" Willa's voice rang out above the amazed gasp which ran around the table. "I saw you running up the hands before when you cleaned Mr. Follinsbee on four planted jacks. That's why I eased myself into the game."

Shirley obeyed, with a sickly smile.

"Really, this is most extraordinary!" he drawled. "Is

your charming cousin about to entertain us with a bit of wild-West melodrama, Vernie?"

"No," Willa interposed. "I'm going to show you what we do with a crook below the border.—Mr. North, will you take this pack and deal face up for Mr. Shirley? You'll find that somebody will have a hand to go the limit on, but our friend over there will top him, pat."

Mechanically, Winnie North complied, and, in a silence broken only by the whispering fall of the cards, he dropped before Willa herself a king full, and at the erstwhile dealer's place, four damning eights.

"You infernal scoundrel!" They were all on their feet, but it was Vernon's voice which rumbled in unexpected strength. "If my cousin weren't here, I'd thrash you within an inch of your life!"

"Don't mind me!" The revolver wavered regretfully in Willa's fingers. "I'd have winged him at the start, but I reckon shooting don't go in New York. I'll take a chance, though, if he don't loosen up with every peso he's stolen."

The threat was wholly unnecessary. With shaking hands the cheat made restitution, his sallow face graygreen and distorted with silent rage.

"Now, vamoose!" Willa commanded. "If I don't hear the front door slam in just thirty seconds, you'll be the deadest hombre this side of Kingdom Come!"

There were a few seconds to spare from her ultimatum when the scurry of feet ceased in a thud which echoed through the silent house.

Willa slipped the revolver back under her belt and turned with a little rueful smile to her cousin.

"I—I suppose it wasn't just what a lady ought to have done——" she began, apologetically.

"It was wonderful!" Winthrop North's eyes shone. "You saw him stack up the cards on Pete Follinsbee, and then dug up that revolver and came in here to expose him! It's the gamest thing I ever heard of a girl doing! Congratulations, Miss Murdaugh!"

Vernon pulled himself together, and held out his hand.

"I'm proud of my cousin! Only—what in thunder will the mater say if this gets out?"

"I know what Dad would have said." Willa flushed. "But I suppose I've made a regular hash of—of my début!"

CHAPTER IX

BIRDS OF A FEATHER

"WHAT in the world are you doing, Vernie?" Angie paused in the library door, stifling a yawn daintily as she slipped her evening cloak from her shoulders.

Vernon looked up from his book with raised eyebrows.

"I should think that was self-evident," he observed. "What brings you home so early?"

"The dance was insufferably stupid." She dropped into a chair and began stripping off her gloves. "The music was awful and you know what the Erskine's ball-room floor is like; domestic champagne, too, with frilly serviettes around the labels and half the boys drank quite too much of it. Ghastly bore, the whole affair."

"It seems to me everything is a bore nowadays, according to you." Vernon grinned. "When is Starr Wiley coming back?"

"I haven't the least idea." Angie flushed. "What has he to do with it?"

"A good bit, I imagine," responded her brother. "You were playing him pretty strong before he left."

"Heavens! I wish you wouldn't use such horrid coarse expressions! That's Willa's influence, but I knew just how it would be. I warned mother it was a hopeless job to try to make anything of her the very night she came, and I'm simply dreading next Tuesday!"

"I wouldn't worry on her account if I were you," Vernon returned. "She may be a little green yet, but she's learning fast, and I wouldn't be surprised if she were the hit of the season. That black hair and dead-white skin and those deep blue eyes of hers are going to make a sensation right off the bat. You'd better look to your laurels, my dear sister."

"Tommyrot!" retorted Angie, inelegantly. "She's as awkward as a calf, and hasn't a word to say for herself, though if she'll only continue to keep still, I'm sure we shall all be thankful. Mother is in despair over her studies; she simply refused to go on with the tutor, you know——said she could read all the history and literature she wanted, and it was a waste of time to study geography until the war was over and the map settled. Moreover, she told Mr. Timmins to his face that she knew more about practical mathematics and executive finance than he did, and the dead languages could stay dead as far as she was concerned."

Vernon chortled.

"Bully for her! I think she's a corker. She dances like a dream already, and old Gaudet is ready to weep with joy over her fencing."

Angie compressed her lips, in the fashion she had inherited from her mother.

"She ought to come naturally by the dancing, I'm sure," she sneered. "And she rides in rotten form, like a Western cow-girl. It was wise of mother to introduce her first at a small dinner instead of giving her a formal coming-out party, where she would be the center of observation."

"Yes," Vernon teased. "It is rather awkward to

engineer a second début, while the first bud is still lingering on the parent stem. You want to look out or she'll leave you at the post."

"Thank you!" Angie tossed her head. "I'm only afraid she will be a laughing-stock and bring down ridicule on all of us. You and Father are perfectly idiotic about her. You might be expected to make a fool of yourself, but I am surprised at Father's interest in her."

"You wouldn't be if you'd heard them the other night, talking about the oil business; she was actually advising him, and what's more, he took it thankfully. I couldn't quite get the hang of it myself, but you can bet I'm going to!" He flourished the book. "Little brother is going into the oil game!"

"For about two days, I suppose, until something else comes along." Angie yawned openly. "Thank heaven, there won't be many people here Tuesday night."

"Who's coming, anyway?" Vernon demanded. "If I have to take in any giggling idot of a débutante, you and mother can just count me out!"

"Tell her your troubles then," Angie suggested lazily. "Mr. North and Winnie will be here, of course; the Erskines, Harrington Chase, the Judsons, Mrs. Beekman——"

"Me for her!" interjected Vernon. "She's the best all-round sport in the crowd, and the only girl who can win cups at tennis and polo and yet manage to look pink-and-white in the evening. I'll ask mother to let me take her in. What's become of her brother, Kearn?"

"Mr. Thode?" Angie shrugged. "He's out West or down South, prospecting about, I imagine. Awful bore, I thought him, and so silly to spend most of his time in the wilds when he could stay in the New York office and live like a gentleman if he chose."

"A society hanger-on, grafting dinners and week-end parties because he's good-looking and there with the family tree, but not rich enough to marry? Thode's too much of a man for that, and I fancy he prefers to lead a man's life. I'm getting jolly sick of the whole thing myself, and I'd like to cut it as he has!"

"By the way—" Angie's negligible thoughts had flown off at a tangent—"isn't it funny about Cal Shirley?"

"What?" Vernon frowned. "Haven't seen him for ages."

"Nor has anyone else. He's simply dropped out of everything, and to-night I overheard his mother tell Mrs. Erskine that he was going to winter at Coronado, for the polo. It's odd, when he was rushing Suzanne so violently. Perhaps she turned him down."

"Lucky for her if she did," growled Vernon. "He's a pretty-average cad, if you want to know; I don't believe he'll show up again in a hurry."

"Why——!" Angie's eyes gleamed. "What has he done, Vernie? Is there going to be a scandal?"

"Sorry to disappoint you, my dear girl." He rose. "The incident is closed, and there won't be even a whisper to delight your ears. However, you can take it from me that Suzanne has seen the last of one little playmate. I'm going to bed; you have interrupted the flow of—of oily meditation."

"Wait a minute, Vernie. You and Father are so prejudiced that it's scarcely worth while trying to talk to you, but mother has enough to worry about as it is, with Willa on her hands. Besides, I—I couldn't very well explain how I happened to see her, but I should like to know what Willa was doing in a horrid little frame house out on the Parkway at five o'clock this afternoon."

Vernon stared.

"Don't believe it. Someone's been stringing you. She doesn't know a soul in town—er, that is, no one but the few she has run into informally here."

"But I tell you I saw her myself! She was just coming out as I motored past."

"I say, what were you doing out there yourself? I thought you went to a matinée."

Angie grimaced.

"I went out to the Bumble Bee Inn for tea. You needn't be a prig about it! Lots of really nice people go, and what's the harm?" She picked up her gloves and trailed to the door. "I suppose you'll ask who I was with next, and I sha'n't tell you, my dear. I'm bored to death doing the same old proper thing all the time! Sweet dreams!"

Vernon looked after her for a moment with real anxiety in his eyes. One of them was enough to be kicking over the traces; it wouldn't do for Angie to start. However, that was her own affair. . . . He shrugged, and, picking up his book, switched off the light.

Life was beginning to round out for Willa, if a multiplicity of demands upon her time and interest could satisfy her eager impulses. There were still moments of homesickness, and crises of unrest when she would gladly have forsworn the stifling hot-house existence and gone back to the joyous freedom of Limasito days, had it not been for her secret project. That alone held her to her course and would so hold her until her purpose was achieved.

The eventful night which was to mark her first appearance in her cousins' circle came at last, and she smiled whimsically at herself in the mirror as her new maid added the finishing touches to her toilette. She still clung stubbornly to black, but Mrs. Halstead had seen to it that no awkward suggestion of mourning marred the effect of her shimmering sable gown. It brought out her waxen, lily-like pallor and the midnight luster of her hair, accentuating her height and slimness, and her eyes glowed like sapphire stars.

The reflection which met her eyes was a far cry from the khaki-clad girl who rode man-fashion about the dusty white roads of the Limasito country, and rallied the gamblers in the Blue Chip. Oblivious of the maid's presence, Willa bowed solemnly in acknowledgment of the transformation, and pinning on the orchids Ripley Halstead had thoughtfully provided, she descended to her fate.

At first she was conscious only of a great many people; very bored, very languid people who touched her hand limply and then turned away as if to pursue some interrupted conversation of their own. Then all at once Willa was aware of a handclasp more vitalizing, and looked up into a pair of familiar laughing eyes.

She smiled infectiously.

"How do you do, Mr. North?"

"By Jove!" Winnie beamed at her. "How do you girls manage it?—to change your type, I mean. I thought you were wonderful that night, but now you've eclipsed the memory of it, and I didn't believe anything could ever do that. Somehow, you make me feel as if that girl never existed, and I don't know that I like it. She might have been a real pal, but you are much too stunning and gorgeous for one to dare such a thought."

"I don't quite know which the real girl is." Willa eyed him gravely. "She seems like a stranger to me, sometimes, but I reck—I think the one you met first is down underneath, just taking a siesta, and she's apt to wake up any time. Who is the man with the lock of hair shot away over his right ear?"

Winnie started, and eyed her curiously.

"You mean Harrington Chase? He says his hair grew out that way after an attack of yellow fever."

Willa pursed her lips.

"It is only a bullet which leaves a scalded furrow like that, as clean and clear as a line drawn on paper. Who is he, anyway?"

"Funny you should have asked that. He's one of the biggest oil-operators on the Exchange; owns a lot of leases somewhere in Mexico. His partner is down there now, Starr Wiley. I don't suppose you ever ran across him."

"Yes, I think I have." Willa's tone was quite colorless. "At any rate, I've heard of him.—Oh, there's your father!"

As it happened, the senior Mr. North had been just behind her when she greeted his son and the latter's opening remarks had given him food for lively conjecture. Dexterously, considering his bulk, he had insinuated himself into and through a screening group of people and rejoined his hostess near the door. Where and when could that boy of his have encountered Willa Murdaugh?

The man with the scarred forehead took her in to dinner and Willa listened politely to his rather heavy pleasantries, studying him the while through narrowed eyes. Of a type foreign to the frequenters of the Blue Chip, he had not crossed her path in Limasito, but his previous activities there were an open book to her. She knew that his methods in acquiring more than one lease had been unscrupulous and his reputation none too good, yet the man interested her.

"Your cousin tells me that you've been in Mexico yourself." He turned his small eyes, sleepily bright, upon her. "Says you've picked up an uncommon lot of knowledge about the petroleum industries."

"I've heard them discussed, that is all," Willa deprecated. "Naturally, they're the main subject down there, after government upheavals, of course. It would be a good thing if the States took the oil lands under protection, wouldn't it?"

He laughed shortly.

"Good for us. It will come in time, too. A few more outrages——"

"Yes." Willa interposed softly. "Even the less important disturbers, like El Negrito for instance, have their uses."

"El Negrito?" He laid down his knife and fork. "That's what they call Alvarez, isn't it? I didn't know his fame had spread all over Mexico. You were at school there, I understand."

Willa shook her head.

"Not lately. I happened to be among those present when El Negrito made his last sortie from the hills."

"The deuce you were!" The small eyes filmed craftily. "I beg your pardon, Miss Murdaugh, but you astonish me! I had no idea——! Most disastrous affair, that."

"Very." Willa dropped her eyes. "That is the worst of the country down there, those bandit raids. Creatures like El Negrito know no law but their own; they can't be hired or bribed or coerced and no one knows when they will take it into their heads to appear, murdering and looting and burning. It's a picturesque country, but bad for the nerves."

She turned as the man on her right spoke to her, and apparently was deaf to the sigh with which Harrington Chase drained his wine-glass. She had piqued his curiosity, aroused his interest and disturbed by just a pin-prick his pachydermatous equanimity; she would not raise again before the draw.

Later, Winnie found his way to her side in the music-room.

"Chase has been telling us over the liqueurs that you've had some exciting experiences down in Mexico. That's where you learned to play poker, isn't it? Jove, I envy you!"

"Poker isn't so difficult!" she laughed. "If you'd stop betting your head off on two pairs, Mr. North, you wouldn't find it so expensive."

"Oh, you know I don't mean that! I was thinking of your adventures. Father told me he found you living with some old friends on a big fruit-growing estate near a small town, and I supposed it had been all rather lonely and humdrum, until that quiet little game a few weeks ago made me realize that you must have seen a bit of the strenuous side down there. That would be the life for me!"

She glanced at his round, innocuous face, with the downy mustache and ruminative eyes, and smiled irrepressibly. Then her own face grew grave.

"I wonder! You see, Mr. North, it isn't all like a movie; there's an element of uncertainty that keeps a man quick on the trigger. I was living with friends at the Casa de Limas, as your father told you. But if he had arrived on a certain night just a week or so before, he would have found me barricaded in a—a great hall in town, with men shot to pieces and dying like flies all around me, and three hundred butchering rebels from the hills battering in the door."

"Great guns!" exclaimed Winnie. "Fancy your living through that! What happened—did your friends manage to beat them off?"

"No, the government troops came; the Carranzistas. But they were only just in time."

"Phew! No wonder you spoke of the movies! It sounds like a melodrama, doesn't it?"

"It was a tragedy." Willa's voice was very low. "We would all have been wiped out, if it had not been for one man. He was with us when the raiders came, but he fought his way through them, took one of their own horses and rode to the barracks for the troops; ten miles each way, and he made the whole trip in an hour, wounded as he was. He reached us just as the door went down, and I'll never forget him cutting his way through that crowd of fiends to fall unconscious at my feet."

"I shouldn't think you could!" Winnie's breath came

fast. "What a magnificent stunt for a chap to do! Was he a Mexican?"

"No, an American. His name is Kearn Thode."

"What! Who?" Winnie exploded. "You can't mean——! For the love of Pete!"

Willa stared at him in dawning comprehension.

"You don't mean that you know him?"

"'Know him'?" he repeated, jubilantly. "I should rather think I do! Classmate of mine at college and the best fellow that ever lived. So old Kearn's been pulling off heroic stuff in Mexico! I never thought he had it in him; he was always one of the quiet kind, but at that he was right there when it came to a show-down. He's an engineer of some sort and forever wandering over the face of the earth. I haven't seen much of him consequently in the last three or four years, but I ran into him about six months ago, and he told me he'd been out in Oklahoma. I wonder what he's doing in Mexico!"

"Tell me about him," Willa invited. "I'm interested after what he did, although I really liked him before that; he is so strong and clean and straightforward."

"Yes, he's all of that," replied Winnie. "There isn't very much to tell about him, though. We were at St. Paul's together and then college, and we were pretty thick in those days, although he never cared much for the society racket. His sister is his only living relative; that's she, Mrs. Beekman, in the gray gown over there."

Willa eagerly followed his eyes. Why had she not guessed? He had spoken only of "Edna" to her, but the likeness was unmistakable; the same smooth brown hair, clear-cut profile with the firm, rounded chin and frank, steady, laughing eyes. She remembered vaguely having been presented, but the conventional tone of the other's greeting had awakened no memories. Willa drew a deep breath.

"I'd like to really know her," she said wistfully.

"She's a rattling good sort; you'll like her, when you do.—I say, was Wiley anywhere around when that raid took place?"

"I don't know." The eager light faded from Willa's eyes. "Why?"

"Oh, well, I can't just imagine him doing what Thode did, that's all. But perhaps I shouldn't have said that. Even if you haven't met him yet, you will probably see a great deal of him when he returns."

"How do you mean?" Her tone was oddly constrained, but Winnie was impervious to subtleties.

"I really haven't any right to discuss it since it hasn't been announced, but I thought you knew." He nodded toward the group of callow youths who surrounded Angelica. "It's an open secret that he's going to marry your cousin."

Still later, as the two Norths rode homeward, the older turned a speculative eye on his son.

"Win, how did you meet Miss Murdaugh?—Don't look at me like that, you young pirate! I mean the first time. I overheard some of your conversation before dinner."

"I refuse to answer, not on the ground that it would incriminate either the lady or myself, but merely because it is against the rules of the game." Winnie responded glibly, throwing an affectionate arm across his father's shoulders. "Governor, she's a peach of a girl!"

"She is a most extraordinary young woman." Mason North agreed, with conviction. "Fine-looking, too; I don't believe I noticed it before to-night. You seemed to be getting on famously with her later in the evening. Except when she is angry, I have never seen her so animated."

"Yes." Winnie sobered. "We were talking about another fellow."

CHAPTER X

An Ace in the Hole

NOVEMBER was well advanced, and the first snow of the season was falling when Starr Wiley reappeared in New York. His coming was unheralded, but Harrington Chase was on hand when the train crawled into the station at midnight and the two partners repaired to the room of the returned wanderer, where they held an absorbing conference until the small hours.

Nevertheless, Wiley was stirring bright and early. He appeared thinner than a month or two previous, and he was tanned as with much roughing it on the open trail; his eyes, too, were clear, but there was an odd, furtive droop to their lids which had not been noticeable before.

Abstractedly he drank his coffee, and then, ignoring the tray piled high with its accumulation of mail which his valet had placed on the table, he drew his lounging-robe about him and picked up the telephone.

When his number was connected a respectful male voice replied to the summons.

"Mr. Halstead. Mr. Vernon Halstead, please. . . . Well, wake him, then. . . . I can't help that, it's important."

There was a full minute's pause and then a querulous, sleepy voice grumbled over the wire.

"That you, Vernie? This is Starr. . . . Just last night. . . . No, you won't, either, you're not supposed to know I'm in town till someone else tells you later in the day, do you understand? . . . The racket is this: I've got to see you at once, privately. I'll wait here just twenty minutes for you. . . . Yes, you can and you will! You seem to forget, my friend, that I hold the whip hand. . . . No hard feelings, Vernie, but you know what's in store for you if you don't do what you're told. . . That's better! In twenty minutes? Right!"

Willa, meantime, had plowed her way through the slush in the Park on her early morning canter, and surrendered herself listlessly to the hands of her hair-dresser. A morning musicale, a luncheon, four teas, a dinner, opera and a dance formed the program of the day before her and she quailed in spirit. The novelty of the first few weeks following her initial dinner party had worn off, and greater ease and familiarity with the social round brought with it only an added restlessness and contempt.

There had been no clash, of late, between her will and that of the wary Mrs. Halstead, but the latter watched her every move with argus eyes and directed each detail of the day so implacably that Willa had followed the line of least resistance, save in one particular: she still slipped away at odd moments and left no trail.

Mrs. Halstead was therefore suspicious when, after the luncheon, Willa pleaded a headache, and announced flatly that she would take a siesta in lieu of attending the receptions.

"But, my dear, surely you will make an effort to put in an appearance, at least at the Allardyce's. I am particularly anxious that you make an impression there; they are most exclusive, and if they take you up your position is assured. You cannot afford to miss this opportunity."

"Oh, yes, I can." The smooth, dominant voice roused Willa swiftly to white heat. "I haven't seen anything about this outfit yet that comes too high for Grandfather Murdaugh's money."

It was the first cynical remark that had ever fallen from the girl's lips, but she was learning fast, and Mrs. Halstead recognized the storm signals and withdrew.

In the hall, she encountered Willa's maid, a bright-eyed, hard-featured Frenchwoman.

"Liane, if Mademoiselle goes out before I return, you know what to do?"

"Bien, Madame, pairfectly." The woman smiled quietly, and, turning, reëntered her mistress' room.

"Go away, Liane. I'm going to try to rest. No, don't pull the curtains, I want the air. You may call me at six."

Willa waited half an hour, then, dressing quickly in plain, dark clothing, she slipped from the house.

A taxi' stand was two blocks away on the Avenue, and as Willa stepped into the first cab, a taller, portlier figure entered the second, and followed slowly but persistently through the maze of traffic. The girl glanced from the window at the back to make sure of her espionage, then took up the speaking-tube.

"Never mind that address I gave you. Drive into the Park, to where you can find a sharp turn in the road; get around it as fast as the law will let you and then stop, but keep your engine going. There's a good tip in it for you if you obey instructions."

"Right, Miss."

The car swerved into the Park entrance, and Willa sat back with a peculiar light in her eyes. When it stopped abruptly she sprang out, and, walking rapidly back to the turn in the driveway, waited beside a screening clump of shrubbery.

In a moment the second taxi' hummed about the corner. The girl stepped forward with her arm thrown up and the chauffeur, bewildered, brought his car to a stop with a grinding jar of the brakes. In a moment Willa had the door open.

"Get out, Liane," she commanded briefly, and with one look at her blazing eyes the woman meekly obeyed. Willa turned to the chauffeur. "How much does your meter register? Take it out of this, keep the rest for yourself and go. Your fare will not need you any longer."

The man hesitated, but his late passenger made no move, and the proffered banknote was a tempting one. He took it and went.

When the humming of his engine had died away Willa addressed herself to the cowering maid.

"You can walk back now, and tell your employer that you have failed. Tell her, too, that your services are no longer required, and mind you stay only long enough to pack your things, for if I find you there on my return, I'll show you what we do to spies where I come from!"

"But, Mademoiselle, I was obeying my instructions!" The maid gesticulated vehemently. "Madame commanded that I follow and observe who is at the rendez-vous. If Mademoiselle will be calm and tranquil we may come to an understanding, is it not so? I would prefer to be wholly in the service of Mademoiselle, and we might together arrange a little story for Madame——"

"Sell her out, would you, you treacherous Jane!" The old vernacular returned unbidden to Willa's lips. "You'd

play both ways from the ace and take in the look-out?
If I had you down in Mexico I'd shoot you full of holes!
You heard me! If I find you at the house when I get
back, look out for your wretched skin!"

She sprang into her own taxi' with a swift word to the
chauffeur and bowled away, leaving her erstwhile guard
wringing her hands in the road.

At the gate of the neat little frame house far up on the
Parkway, her driver hesitated.

"Excuse me, Miss, but it's only fair to tell you this car
can be traced here from the stand. I wouldn't double-
cross you, but if the police get after me I'll have to come
through."

Willa smiled and then her face grew thoughtful.

"This isn't a matter for the police. You look like a
white man. What's your job worth to you a week?"

"Anywhere from fifty to seventy-five; depends on the
fares I get," the chauffeur returned promptly.

"I think I can use you. What is your name?"

"Daniel Morrissey, Miss."

"I'm Willa Murdaugh." She gave no heed to the man's
respectful stare. "I'll give you a hundred a week flat.
You throw up your job, meet me to-morrow at the Circle
at ten in the morning and we'll go and buy a good car,
light and strong and fast. Can you drive a racer?"

"Anything on wheels but a locomotive!"

"All right. I'll pay you for six months, whether I use
you that long or not, and make you a present of the car
when I'm through with you. Is it a go, Dan?"

Then ensued the spectacle of Miss Willa Murdaugh,
most important débutante of the season, and Daniel Mor-

rissey, chauffeur, binding the bargain with a solemn handshake.

While her new ally waited, she mounted the steps of the porch and rang the bell. Hurried footsteps thumped along the hall within, and a weazened, hunch backed lad smiled eagerly in the doorway.

"Greeting to thee, José." Willa spoke in soft, liquid Spanish. "I have come to tell thee that we are safe here no longer. We must seek another casa this very day."

Dinner-time came and passed, and the Halstead family sat in strained silence, their engagements forgotten in the new enxiety which enshrouded them. Mason North, hastily summoned to the conference, paced the floor restlessly.

"It was a mistake, Irene!" he said at last. "If you had told me I would never have sanctioned it. You can't treat a girl of Willa's type that way."

"But something had to be done!" Mrs. Halstead cried. "You and Ripley were both powerless to combat her, and we must know what scandal these mysterious errands of hers are likely to portend. This is what comes of putting a beggar on horseback!"

"And there is nothing to prevent her riding straight back to Mexico, renouncing the inheritance and daring us to go after her!" the lawyer retorted. "Where would your share of your uncle's estate go then, my dear Irene? The girl's never been too keen on this proposition, anyhow, as I've tried to make you realize; drive her too hard, and she'll throw the whole thing to the four winds."

"I'll master her yet." Mrs. Halstead spoke through set teeth. "No insolent chit of a girl can defy me! The conditions of the will give me a certain amount of authority and I shall exercise it to the limit. Willa must be controlled."

"Then play fair!" A voice sounded from the doorway, and Willa herself looked in on them. "Don't set your servants to spy on me and try to interfere with affairs which are my concern alone."

"My dear child! What a frightful hour you have given us!" Mason North wrung her hand in hearty relief. "Come in and sit down, and we will talk it all over. We are willing to admit that an injustice has been done you, but we must clear the air once and for all."

Willa complied.

"I think it is about time for an understanding," she said. "I don't want any admissions or recriminations, and I don't intend to submit to a lot of questions. Let's get right down to business. Do you want to start?"

The lawyer hesitated, taken aback by her cool, matter-of-fact manner. It bore no trace of insolence, yet conveyed a serene poise and grasp of the situation which was disconcerting.

"No, Willa." It was Ripley Halstead who replied mildly. The two younger Halsteads merely stared. "Tell us just what is on your mind. I want you to be happy here; that is the first consideration."

"I'm not thinking about that just now." Willa's calm, direct gaze moved from one to the other of them. "I'm going to speak plainly; it's the best thing for all of us. This thing is a business proposition, pure and simple. If it were not for the terms of Grandfather Murdaugh's will no one would ever have tried to find me; no one made the least attempt to help my father and mother, or even see that they were given a fair chance to help themselves. I'm not unmindful of the kindness you've all shown me here, however. Cousin Irene has been very conscientious in trying to make a lady of me, but that was a part of her bargain, wasn't it?"

Mrs. Halstead glared, but made no comment, and after a moment the girl went on wistfully:

"Of course, if we could have grown fond of each other it would have made things easier, but I'm so different from you-all that I guess you couldn't really like me. It looks to me as if we were all sort of in partnership to carry out the terms of Grandfather's will, and whether we like each other or not we've got to stick or get out of the game. Whether we're civil to each other or not, too, depends on our own decency, I expect, but we've got to play square."

She paused, and the lawyer remarked:

"We are all ready to, my dear Willa. We are only trying to safeguard your interests, and yourself. You are very young and unsophisticated and you know nothing of the city. We feel that you should be frank with us and tell us where it is that you go by yourself and what errand takes you. What are we to think if you do not explain?"

"I don't know," Willa replied simply. "Partners trust each other, don't they?"

Ripley Halstead smiled.

"Not always, Willa. But in this case we do not distrust your good intent, only your impulsiveness and inexperience. We really need not have made a family matter of this; do you wish to speak to your Cousin Irene alone, or to Mr. North and me?"

Willa opened wide eyes.

"Why should I? I have nothing to tell anyone. I suppose I seem awfully young and foolish to you, but I'm not afraid New York has much danger for me; I've taken care of myself in all sorts of situations, among the roughest hombres that ever crossed the border. You must trust me now. I am not doing anything wrong, I give you my word; anything that would create scandal in the way Cousin Irene fears. It's just an affair of my own, that started before I ever knew I was Willa Murdaugh; it's a kind of a trust laid on me, and I must fulfill it alone."

There was a ring in her tones that was almost solemn, and as the lawyer looked into her clear, young face his former vague hypothesis that his ward was being blackmailed faded forever from his mind. Whatever the situation confronting her might be, she was the prime mover and the initiative was hers. What strange motive could lurk behind her calm surety and singleness of purpose?

"I can tell you where she goes, if you want to know!" Angie said suddenly and turned with a mendacious inspiration on her brother. "So could Vernie. He saw her! It's to a little frame cottage away up on the Parkway."

"*I* saw her!" ejaculated Vernon, glowering at her. "I like that! I never said anything of the kind, and it isn't true, anyway!"

"What does it matter?" Willa asked wearily. "I will not be shamed by being spied upon by servants. Am I to be trusted on my word of honor that I am doing nothing wrong, or shall I go away?"

"Certainly not, my dear girl." Ripley Halstead rose

and held out his hand. "I'll apologize, if my wife does not, for the trick that was attempted to-day. We will trust you absolutely, but I should like to have your assurance that if you find yourself in any difficulty you will come to either Mr. North or me."

"I'll gladly promise that." Willa turned hesitatingly toward Mrs. Halstead. "I am really very sorry if I have been insolent, but Liane's behavior this afternoon aroused all my fighting blood."

Mrs. Halstead kissed her coldly.

"I hope you realize that I thought I was doing only my duty. There is one question I must ask you, though, and since you refuse to discuss this with me privately you must take the consequences. In justice to yourself I will say that I do not believe you capable of carrying on a vulgar flirtation or intrigue, but remember we knew practically nothing of you when we took you into our home. If you are interested in anyone, if you are secretly engaged, you should tell us and your fiancé must present himself here. Willa, is there a man in the case?"

The girl smiled slowly and gazed off into space. Watching her, Mason North drew a deep breath, for into her changing expression there came a look of implacable, passionless vengeance which made her for the moment the personification of Fate.

"Yes," she said at last. "There is a man in the case, Cousin Irene, but not as you imagine. I have not seen him since I left Mexico and personally he is nothing to me; in fact, I scarcely know him, as you count knowing a person. I have a little matter of business to settle with him, that is all."

Mrs. Halstead sighed and turned to the door as the butler appeared.

"What is it, Welsh?"

"A gentleman, Madam." He extended the salver.

Mrs. Halstead glanced at the card and then quickly toward her daughter, and her face broke into an exultant smile.

"Of course, we are at home!" Then, as Welsh withdrew. "Fancy, we did not even know he had returned! It's Starr Wiley!"

CHAPTER XI

A Change of Front

THE following morning, Willa and Dan Morrissey went motor shopping. The latter was still slightly bewildered by his sudden change of fortune, but it was plain to be seen that he regarded his new employer with worshipful admiration and respect, and she in turn was satisfied, from his discussion of technical details with the several automobile salesmen, that he was sufficiently expert for her purposes. His loyalty remained to be proven, but she had learned to read faces swiftly and surely, and she had formed an instinctive belief that he was worthy of trust.

The car she decided upon was a gray roadster, light and high-powered with long low lines like a racer and a multiplicity of cylinders which made Dan fairly delirious with joy. This important matter settled, she gave him his initial instructions.

"You are simply to hold yourself in readiness for a call from me at any hour of the day or night. You are to obey no summons unless you hear my voice over the telephone, or a written order in my handwriting is brought to you—unless a hunch backed boy about sixteen, a foreigner with very dark skin, should come to you. In that case, you are to accompany him wherever he directs. Do you drink, Dan?"

"Only beer, and not that when I'm on the job, Miss."
He eyed her straightforwardly. "I don't go joy-ridin',
and I keep my mouth shut, and ask no questions. I'll be
on the spot when you want me, Miss, and there till the
finish."

"I'm sure you will!" she smiled. "I sha'n't mind your
asking questions so much as answering them. There are
apt to be quite a few people interested in our doings, Dan;
a young man and two older ones particularly, and they
will try all sorts of methods to get information from
you."

"Let 'em," he responded, briefly. "It's precious-little
dope they'll get out of me! But have you forgotten the
registry, Miss, and the license?"

"No." Willa drew a roll of bills from her purse. "It
had better be attended to at once, for I don't know how
soon I may need you. That's why I insisted upon having
their exhibition car, without waiting for delivery. Take
this and get yourself an outfit; something dark and neat,
not noticeable so that it could be easily described. Then
can't you take out the license in your own name? You
can refer to me if you like, and say that I gave you the
car."

"As if you'd set me up in the renting business, maybe,"
he observed shrewdly. "I guess I can put it over, Miss.
I've got a good, clean record in taxi'-driving, and I know
most of the cops. You'll 'phone when you want me?"

Taking leave of her new henchman, Willa crossed the
Park on foot and swung down the Avenue, so intent upon
her own thoughts that she all but collided with Vernon,
descending the steps of his club. He appeared troubled
and morose, but his brow cleared at sight of her.

"Hello! May I walk a bit of the way with you?" He fell into step beside her. "I say, you aren't angry with me about last night, are you?"

"Indeed no, Vernon. Why should I be? You did nothing."

"That's just why." He reddened. "Perhaps you think I might have taken your part after what a bully pal you proved yourself the night you showed Cal Shirley up, and I did feel like telling the whole bunch to stop hectoring you, the mater included, only—well, we can't do just what we'd like, always!"

"There wasn't anything you could have said, really," she assured him. "I was the only one involved and I had to see it through."

"At least, I want you to believe I never mentioned any house on the Parkway, or saw you there. Angie made a mistake. Someone did say something about it once, but I didn't repeat it." He gave her a curious sidewise glance, but her face was inscrutable.

"I believe you, of course, but it doesn't matter anyway, Vernon. I'm sorry everyone was so worried about my absence last evening, but it was unavoidable. Don't let's discuss it any more."

"All right," he sighed. "I only wish, though, that I'd learned to stand up to the family the way you can. You're so different to the girls up here, but I suppose that is the result of the wonderful, free kind of a life you led in Mexico. You must have had some great experiences down there."

It was Willa's turn to glance curiously at him, for Vernon's tone was oddly constrained and hesitant as if he were endeavoring, awkwardly enough, to lead up to some point in his own mind.

"Yes," she assented quietly, and waited.

"Starr Wiley was disappointed last night at not seeing you," he pursued. "I never knew you had met him down there."

"You never asked." Her tone was serenely noncommittal.

"He was telling us of some of the queer characters he has run across in that part of the country." Vernon paused, and then plunged in desperately. "He said you knew one old woman who was a wonder; a half-caste hoodoo-worker who brewed magic potions in a big pot, and knew all the legends of the countryside. 'Tia—' something, her name is. Do you know what has become of her?"

He blurted the question point-blank, and Willa smiled in spite of herself.

"Tia Juana, you mean? Did Mr. Wiley say she had left her home? I never heard of her doing that before," she remarked innocently enough.

"It seems she disappeared some time ago, and no one knows what happened to her. She must have been a queer old bird."

"Why are you so interested in her?"

He started, blinking at the swift directness of the question.

"Oh, I was thinking what a hit she'd make telling fortunes at some of the charity bazaars, if she ever came up here. People are always so nutty about anything new and a genuine witch would be a sensation."

"Tia Juana is not a witch and she doesn't tell fortunes.

She is a little bit peculiar, perhaps, like many other very old people, but that is all." Willa laughed lightly. "Mr. Wiley must have been stringing you! What else did he tell you about Mexico?"

But Vernon's mind was apparently hazy on the subject of his friend's further reminiscences, and he left her at the door with ill-concealed alacrity. She knew that the conversation had not been uninspired, and his otherwise futile questions had served a useful purpose in forewarning her.

"You will go to the opera with us to-night?" It was more a query than a command which Mrs. Halstead addressed to her. "We are going on afterward to the Judsons', but we can drop you at home if you don't care to accompany us."

"Thank you, no," Willa responded. "If you don't mind I think I will stay quietly at home this evening, but I'll try to keep my engagements in future. I wish there were not quite so many of them!"

"That can be arranged," Mrs. Halstead assured her stiffly. "I wish to give you every opportunity to meet all the eligible people in our circle and then you must select your own friends."

The truce between them was evidently to be an armed one, but it was a respite at least. Willa realized that her cousin would not soon forgive defeat at her hands, but her attitude was more fortuitous than open war.

She had intended to write a long-delayed letter to Jim Baggott, but after the family departed and she settled herself at her desk, the words would not frame themselves in her thoughts. A spirit of unrest took possession of her, a sensation of suspense which did not lighten with the dragging minutes, and in despair she flung down her pen and wandered into the music-room.

Piano lessons had appeared to Willa to be a sheer waste of time and patience in this era of mechanism, and she had not responded with any degree of enthusiasm to Mrs. Halstead's suggestion made shortly after her arrival, but now she touched the keys wistfully. Oh, for one of Mestiza Bill's tinkley old tunes on the piano in the Blue Chip!

She was turning blindly away, when the phonograph in the corner caught her eye and on an idle impulse she started it. By chance, the record left on the machine had been that of the latest tango, and as she listened to the pulsing, languorous strains, Willa commenced half-unconsciously to sway in rhythm with its lilting harmony.

The next minute she was dancing, but not in the dull, mincing fashion in which she had so recently been coached. The music caught at her homesick heart-strings, the old familiar scent of blossoming gardenias was in her nostrils and she was out under a Mexican night. Her pulses leaped to the throbbing notes, and she flung herself sinuously into the measures of the tango, snapping her fingers in lieu of castanets.

All thought of her present environment had slipped away from her, but she was recalled sharply to herself when the music stopped and she halted, flushed and panting.

"Brava!" a cool, slightly mocking voice called from the doorway, and the soft pad of gloved hands sounded upon her startled ears. Whirling about, she found herself face to face with Starr Wiley.

"Brava!" he repeated. "Charming, Miss Murdaugh! I would not have missed it for worlds!"

"How did you come here?" she stammered.

"By way of the front door, most conventionally, I assure you. I heard the phonograph and told Welsh not to announce me." He shrugged, and drew off his glove. "Aren't you going to greet me, Miss Murdaugh?"

There was a covert sneer in the repetition of her name, and Willa made no advance.

"My cousin is not at home."

"I did not come to see your cousin. I came to renew my acquaintance and make my peace with you. Are you going to punish me still for my temerity in Limasito?"

"No." A little, quizzical smile hovered about her lips. "I think you were quite sufficiently punished for that."

Ignoring the dull red which swept up into his face, she led the way to the drawing-room and dropped into a chair, motioning him to one on the opposite side of the glowing hearth.

"I thought you would be at the opera to-night; I looked for you there, but Mrs. Halstead said you did not feel quite up to it, so I came on the chance that you would say 'How do you do?' to me. We have all missed you in Limasito."

"You have become quite a native, then?" She raised her eyebrows. "You find the life there more congenial, perhaps, than at first."

"Not since you left, my dear Billie. Or is that name forbidden?"

"It is forgotten. Only my friends may recall it, and you were never of their number, Mr. Wiley."

"I beg your pardon. I, too, had forgotten for the

moment that it must bring you tragic memories." His voice was lowered to the tones of conventional condolence. "Believe me, I would not have grieved you, Miss Murdaugh. I meant it for a jest, but it was lucklessly ill-timed."

"I would rather not speak of what is past, Mr. Wiley. It is still too fresh in my memory." Willa's eyes, fixed on the flames, were dry and very bright.

"But now that you are here, perhaps you will tell me something of my friends."

"Gladly, but there is little news," he responded hastily. "I have been very busy and, as you know, nothing interests me below the border now but my work. Your friend, Jim Baggott, is flourishing, the crowd that bought out the Blue Chip are bringing new life to Limasito—but I have hurt you again. I am sorry."

Willa had winced uncontrollably, but she recovered herself and smiled.

"And Mr. Thode?" She voiced her query blandly, and Wiley flushed.

"I have seen nothing of him," he responded. "To tell you the truth, I've forgotten the very existence of the fellow. He took care to keep out of my way after your departure until I myself went West."

"You have not come, then, directly from Mexico?"

"No. I little matter of business took me to Arizona. I may tell you of it sometime, I am sure it would be of peculiar interest to you." He smiled, with an odd light in his eyes. "As for Kearn Thode, if you'll permit a little friendly advice, Miss Murdaugh, I wouldn't waste any thoughts on him. I don't believe in discussing a chap's affairs behind his back, but I can assure you his own memory is very short."

"Still, I do not forget my friends, Mr. Wiley, nor my enemies."

"There is much else that I would like to ask you to forget," he said slowly. "I was a cad, I know, but I fancied that you were too broad and generous to hold the madness of a moment against me. I hoped you would be more kind to me when we met here in the environment in which we both belong. I even dreamed that we might be friends."

"Are we enemies, Mr. Wiley?" She raised her eyes to his. "I assure you I have not given that little scene on the camino a second thought."

"Then shall we start all over?" he asked eagerly. "Since you deny me a former one, won't you let our friendship date from this hour? I cannot tell you how delighted I was when I learned that your relatives had found you and that you had taken your rightful place. I knew from the first that you were different to the rest; you were the only one I cared to know, and you would not——"

"Play about with you?" She smiled dryly. "I don't think I have ever learned how to play, and now I am more serious than ever. There are responsibilities, I find, attached to my present situation of which that other girl in Limasito never dreamed."

"Naturally," he conceded, adding quickly: "But you are fortunately not troubled with the details of your estate, while you have two such efficient guardians as Mr. North and your cousin."

The rising inflection in his tone seemed to demand a

reply, but Willa vouchsafed none and after a moment he went on:

"You must find the social life very engrossing. I know that I am always glad to get back to civilization after a few months in the wilds. I would have returned earlier in the season, but my work was not completed."

"And is it now?" she asked with studied carelessness.

"Almost. I came to consult my partner, Harrington Chase—I believe you know him, by the way."

"He dined here, but he said nothing about your return. My cousin was quite agreeably surprised. She is going on to the Judsons' after the opera, did she tell you?"

The hint was unmistakable, but he shook his head, smilingly.

"I really don't remember. I only had a moment's chat with her after the curtain fell on the first act. I saw that you were not in the box with them, and I went to it merely to inquire about you. You were not in evidence when I called last evening——"

"You came to see Angie, did you not? At least, that was my impression."

"I came to see the whole family, of course, but particularly you." He smiled constrainedly. "Your cousin is a very charming girl, and we were great pals before I left for Mexico, but I assure you she does not regard me with any more warmly personal interest than she grants to a host of her other friends."

"My cousin does not discuss her affairs with me, but I have heard rumors which led me to believe you were to be congratulated."

Starr Wiley writhed.

"I have not that good fortune," he said stonily.

"Perhaps my remark was premature?"

"No. Your cousin is quite too clever and worldly to have misunderstood my interest. We were congenial, and it happened that we were thrown together a lot, but I am sure she never thought of any serious outcome of our companionship. I would not have mentioned this to you, but you seemed to be laboring under a false impression. Rumor is never at rest in our set, and I want you to be assured of the truth."

"Why?" Willa sat straight in her chair. "What possible difference could it make to me? I am interested, naturally in anything pertaining to my cousin, but her affairs are her own."

"I want it to make a great deal of difference." He leaned toward her with a swift, avid light in his eyes. "Ever since I first saw you in Limasito I knew that you were the only girl I had ever really wanted, the only girl who could hold me, who was worth working for and waiting for. Gad! I loved everything about you, even that furious, blazing temper of yours, and I determined then that I would make you care!"

"You!" She shrank from him in horror and amazement. "You dare to speak to me of such a thing?"

"Why should I not?" he cried eagerly. "These other girls, these pretty stuffed dolls who preen themselves and go through their conventional paces like marionettes on a string; they are fitted perhaps to preside at a man's table and hold up the social end of the game, but it is women like you who fire a man's soul as well and drive him to madness! I knew there in Mexico that you were the one woman who would ever be my wife!"

"You were so sure?" Willa had regained her com-

posure now, and her quick brain was probing the possibilities of this unexpected situation. "That is why, I
suppose, you brought your cave-man method into play?"

"I lost control of myself," he admitted. "Can you
blame me, now that you know the truth? Your scorn,
your refusal to accept even my friendship, drove me to
desperation. I could not endure it that you should turn
from me——"

"Was it not rather that you could not brook defeat at
the hands of a product of the Blue Chip, a mere gambler's
daughter? It piqued you that I did not faint with delight
because I had found favor in your eyes!" Her scorn
bit deep. "Now that conditions are reversed, you call it
love!"

"You are horribly unjust!" He sprang from his chair
and towered over her. "You have listened to the lies of
that braggart, Thode, and condemned me unheard! His
grand-stand play at the time of the raid has blinded you
and you will not be fair. You do not even know what
love is, but I can teach you and I will! I offended you
by my impetuosity when you provoked me to madness,
but now I will be in the dust before you! Only tell me
that you don't quite hate me, that I have a fighting
chance!"

Willa realized the truth of his sudden change of front;
the granddaughter of Giles Murdaugh would be a more
desirable asset as a wife than Ripley Halstead's daughter.
His audacity in attempting to woo her in the very home
of the girl he had so lately made love to, and with his
former conduct still fresh in the minds of both, filled her
with disgust and loathing, but she held herself with an
iron hand.

"What can I say to you, Mr. Wiley?" She forced a smile. "I can scarcely believe you serious!"

"I will prove it to you!" he exclaimed, bending until his impassioned eyes were close to hers. "I will show you how patient I can be, and devoted. I will wait, I will not try to rush you into a decision, but you are going to care for me, Billie! You are going to be my wife."

"Upon my word!" A light voice, oddly shaken, came from behind them. "You two look fearfully intense! Do I intrude?"

Angie, her face aflame, stood in the doorway.

"On the contrary!" Wiley was the first to recover himself. "A delightful surprise, my dear Angelica! Had I known you were coming directly home from the opera I would have offered my services."

"I—I thought you were going on to the Judsons' dance," Willa stammered.

"Evidently." Angie sneered, looking from one to the other of them. "I was mistaken also, it appears. I fancied you were indisposed, but that was a mere façon de parler, no doubt.—My cousin is getting on, isn't she, Starr?"

Willa flushed, but Starr Wiley replied easily:

"We were just renewing our acquaintanceship, Miss Murdaugh and I met in Limasito, you know."

"How unfortunate!" Angie tittered. "Just when Willa was so successfully living down the past, too! It really wasn't tactful of you, Starr—"

"You are mistaken once more, Angelica!" Willa had risen and her very lips were white. "I am not trying to live down the past, but to live up to it! If you will excuse me now—"

"Oh, don't let me interrupt your charming tête-à-tête," shrugged Angie. "I only stopped on my way to the Judsons' for my vanity case. The car is coming back for me."

Wiley glanced quickly at Willa, then turned to her cousin.

"I am going on also. Will you give me a lift? I really dropped in just to say 'How-do-you-do'."

"Good-night, Mr. Wiley." Willa held out her hand to him.

"Good-night. Remember my prediction." His eyes rested upon her daringly, their ardor for a fleeting instant unmasked as the other girl turned away. "I am willing to stake my life that it will come true."

She smiled, adopting his own light bantering tone.

"Is it worth so high a stake? Good-night, Angie."

Without waiting for a reply, she bowed, and, turning, left them together.

CHAPTER XII

COALS OF FIRE

WILLA paused in the vestibule of the shabby apartment-house and looked carefully up and down the street before venturing forth. The early dusk had fallen and the lamps were not yet alight, but the passers-by were still clearly discernible in the gloom. The girl studied their movements for a time, and noting that none loitered or retraced their steps, she descended and made her way around the corner to where her car was waiting.

Dan Morrissey touched his cap with alacrity.

"One guy in a taxicab down the avenue there, Miss, and another across the street. Where to, now?"

"The little house on the Parkway, where you took me the first time," she directed on a sudden impulse. "When you drop me there, go straight back to the garage and wait until you get a call from me."

"They're both stringing out behind us," he announced, when they had traversed a mile or more in silence.

"That is what I wanted them to do," Willa responded. "Don't look back again, Dan; just go along as if you didn't know anyone was trailing. I'm glad you lighted up while you were waiting for me."

The long, low car seemed to stretch out over the road like a lean horse in a speed that ate up the miles and more than one motor-cycle policeman gazed appraisingly after them, but they drove steadily ahead and drew up at length before the sagging gate.

Darkness had come and the little house looked bleak and deserted. As Willa sprang out of the car, Dan hesitated, and then volunteered:

"Looks as if there wasn't anybody there. Sure you don't want me to wait, Miss? The first taxi' is coming now."

"No. Don't worry about me, Dan." She smiled understandingly. "I don't think I'll need you any more to-night, but wait at the garage until ten. Now go quickly, please."

Without a backward glance, she mounted the path and inserted a key in the door. All was silence and gloom within, but she fumbled her way to a mantel in the small front room and found a box of matches. Lighting them one after the other as they burned out, she made her way from room to room on each of the two floors. They were bare of furniture, but the débris of a hasty exodus was visible everywhere, and half the windows were unfastened.

Willa wasted no time in looking about, but made her way quickly to the heat register let into the floor of each room, and opened them wide. Then she fled down the creaking stairs to the cellar, heedless of the mice which scurried in droves before her, and opened the door of the cold, empty furnace.

The chill dampness of the low, cramped vault no less than the animate darkness made her shiver, but she resolutely crawled into the furnace and pulled the door close behind her. She was scarcely settled in her place when footsteps sounded on the porch above and an indistinguishable murmur of male voices.

Presently the footsteps retreated, there came the rasp of an opening window and then the tramp of feet within the house. There were two distinct treads; one light and springy as a cat's, the other dragging heavily and in apparent reluctance from room to room in the wake of the first.

The voices reached her, now raised as the intruders called to each other, now lowered in an earnest monotone, but to Willa's disappointment the registers did not carry the sound to her as she had hoped and the tones alone reached her ear in a confused rumble.

It was evident that a complete search of the house was in progress, but at last the two men came to a halt beside the register in the room directly above that part of the cellar where the girl crouched and the words floated down to her, sharp and distinct in the silence.

"They've flown the coop, all right, whoever they were." It was Vernon's voice. "I don't see why Willa came up here now, though, if she knew they had gone. Where do you suppose she is?"

"She may not have known." Starr Wiley replied thoughtfully. "Finding the place deserted and hearing us on the porch in all probability, she may have slipped out the back door and taken the subway down-town. Remember that burnt match I found in the hall was still warm. I wonder if it's worth while to have a look in the cellar?"

"In the darkness, and filth, and rats, too, for all you know? No girl would take a chance." Vernon's tone was lofty with contempt, but it changed as he burst out:

"Who are these people, anyway, and why are they hiding and what are you so keen after them for? I hate fooling around blindfold like this, and how do I know it's fair to Willa? What is her connection with them?"

"You don't have to know, my dear fellow!" Wiley spoke with the bland mockery the listening girl remembered. "It's up to you to do what you are told and ask no questions. Why this sudden chivalry?"

"Well, you know, Willa's one of the family now. Hang it, I like her, anyway, and I'm not going a step farther in this till I find out what the devil you are up to!"

"A perfectly square business deal, if you must know. Your conscience is waking up rather late in the day, don't you think?" The mockery changed to a swift menace. "As to how far you will go, that will be as I direct, or you, my dear Vernon, will find yourself in a position where the going is distinctly not good."

"Gad! I'd rather face it than stand any more of your domineering!" Vernon's faltering tones belied his words and the other laughed shortly.

"All right. The money is earning no interest for me. I'll put through the check to-morrow."

"Oh, I say—!"

"Then come along, you young puppy, and no more whining, or I'll——"

The steps moved away and the voices again sank to an indistinguishable murmur, but Willa had learned enough. Waiting only long enough to make sure of their departure, she crept from her hiding-place, and, heedless of the soot which clung to her boots and skirt, she acted upon Wiley's inadvertent suggestion.

From the subway station she took a taxicab and

reached home just in time to dress for dinner. A not wholly disinterested plan was forming itself in her mind and gained added strength of purpose with each glance at Vernon's pale, troubled face across the table.

Angie, who had been cold and distant all day, departed for the theater; the elder Halsteads went to a bridge party, but Vernon wandered aimlessly into the library where Willa found him staring into the fire in profound dejection.

"What is the matter, Vernon?" she asked abruptly. "You haven't been at all like yourself these last few days. We're pals, you know; tell me."

He glanced up, hastily shifted his eyes, and then blurted out desperately.

"If you'd ever been an absolute rotter and then got on to the fact when it was too late, I guess you wouldn't be very much like yourself, either. I'm a confounded cad, Willa, and worse!" He dropped his head on his hands with a groan. "I ought to be shot!"

"Well, that's a healthy sign," Willa observed cheerfully. "Lots of people are rotters and never find it out. It's like a disease; when you know what is the matter, you can usually find a cure."

"Sometimes it's incurable." His voice was muffled. "I'm in a hole and there's no way out."

"Then climb up again." Willa paused and added deliberately: "Don't try to burrow a passage-way through slime, Vernon. You'll only get in deeper and deeper."

That brought his head up with a suspicious start.

"I say, what do you know about it?"

"Suppose you tell me?"

"You, Willa? You're the last person in the world—!" He broke off hastily.

"Why? If you are in a scrape perhaps I could help you out of it."

"It's worse than a scrape! It's something beyond the pale; it's the sort of thing they shoot a man for, down where you came from! Now you know!"

"Yes," responded Willa slowly, "I do know. Now tell me what that check is, which Starr Wiley is holding over your head."

Vernon rose with blanching face.

"You heard! Good Lord, where were you?"

"In the furnace!" Willa dimpled irrepressibly. "Right in it, with the ashes and all! And you stood talking straight down into the open register, like a speaking tube."

Vernon cringed away from her in bitter shame.

"Then if you heard the whole thing, you know what a wretched cad I've been, spying on you and trying to get information from you for that bounder."

"I knew about that before, Vernon. When I met you leaving the club yesterday and you tried to question me about Tia Juana, you made a dreadful mess of it. I saw right through you and I realized for whom you must be acting, but not why, of course." She drew a deep breath and added in a matter-of-fact tone: "What's the matter with that check Wiley has? Is it a forgery?"

He nodded dumbly.

"Whose name did you sign? I might as well know the rest, don't you think?"

"Mason North's." His voice was a mere strained

whisper. "I must have been crazy to do such a thing!"

"What sum did you make it out for?"

"Four thousand dollars." He gazed at her as if hypnotized, replying mechanically under the sheer dominance of her will.

"Was it for speculation or in payment of some sort of debt?"

"A debt of honor!" He laughed in measureless self-contempt. "Poker."

"I see. But, Vernon, don't make me drag it out of you like this. Tell me the whole story."

"It was before Starr went to Mexico." Vernon hesitated and then the words came with a rush from his overburdened breast. "He was playing up strong to Angie, and he saw I didn't like it. Father is hipped about him and so is old North; they think he's the coming man in the oil game, and he may be for all I know, but I'd heard other things about him and I wasn't keen on having him for a brother-in-law. He began to jolly me along; made up parties and wanted me to pal around with him. He's older and he goes with the swiftest bunch in town, and, like a regular saphead, I was flattered. He put me up at his club, and I got into some pretty high play, away over my head, but I wouldn't have him or his friends think I was a piker, so I stuck.

"He won usually, and I almost got writer's cramp making out I. O. U.'s for him. Then his manner changed a bit and he began kidding me. He was good-natured with it at first, but after a while he grew nasty, and one night he taunted me before the whole crowd about my four-flushing.

"I'd been drinking and it made me wild. I don't

know what put the idea in my head, but I brooded over it and I couldn't see any other way out. Father had said when he paid my debts before that it was the last time, and he meant it. I—I took a check from his desk—he and Mason North have accounts in the same bank—and I made it out, copying the signature from an old letter."

His voice was getting lower and lower, and finally it halted, but Willa prompted him firmly.

"What happened after you gave it to Starr Wiley?"

"Nothing. I realized what I had done when it was too late, of course, and I lived in just plain hell for the next four weeks, waiting for the blow to fall, but it didn't. At last I couldn't stand the strain any longer; I went to Starr and asked him if he'd put it through, and he said he hadn't. He knew when he accepted it from me that it was forged. I had given him a song-and-dance about it being some money coming to me from your grandfather's estate, but it hadn't fooled him for a minute.

"I groveled at his feet and told him I'd work my fingers to the bone to pay it back, but he said I could do that in his way, at his own time. He's held me under his thumb ever since, and when he got in town a few days ago he sent for me and forced me to try to get a line on this Tia Juana woman through you. I hated it, Willa, but, God! what could I do?"

"What you are going to do now." Willa rose with decision. "You're going to Mason North at once, and make a clean breast of the whole thing."

"I couldn't! I thought of that, but you don't know the old boy—"

"I know he's square, and I guess I can handle him, if

you can't. I'm going with you and I'll reimburse him for the four thousand, to let the check go through. Then you can tell Wiley to go—to go ahead and show you up."

"Willa!" Something very like a sob welled up in his throat. "You would do that for me, after——after—"

"You didn't do anything very dreadful to me, Vernon."

"But I promised to spy on you."

"That's all right. Wiley is in this affair simply on a business deal as he told you to-day, although I doubt the squareness as far as he is concerned. But I'm out for higher stakes—" She paused, clinching her hands. "Never mind about that. I'm going to 'phone Mr. North, and see if we can catch him at home."

"Look here." There was a ring of strength in Vernon's tones. "I appreciate, no end, what you've offered to do, Willa, but it can't be! I'm pretty low, I'll admit, but I'm not such a rotter as to take that kind of help from a girl!"

"Why not?" Willa asked quickly. "You said yourself this afternoon that I was one of the family, and, besides, you can pay me back, you know."

"I wonder if you really believe that I would!" he remarked wistfully.

"I know you *will!*" she retorted. "I'm putting up that money on a bet with myself, and it's a sure thing. You'll make good, Vernon."

Mason North was comfortably ensconced in his own library, with a Life of Disraeli and a malodorous pipe, when Willa burst in upon him.

"Mr. North, you told me to come to you if I was in any difficulty, and—and I'm here!"

"Certainly, my dear!" He was plainly startled. "I

shall be delighted to be of any service that I can. What is it that you wish my advice on?"

"I don't want any advice! I want you to help me compound a felony."

"My dear Willa!" His rotund face paled. "Are you serious? You cannot realize what you have said!"

"Oh, yes, I can!" she affirmed. "A friend of mine signed a check with a name that wasn't given to him in baptism, and I want you to see that it goes through all right, and nothing happens. I'll give you my own check out of Dad's money to cover the amount, and that'll be a comfort to you; you'll know where some of it is, at any rate."

"Forgery!" he groaned. "It is outrageous, Willa! Scandalous! A young woman of your position consorting with a criminal! Oh, we have all been too easy with you; we permitted you to defy us, and now you will disgrace the name you bear! I knew that you had been associated with desperadoes of the lowest type, but I thought that now—"

"Just a minute, Mr. North!" Her tone was ominous. "We'll leave my old friends out of this, if you don't mind."

But Mr. North was far too agitated to take heed.

"This will kill your Cousin Irene—!"

"I expect it would," she interposed soberly. "But she will never know it, Mr. North. What I tell you now must never go beyond this room."

Forthwith, Willa related the whole story just as it had fallen from Vernon's unhappy lips, and the attorney listened in consternation. She eliminated, however, all mention of Wiley's knowledge that the check was a forgery and his attempt to drive a bargain on the strength of it.

"Mr. Wiley meant to put the check through, of course, but he mislaid it," she substituted. "When he returned a few days ago, he came upon it among his papers and told Vernon this afternoon that he was going to turn it in at his bank. Vernon couldn't tell him the truth, because—well, you wouldn't want a thing like that to be known outside the family, would you? You are different, you know."

"Why didn't that young whelp come to me?" North snorted. "It's a wonder his sly wits didn't grasp the fact that I wouldn't prosecute, because of his father, but I might have started something I couldn't stop short of a scandal if the check had been put through and I not known he was at the bottom of it."

"He was afraid," Willa explained simply. "He isn't really bad, he's only weak, and I guess you-all have hounded him so that he's just about ready to stick up a train! He's out in the drawing-room now, and just as soon as you let me write a check for you I'll bring him in."

"You'll write no check!" thundered North. "Just you send him in here to me."

"But I must!" Willa pleaded. "Don't you see, it's the turning-point for him. Let him realize he owes me that money and if he hasn't got a yellow streak a mile wide, it'll be the making of him. If you just blow him up and then forgive him, he'll be back where he was before it happened, and liable to repeat it. I've known some pretty rough characters, as you said a while ago; you learn a lot about human nature in a place like the Blue Chip,

Mr. North, and I've seen men going the way Vernon's
headed for, just because nobody believed there was anything in him to hold him back. I'm trusting Vernon to
pay it back and that's the very reason why he will."

Mr. North cleared his throat.

"You're a—a damn'-fine young woman, Willa Murdaugh—and an uncommonly wise one! We'll give the
boy a chance. I hope he will realize some day what he
owes to you."

Willa hesitated and then her native honesty came
uppermost.

"I haven't done this for him alone. I can't say that I
wouldn't have, of course, but I'm just freezing him out
this hand." She smiled at the other's bewilderment. "It's
funny how everything reduces to poker terms, isn't it?
I'll send Vernon in."

"Wait! Let me understand this." North put out a
detaining hand. "If you're not doing this for that young
scapegrace in there I'd like to know in whose interest it
is. Is there something else back of it?"

"If I tried to explain, Mr. North, you'd be in a worse
muddle than ever," Willa told him candidly. "Dad
always said you could take care of the pat hands against
you if you froze out the four-flushers.—Don't scold Vernon, please. Remember, he's just balancing; a push
either way will determine his course for the future. I'll
wait for him."

A long half-hour passed, but when she heard her name
called in the attorney's strangely subdued tones, Willa
reëntered the library to find the two standing with
clasped hands. Both were flushed and seemed to find
difficulty in speech, but at length Vernon burst out:

"Willa, he's a trump! I never realized what an utter beast I was until now and it's just because he hasn't said anything that he might well have! It isn't only the money, though I'll work like a dog to pay that back——"

"I know you will, my boy!" North found his voice, although it was suspiciously husky. "Willa's sure of you, too."

"That's it, that's what counts! A fellow couldn't help but be straight with two such friends believing in him!" Vernon choked, but he squared his shoulders. "Will you shake hands with me, too, Willa? I'm not going to talk, I'm not going to try to thank you, but I'm going to show you! I know what friendship means now, and I mean to be worthy of it!"

Their hands clasped, and, looking into his eyes, Willa said with conviction:

"I'll bank on you, Vernon. Go in and win. It'll be a stiff game, but you can't lose for you're on the square now."

CHAPTER XIII

The Challenge

"WHAT do you think about this?" Harrington Chase growled as his partner entered the private office the next morning. "Somebody's getting after us good and plenty!"

"Let them come!" Starr Wiley shrugged. "We're on the right side of the fence now, nobody can touch us. Anything from Cranmore?"

"Yes. Whoever it is that is trying to get a line on us isn't overlooking any bets. Our men have been keeping me posted on the inquiries up here, and they've got the dope so straight that it's my opinion they have reached one of the inside staff." His tones lowered and he glanced significantly toward the ground-glass partition which separated them from the small army of clerks in the outer office. "It doesn't matter, of course, but it would be just as well for the future to know if we have an enemy in camp.—Now, Cranmore wires me in code from Limasito that someone down there is mightily interested in our titles and leases and particularly in what new fields we're opening up. I tell you, if you don't get in touch with that old woman soon, somebody will beat us to it as sure as you're alive."

"I have got a line on her." Wiley paused to light a cigar. "I told you I suspected she'd been brought up here, and I've verified it. I know where she and that hunchbacked kid were living two days ago. They've cleared out, but I've put a couple of men on the party that will lead us straight to her. I'd like to know, though, who is so devilishly interested in our affairs."

"It is Larkin's outfit, of course. That young engineer they've got down there has spudded in the Consuegra, that you passed up, and it's producing seven hundred and fifty barrels a day as a starter."

Wiley thrust out his jaw.

"That's all right. I know Larkin's man; Kearn Thode, his name is. I met him before out in Oklahoma, and I've no use for him. He's had little use for me, either, and between you and me, he's got less now than ever before, only he doesn't know it!" He laughed shortly. "You might be surprised to know that Larkin himself was after the Lost Souls."

"What?" Chase swirled about in his chair to face his partner.

"Fact. I don't know how he got wind of it, but as soon as Thode showed up and began nosing about I knew what his game was."

"No wonder they're butting in on our affairs! We'll have to do some quick work——"

Wiley laughed again.

"No fear of trouble from Thode. I beat him to it and spiked his guns at the same time. He's given it up as a bad job; that's why he tackled the Consuegra. Wait till we pull off the big noise and he'll be welcome to all the jitney gushers below the border."

"When we do," Harrington Chase observed with emphasis. "We'll have to get hold of the old dame first."

"We'll land her." Wiley smote his desk. "There isn't a woman living, young or old, who can cut the ground out from under my feet!"

But a distinct shock awaited him when he entered the club that evening, in the attitude of his erstwhile ally, Vernon Halstead. He had difficulty in locating the young man at first; a survey of his usual haunts, the bar and card-rooms, failed to disclose him, but Wiley ran him to earth finally in the library, deep in a bulky and serious-looking volume.

"Improving your mind?" he sneered.

Vernon raised his eyes serenely.

"Never too late to learn, is it?" he observed. "I've found out a lot in the last day or two."

"You mean—?" Wiley dropped into a chair beside him. "Any new developments? Did she go out alone to-day?"

"My cousin?" Vernon closed his book, and rose. "I haven't the least idea, I assure you. I ran out to Mineola myself, with an aviator chap I know."

He had paused, looking down at his interrogator, and at the expression in his eyes the latter half rose also, then sank back.

"And just what am I to infer?" Wiley spoke through set teeth.

"Anything you like, my dear fellow. Help yourself."

"Ah! You're going to renege, are you? You're prepared to take the consequences?"

"You've guessed it." Vernon nodded. "I'm off the dirty work, Starr. You'll have to do your own sleuthing in future."

"You realize what it means? I've never bluffed in my life, Vernon, and I'll push this thing to the limit!"

"Go as far as you like." Vernon waved his hand airily. Then his expression hardened. "But whatever happens, leave my cousin out of your future plans. Do you understand? Play your game with men if you like, but leave the women of my family alone."

"Indeed?" This time Wiley rose, and the two looked levelly into each other's eyes. "When you go up for forgery you won't be in a position to interfere with any game I choose to play. I've told you this was a straight business proposition, Vernon, there is no use getting melodramatic about it. I've taken a lot of insolence from you, and I'm prepared to teach you a lesson."

"And I am always willing to learn, my dear Starr. It's up to you." He bowed formally, and, turning on his heel, left the room.

For a time Wiley communed with himself. The worm had turned, with a vengeance, and the maneuver was beyond his comprehension. In spite of his declaration anent a bluff, he was not prepared to push the matter of the check to the end he had threatened. A scandal was farthest from his desire and other considerations were involved; his matrimonial ambitions not the least of them, if he antagonized the Halstead family. Then, too, what could have been back of Vernon's sudden independence? Was it an idle bluff, or had the young scamp managed in some way to protect himself?

The conclusion of his cogitations led him to the telephone and a half hour later found him confronting Mason North in the latter's home, much as Willa had done on the previous night.

"Sorry to have disturbed you, Mr. North, but this is a strictly confidential matter, and rather urgent. I have your assurance that it will go no farther?"

"Certainly!" Mason North was suspiciously affable. "Take a seat and try one of these cigars. They're made especially for me in Porto Rico and I know you to be a connoisseur. You were saying——?"

"I have a check in my possession signed presumably by you." Wiley chose his words with evident care. "It was made payable to bearer and of course I do not know whether it changed hands or not before reaching me. I wish to insinuate nothing, but I should like your assurance that the signature is genuine before depositing it."

"You have it with you?" the attorney asked crisply.

Wiley nodded, and, taking an oblong slip of paper from his bill-case, he presented it for the older man's inspection.

"Um! Four thousand dollars, eh? The signature looks all right to me, but I don't quite recall making it out. I have my old stubs here in the desk, and if you will wait I'll look it up."

Secure in the outcome, Wiley was more than willing to wait. He sat with a half smile on his face, puffing at his fragrant cigar and formulating his next move, when the storm should break.

But the other's voice cut short his pleasant reflections and the words themselves brought him up standing.

"Yes. Here we are! I gave that check to young Halstead. It is quite correct; 'four thousand'. Little matter of an inheritance. I—I trust he hasn't been speculating, but I suppose I must not ask, eh? Sad young dog, Vernon!"

"It was a business transaction of rather a private nature, but I can assure you that Vernon was not a loser by it." Wiley's tone was quiet, but he had gone white to the lips "I would not have doubted the signature, except for the fact that I thought it an unusually large sum to be payable to bearer, and, as I said, I did not know to whom it had been issued originally. I am sorry to have troubled you."

He took his leave amid the other's cordial protestations, with outward composure, but his expression changed savagely as he descended the steps of the house and started up the Avenue.

The attorney's attitude had not deceived him for a moment. Someone had checkmated him, that was plain; had disclosed the truth and persuaded North to shield Vernon. Could that young man have confessed voluntarily and thrown himself on the attorney's mercy rather than play the game? But such a step would have involved courage of a sort, and he was sure Vernon did not possess enough of that commodity to carry him so far. Someone must have interceded for him—but who?

Then an inspiration came and under its goad Wiley almost cursed aloud. That girl, again! He recalled Vernon's swift, unaccountable championship of his cousin at the club an hour before. That was the answer, of course! The young cub had double-crossed him and placed himself in Willa's hands—and incidentally landed his erstwhile tyrant in the same position.

So be it. He would carry the game into the enemy's camp and then, if necessary, arbitrate. Wiley had fought many duels with the fair sex, but never a financial one before, and the prospect was not without an element of sport. She had outwitted him at the start and borne off the spoils, but he would wrest them from her, and tame her into the bargain.

The morning dawned clear and crisply cold, and Willa started upon her early gallop in the Park with every nerve a-tingle and the blood racing in her veins. Her perplexities were forgotten, her slow, waiting game put aside and she gave herself up joyously to the influences of the hour. After all, it was good to be alive!

Her mount was fresh, but she rode him hard until she had taken the edge off his spirits and he was willing enough to drop into the easy, loping canter for which she had originally chosen him from her cousins' stable.

Her clear, pale cheeks bore an unwonted flush and her eyes were dancing when she came face to face with Starr Wiley around a bend in the bridle path. Willa would have passed him with a gay little nod, but he reined in his horse and, wheeling, fell into pace beside her.

"May I take the trail for a little way with you?" he asked. "Glorious morning, isn't it?"

"Yes." She smiled, but the brightness had fled from her face and her eyes narrowed as she gave him a side-long glance. "I didn't know you were given to an appreciation of them, though. What brings you out so early?"

"Do you want a confession? It was with the hope of meeting you that I came. One can see you alone so seldom in these crowded days, and I want to grasp every opportunity. Can you blame me?"

"Your judgment, perhaps. My cousin is a far more attractive spectacle than I, Mr. Wiley."

"Still unkind!" he exclaimed ruefully. "I have told you, I have explained and you will not believe me!

Willa, you cannot have forgotten the other evening, you know what I feel toward you. You permitted me to tell you and you said that at least I might hope. Don't taunt me, dear! It's scarcely fair, is it?"

"I gave you no assurance, Mr. Wiley." Her eyes opened very wide upon him. "You were well supplied with that. I was careful not to commit myself in any way, if you remember. You were in my cousin's house and I listened to learn just how far your effrontery would carry you. It was scarcely an open game, I admit, but it was your deal and you weren't playing exactly fair yourself, were you?"

"I was sincere." His voice shook, but not with tenderness. "You led me on; you played with me from the first!"

"On the contrary, I refused to play with you at all, but you would not be convinced. Let us understand each other, Mr. Wiley. Your protestations are distasteful to me, and there is no longer need of pretense between us. I will be civil when occasion requires, but friendship between us would be an impossibility, and I beg that you will not force me to be more rude to you than you have made necessary now."

"So," he remarked quietly. "We have done with pretense, have we? I will meet your frankness, then. I have offered you all that a man can offer a woman in devotion, but you have thrust it from you. Now I have another kind of a proposition to discuss with you, and I am prepared to offer terms. I want to know where you have secreted Tia Juana; I want an interview with her. If she, of her own volition, refers me to you as I anticipate and gives you power of attorney to act for her, we can perhaps come to an agreement which will be to our mutual advantage."

"That sounds interesting," Willa remarked. "What makes you think I know where Tia Juana is?"

"I thought we had done with pretense?" he reminded her. "I know of the little house on the Parkway, and the beautiful rich young lady who hired it and installed the fierce old Spanish woman and the hunchback there. I know, too, of their hasty departure, and all that happened before in Mexico. You played a very shrewd game, my dear Miss Murdaugh, but your disinterested charity toward Tia Juana is open to question; a legal question, perhaps, if it comes to that, involving undue influence and a dummy title."

"Assuming that I know what you are talking about, don't you think you are taking a great deal for granted?" asked Willa. "I do not admit that I know where Tia Juana is, but in the event that you discover her, what assurance have you that she will receive you? There is a strain of Indian in her blood as well as Spanish. She does not forget, and do you think your treatment of José would inspire her with any confidence in your good faith or with any desire to deal with you except in retribution?"

"Nevertheless, she is the principal I intend to interview. You give me no credentials as her authorized agent, and whether she cares to deal with me or not is a matter I mean to put to the test. It lies between her and me, and I fancy I shall have no difficulty in opening her eyes to much that will be to her advantage, to which she has been kept heretofore in the dark."

"Would you, if you could? I doubt it. However, by

all means make your proposition to her when you have found her, Mr. Wiley. That's the first thing, isn't it? You can't hazard your bet until you have picked your number, can you?" Whimsically, she imitated the croupier's sing-song whine "Make your play, gentlemen! The wheel is about to spin!"

"You vixen!" he muttered wrathfully. Then he controlled himself with an almost visible effort and half turned in his saddle. "Will you permit me to give you a bit of purely disinterested advice? Don't go in for the financial game on your own; you are bound to lose. In your proper sphere you are invincible, but it is a social one. When you pit yourself against men in a contest for financial supremacy your chief weapon, that of sex, is turned against you. Make no mistake! I shall find Tia Juana, I shall obtain her order to treat with you, and you will come to an agreement with me on my own terms. You cannot afford to reject them if you would. You have not the slightest inkling of their nature now, that is a card I am holding in reserve, but when you learn what an indemnity you will be called upon to pay in the event of a refusal, you will jump at the bargain, my dear Billie."

He uttered the old name deliberately, and she flushed.

"I am Willa Murdaugh, if you don't mind."

"Are you?" He asked significantly. "The clock struck twelve for another Cinderella, you may remember, and all the jewels and gorgeous apparel disappeared, as well as the pumpkin coach. I doubt if there would be a fallen slipper or a fairy prince to put it on again if the old story came to be rewritten to-day."

"What do you mean?" Willa turned to him, startled in spite of herself.

He shrugged.

"I will tell you when the time comes to drive our bargain, and I have an idea that it will not be deferred long. You cannot conceal Tia Juana indefinitely, and I shall have more able tools to aid me in my search than the one you so cleverly removed a day or two ago."

"I?" Willa's tone was mechanical, her thoughts centered on his implied threat and what it might portend. "What tool?"

"Vernon," he responded tersely. "He is to be congratulated on his fortunate choice of a confidante. When he told you of our visit to the empty house, close on your heels——"

"You weren't; you were just over my head!" she retorted. "Vernon told me nothing. It was unnecessary, because I heard it all. I scarcely listened, though, for it reminded me so forcibly of another secret interview of yours that my mind wandered. It was a much more significant occasion, Mr. Wiley, with results so far-reaching that they have not yet culminated."

"Indeed?" He frowned. "I must confess I don't recall——"

"It was an interview at night, out in the open, beneath the stars!" Her voice trembled with sudden passion. "It took place near a garage, and you did not know a listener crouched in the shrubbery. The man you met and bargained with there was Juan de Soria, agent of El Negrito, and the next night El Negrito himself came down from the hills! What price did you pay for that raid, Mr. Wiley; that raid which was to force United

States intervention and protection of the leases of its citizens, yours in particular?"

"You are mad!" he cried hoarsely, but she would not be silenced.

"What did you pay in pesos for that slaughter? What will you yet be called upon to pay in vengeance by those who were spared? Don't be too confident of success in your bargaining, Mr. Wiley, until the final reckoning!"

For a moment there was silence, then with an obvious effort he laughed harshly.

"You are disposed to be highly melodramatic, my dear Billie, but unfortunately your attitude is without justification. No such interview as you describe took place. I suppose it is useless for me to assure you of this, but it must have existed solely in the imagination of your informant—if you had such an informant! I will leave you now, but I beg that you will reflect upon the bargain I have offered you. Wild accusations will not serve to turn the point at issue, and for your own sake I advise you to think well. Au revoir!"

He bent to the saddle in a mocking obeisance and his horse leaped forward beneath the touch of the spurs.

Willa watched until he had disappeared between the leafless trees, then slowly moved off down a side-path.

She had warned him now. Her cards were on the table and he knew the strength of the hand she held against him. But what of his own? To what length would he, could he go in the contest which from that moment would be to the death between them? What did his vague threat mean?

CHAPTER XIV

The Knight Errant Once More

"WE'LL be late," Angie observed as she and Willa waited in the drawing-room for the rest of the family. It was the first remark she had voluntarily addressed to her cousin since she had come upon the tête-à-tête in the library. "Not that I care, of course, these dinners are always stupid, but the Erskines are so horribly particular. I've heard that the Bishop was late once and they went in without him."

Willa smiled.

"I wonder who will be there?"

"The same old crowd, I suppose," Angie shrugged. "For heaven's sake, Willa, if they send you in again with Harrington Chase, don't monopolize him as you did at the Wadleighs'. It's horribly bad form; I wonder that mother didn't tell you."

"Did I monopolize him? I wasn't conscious of it," Willa said reflectively. "He interests me."

"Evidently!" Angie sneered. "So do a few others, I imagine, but you shouldn't show it so plainly. I admit that you've gotten on very well so far, but your methods are horribly crude, still."

"My methods?" Willa was honestly puzzled. "I wasn't aware that I had any. When people bore me I let them alone; but those I find interesting for one reason or another. I listen to. Is it crude to discriminate?"

Angie bit her lip.

"You can be very simple and naïve when you want to!" she burst out. "But do reserve it for outsiders, and spare us! I know you for what you are: sly and sneaking and mean! Your cheap, common little airs and graces don't deceive me, they only disgust me more and more! I wish Mr. North had left you where he found you, with your gamblers and horse-thieves and roustabouts!"

"So do I," Willa retorted frankly. "They were men, anyway. You are unjust because you are hurt, and I am sorry for you. I wish you could understand, but I am afraid you will not believe me. Mr. Wiley——"

"Will you kindly leave his name out of this discussion?" demanded Angie. "I am not in the least jealous, I assure you! He is nothing to me, I merely object to the underhand way you maneuvered to receive him alone. That sort of thing may be all right where you came from, but it is a little bit too raw to put in practice here."

The appearance of the others brought the quarrel to a close and they went out to the waiting limousine in a constrained silence. Mrs. Halstead glanced from her daughter's flushed face to Willa's pale one, and her lips tightened. Had Angie been foolish enough to betray herself to this interloper?

Willa was sincerely distressed. There had never been any real congeniality between the two girls, but her heart ached for the other's evident suffering. Her own conscience was not quite clear for she had permitted Wiley to show his hand without stopping to think of Angie, so determined had she been to learn the depths to which this man would descend in his ruthless self-seeking. She had weighed her cousin shrewdly and she did not believe her capable of deep and lasting affection, yet she shuddered at the thought of any girl's heart in Starr Wiley's keeping.

They were late, as Angie had prophesied. The Erskine drawing-room was crowded, and Willa stared about blankly, her mind still burdened with her cousin's resentment. Then all at once she became conscious of a tall figure which disengaged itself from a nearby group and came eagerly forward.

Mechanically she held out her hand, and a voice sounded in her ears which drove all else from her thoughts and sent the hot blood flooding her cheeks and neck in a crimson tide.

"We meet again, Miss Murdaugh. I told you that it would be soon!"

She found herself looking up into Kearn Thode's eyes, and the wonder of it held her dumb. As unconscious as a child of the instinctive movement, she extended both hands, and he caught and pressed them tightly for a moment before releasing them.

"Mr. Thode! I had almost given up hope." The words sprang to her lips. "I thought you would come before and I used to look about for you everywhere we went at first. It was silly, of course, for I knew that you had your work to do down there, but it would have been nice to see a really familiar face."

The young engineer, too, flushed.

"I meant to come before, but I was delayed——" He broke off. "Was it so awful then, the first plunge? May I remind you that you have fulfilled my prophecy? Just to look at you now makes me half believe those Limasito days were a dream!"

"They're still real to me," Willa said gravely. "They are the only real things and real people I have known. All this up here—oh! it's very pleasant, of course, and new and amusing, but it doesn't reach deep down. It doesn't seem to mean anything."

"So soon?" He raised his eyebrows in whimsical dismay. "My sister wrote me of your success and I was very glad. I knew it would not change you, but I did not think the glamour would wear off so quickly."

"Your sister?" Willa cried. "I'm so sorry that I only met her once. She dined with us, but since then I have not seen her. I should like to have known her better."

"She called twice, but you were not at home. After that she went South and she has only just returned. May I bring her to call to-morrow?"

"I shall be delighted," Willa paused, regarding him with a little, puzzled frown. "Do you know you have changed, somehow, Mr. Thode? You are ever so much thinner, and pale beneath your tan, and you look—oh, almost as if you had been suffering! Am I imagining things, or have you been ill?"

"I had an accident just after you left Limasito. It was nothing serious, just a slight concussion, but it laid me up for some weeks," Thode replied easily. "That is what delayed my work and prevented my return before."

He looked beyond her as he spoke, and his face darkened swiftly. Willa, noting the transition, glanced over her shoulder to see Starr Wiley, smiling and urbane, standing just within the doorway.

"Another reminder of Limasito," she remarked. "A most unwelcome one. But tell me about your accident. I am so sorry——"

His hostess claimed Thode at that juncture and bore him away to fresh introductions, and Willa started across the room to Mrs. Halstead when Starr Wiley intercepted her coolly.

"How do you do?" he asked. Then, without waiting for her reply, he went on: "But that is a superfluous question, isn't it? You are looking as distractingly charming as ever. So our knight errant has put in an appearance once more! He looks a little the worse for wear."

"Mr. Thode has been ill," Willa remarked through stiffened lips. "There was an accident——"

"A hootch bottle in the hands of a jealous Señorita becomes an effective weapon, but I would call it more like fate than accident." Wiley laughed unpleasantly. "There were some interesting rumors afloat about our friend's conquests after your departure from Limasito. He'd be an expert porch-climber if his practice in gaining access to certain balconies on certain back streets counted for anything. I could have told you before, but I did not want to shatter your illusions concerning the local Paul Revere."

"You are trying to now, however." Willa looked straight into his eyes and then quickly away in immeasurable disdain. "I have no ears for idle, malicious slander, Mr. Wiley. Please, let me pass."

"It does rather jar on one, doesn't it? A reminder of the low, primitive life down there is out of place in this highly esthetic atmosphere." He made no move to step aside, and a shade of deeper meaning crept into his tones. "It would be a pity if one were compelled to return to it.

The charms of Limasito would pall, I fancy, after all this; yet such things sometimes happen."

"I trust not, for your sake," Willa responded. "You would scarcely find the climate of Limasito a healthy one, if your activities were fully comprehended there."

"I was not thinking of myself——" he smiled once more—"but of an old fairy tale which I mentioned to you in the Park. You look a very confident Cinderella, but midnight is not far off, and only you can stop the hands of the clock, remember."

"I am not fond of riddles." Willa shrugged and turned away to greet her host, who came forward with one of the inevitable callow youths in tow.

Dinner was announced almost immediately and Willa sat through it with the food untouched before her. Wiley's insinuations against Kearn Thode she had dismissed utterly from her thoughts, but his renewed taunt of the morning filled her in spite of herself with dread foreboding. Could fate have indeed been playing with her after all, and was it possible that Wiley held within his hands the strings of her future destiny?

She was Willa Murdaugh, of course. Mason North and the Halsteads had satisfied themselves of that beyond a shadow of a doubt. But what if Wiley had really stumbled upon some facts unknown to them all which might throw a shadow across her title? Was it an idle threat to coerce her or a very tangible menace?

She raised troubled eyes to meet Kearn Thode's smiling ones across the table and her native courage came back in a swift rush. Surely she had nothing to fear; she would meet Wiley and beat him at his own game, and then . . . she smiled again into Thode's eyes. What did anything else matter, now that he had returned?

An informal dance was the order of the evening and Willa and the young engineer gravitated to a seat on the stairs after a romping fox-trot. Both were flushed and sparkling, but when they found themselves alone together a diffident silence fell upon them.

"It must seem good to you to get back," Willa ventured at last when the pause had become oppressive.

"It is." His glance rested upon her with a world of contentment. "I can't begin to tell you how wonderful it seems!"

"And your work down there?" she pursued hurriedly. "You have finished it? You will not have to return again?"

The contentment faded and in its place there came a look of bitterness and dogged determination.

"It has scarcely begun. I wonder if you ever heard an old legend around Limasito concerning the lost location of a marvelous oil well?"

Willa laughed nervously, a little taken aback by the abruptness of the question.

"One hears so many legends in every country of lost or buried or hidden treasure," she parried. "Scarcely anyone pays attention to them except the tenderfoots. You know up in the mining country one is forever hearing such tales of vast deposits of ore, but nobody can ever find the lead."

"This particular one concerns a well in a mysterious pool of water where a massacre is supposed to have taken place. It dates back to the time of the Spaniards' coming."

He paused, but Willa said nothing. She was striving to mask her thoughts in continued composure lest his quick mind grasp the significance of her interest.

"The place is spoken of as the Pool of the Lost Souls," Thode went on. "Surely you have heard of it? The people to whom you were so kind, old Tia Juana and her grandson, knew more than anyone else about it. Did they not mention it to you?"

"Tia Juana?" Willa glanced up quickly, but she could not meet his eyes. "She is very secretive, you know, and jealous of the old legends which to her form the sacred history of her beloved country. Suppose you tell me the legend yourself."

Briefly he recounted it to her and she listened until the end in a dismayed chaos of mind which culminated in a staggering blow.

"I have found it." There was no jubilation in his tone, but paradoxically a note of defeat.

"You!" she stammered breathlessly.

"Yes. You seem surprised?" he added with a quick glance at her. "I know these old legends are mostly regarded as bunk, but now and then one proves to be a straight tip. Generations have searched vainly for the Pool, as I thought you must have heard, but they did not know where to look."

"Then how did you, a newcomer, discover it?" Willa scarcely recognized her own voice.

"By the simple expedient of following someone else who had stolen a march on me in a despicable fashion." His jaw set in the old characteristic way she remembered. "I don't mind admitting that I would have taken almost any means to locate it; that was my main objective in

Mexico and I was acting under instructions from my chief. But I would scarcely have stooped to the method employed by the man of whom I speak."

"Starr Wiley?" The question was wrung from Willa's lips.

He stared at her.

"You know, then?"

"I—I guessed," she countered hurriedly. "I knew that you two were enemies, of course, and it came to me that if anyone had played a false trick upon you it must have been he. You say you found the Pool by following him. How did he know where to search?"

Thode hesitated.

"I found a map of its location, but I had scarcely got my hands upon it when I was struck down from behind and the paper stolen."

Willa uttered a startled exclamation, but he continued, unheeding.

"Someone found me, hours later, lying unconscious and carried me into Limasito, where your good friend, Jim Baggott, took care of me. It was weeks before I was able to be about again, but I had time to think it all out. Of course, I had not seen my assailant, but I had had an uncanny intuition all day that I was being shadowed—it was the very day of your departure, by the way—and I knew of only one other beside myself who had taken that legend seriously. Wiley was doing his best to locate the Pool; he was aware that I was there for the same purpose and he would have stopped at nothing to win out, for, as you know, there was bad blood between us. If he did not actually strike the blow that felled me I solemnly believe that he was instrumental in it in some way. Please, don't think me ungenerous toward an enemy that I tell you this, or even harbor such a thought, but events really seemed to bear out my suspicions."

"No." Willa was gazing moodily straight before her. "I do not think you are ungenerous, and I am very glad that you are telling me. I believe, too, that you are right; I feel sure that he must have been responsible for your injury. But I am amazed about the map."

"I found it in the ashes of Tia Juana's fire; the little fire in the grove of zapote trees where she cooked her tortillas, and brewed her strange concoctions. You had told me of it, do you remember? But perhaps you have not heard: Tia Juana and the boy, José, have disappeared. They must have gone on the very day you started for New York, and no one has been able to discover a trace of them, except one. That is a very significant trace indeed, though.—Have you no curiosity about the Pool?"

He turned to her suddenly, but Willa could not raise her eyes to meet his now.

"Of course," she stammered.

"It is located on a grapefruit ranch known as the Trevino hacienda, about two hundred miles due north of Limasito. Wiley made the best of his time while I was laid by the heels, but his treachery didn't do him any good, in the end. He found the Pool, but another had been before him; old Tia Juana, herself!"

Willa's lips moved, but no sound came from them. She was praying that he would not look at her again.

"A few days before Tia Juana and the boy disappeared, the Trevino hacienda changed hands. It was sold for twenty-five thousand dollars, to one Juana Reyes.— Reyes, if you recall, was the name of the old Spaniard who owned the Pool originally and whose daughter, Dolores, was killed by the Indians on her wedding night. Reyes is also the almost forgotten surname of Tia Juana, so it looks as if the old lady had come into her own, at last. It is a mystery, of course, where she got the money to purchase the hacienda, but it may have been hoarded in her family for generations. It is possible, too, that she only then succeeded in deciphering the map, and tracing the location of the Pool from it."

"So you and Starr Wiley both failed." Willa spoke as if to herself.

"Not I!" Thode's eyes flashed with determination. "I told you I had only just begun. I am going to find Tia Juana if she is above ground and buy out her claim. To her it only means the ancestral estate. That is much, to be sure, if she has gone through her long life in poverty and want in order to hoard her riches for its purchase, but it is only a sentimental consideration. When she learns that she has a fortune in petroleum, worthless without the money to develop it, I think she will agree to share her interest. The casa and the land about it can still be hers, we only want to drain and develop the Pool, and my chief will be strictly fair with her. The old lady will be rich beyond her wildest dreams and we will have the greatest producer known since the Dos Bocas gusher went up in flames!"

Willa rose.

"If you find Tia Juana, Mr. Thode, don't build your hopes too high. Should she prove to be indeed the owner of the Pool of the Lost Souls, I am confident that you can never gain possession of it."

"I can try." He took the hand she held out to him. "You seem very sure, Miss Murdaugh."

"I cannot imagine Tia Juana relinquishing anything which she could claim, especially if, as you surmise, the property may once have belonged to her ancestors. Cousin Irene is signaling me. I must go!" she added. "You will come to-morrow?"

Thode promised, but he watched her slender figure disappear with a frown of troubled thought. How much did she know? Could it be that she, too, was interested in the Pool of the Lost Souls? Instead of a mere contest between himself and Wiley had it become a three-corner affair, with Willa the apex of the triangle?

Had he but known it, he was destined not to keep his promise of the morrow, and once more it was Starr Wiley who intervened.

It happened that Thode stopped in at the club after taking leave of the Erskines, and arrived at a most opportune moment. He was emerging from the coat-room when a familiar voice came to his ears through the half-open door of one of the smaller card-rooms, and the words arrested him like a command.

"The little Murdaugh? Very naïve, very charming, but I knew her in the Never-Never Land, you know, and I can assure you she's not as unsophisticated as she seems."

"Oh, come, Starr! You're tight!" a strange voice intervened. "Ladies' names, you know——it's not done here."

"'Lady'?" Wiley hiccoughed derisively. "Who mentioned a lady? I'm speakin' of Willa Murdaugh. Gentleman Geoff's Billie they used to call her; pet of an old card-sharp, and mascot of a gambling-hell——"

He got no farther. Someone had seized him by the shoulders and spun him around like a top and he found himself confronting Kean Thode's blazing eyes. His half-fuddled companions shrank back in consternation.

"Take that back, you miserable cur!" Thode's voice was scarcely recognizable. "Take back your damnable lies or I'll ram them down your throat!"

But an alcoholic courage possessed Wiley and he leered: "The knight-errant, by Jove! You know whether it's true or not! You ought to know better than any-one else——"

A crashing blow straight on his maudlin mouth sent him reeling back against the table. His wildly groping hand found a tall glass and with an oath he hurled it full in the face of the man advancing upon him. A moment later, he was lifted clear of the table by an impact that flung him against the wall a sodden, inert heap with the last ray of dazed consciousness gone.

CHAPTER XV

Gone

A METAMORPHOSIS had taken place in Vernon Halstead. He was distrait and mooned about the house, getting in people's way and apologizing with an air of such profound abstraction that the family were moved to comment.

"I think Vernon must be ill." This from his mother. "The poor dear boy seems very pale and hollow-eyed. Haven't you noticed it, Ripley?"

"I've noticed that he looks as if someone had given him a jolt that he hadn't yet recovered from," her husband retorted. "Maybe he's waking up and getting on to himself at last. It's high time! It would give anyone a shock to find they'd been wasting the best years of their lives——"

"You were never sympathetic with his sensitive highly-strung temperament——"

" 'Temperament,' Irene? He's about as temperamental as an army tank!" Ripley added more mildly: "I don't say there's no good in the boy, but it needs waking up. He asked me last night about a course in petroleum engineering, like young Thode, and that's a promising sign. I wish I felt as easy in my mind about Willa."

"I wash my hands of her." Mrs. Halstead shrugged coldly. "It was to be supposed that she would be quite impossible, coming from such an environment, but I fancied at least that she would want to advance herself. She cares nothing for making acquaintances or getting in with the right people and hasn't the slightest conception of the importance of establishing herself. If I had the proper authority over her it would be vastly different, but you and Mason——"

"We haven't it ourselves," her husband reminded her. "We've got to accept her on her own terms or not at all, it seems. She has too much principle to get herself into disgrace, I am confident on that score, but she has such ultra-democratic ideas that I am afraid she may lay herself open to comment. Have you heard anything, Irene, about a—a gray car?"

"What is that?" Mrs. Halstead sat up very straight. "I've been expecting trouble from her absurd independence, but you know my position. What about a gray car?"

"Nothing much." Ripley looked decidedly uncomfortable. "You are not to mention it to her, Irene, remember. Mason spoke of it and it's up to him to take care of it, but I thought you might keep your eyes open. Mason has an idea that he has seen her more than once running around town in a fast little gray car with a mighty good-looking chauffeur. He's near-sighted and he asked me to find out about it."

"I know nothing of it!" his wife said bitterly. "An elopement with a person of that sort is quite within the possibilities, Ripley. I will watch, of course, but what good will it do? I have tried to guard her, and been insulted for my pains. If I had my way, I should lock her in her room until I brought her to terms.—A chauffeur, indeed! Really, Uncle Giles' money is scarcely worth the strain, and now with poor Vernon acting so strangely, and you so unsympathetic, it is a wonder I am not down with nervous prostration!"

On the morning after the Erskine affair, however, Vernon came in at lunch time with a cheerful air of suppressed but pleasurable excitement which nullified the effect of his former solemnity.

After the meal was over, he drew Willa mysteriously into the library, and shut the door.

"Say! I've simply got to tell you! I don't peddle club gossip as a rule, but this is to good to keep. Starr got his last night!"

"What do you mean?" Willa cried. "He's not——"

"Not dead, you want to say? No, it isn't as good as that, but he got the thrashing of his life and his beauty is pretty well spoiled. Gad, if I'd only been there to see it!"

Willa turned a shade more white.

"Who—did it?" Her voice was a mere whisper.

"Kearn Thode. He is pretty well cut up about the face himself, for of course Starr didn't put up his fists like a man; he threw glassware."

"Oh, is he badly hurt?" Willa caught at her surprised informant's arm in sudden dread. "Is Mr. Thode——"

"Hello! What's the tragic idea? Of course he's not; but you ought to see Starr! The fellows say it was all over in about two seconds, but it must have been great while it lasted!"

"Where—where did it occur?" she asked faintly.

"Right in the club, of all places in the world! The board of governors got together this morning like ducks

in a thunderstorm and held a special meeting. Of course,
they're both suspended until the board can get hold of the
facts, but it's a pretty general opinion that Starr will be
asked for his resignation. Nobody seems to know what
the row was about, or else they are all keeping mum, but
Starr must have said something rather average awful.
The only name he called Thode, though, as far as I can
make out, was 'knight-errant'."

Willa turned away to hide a sudden trembling.

"That isn't so terrible, is it?" she stammered.

"Silly word to start anything! But you never can tell
what's back of it with Starr——"

"Excuse me, Miss. Note for you by messenger."
Welsh stood in the doorway.

Willa took the envelope from the salver the butler
presented. The superscription was in an unknown hand,
but a swift intuition came to her as she broke the seal.

"My dear Miss Murdaugh," she read silently.

"Will you believe me when I tell you that I am more
than sorry I shall not be able to come to you to-day? I
was caught in an annoying but superficial motor smash-
up last night and the broken windshield has made a
bizarre spectacle of me, but I shall be my normal self
again in a few days. My sister, Mrs. Beekman, will call
to-morrow and I shall present my apologies in person at
the earliest possible moment, if I may.

"Very sincerely and regretfully,
"Kearn Thode."

Willa mused so long that Welsh finally asked, with a
deferential cough:

"Any answer, Miss? The messenger is waiting to know."

"No.—Yes! Just a moment!"

She seated herself at the desk and wrote rapidly:

"My Dear Mr. Thode:

"I am deeply sorry to learn of your motor accident. Knights-errant rode on chargers in the old days, I believe, but the spirit remains the same, doesn't it? I scorned it once to my shame, but it is a spirit for which I am now profoundly grateful. Come to me when you can; I shall be at home.

"Hasta la vista,
"WILLA MURDAUGH."

"Well, for the love of Pete!" Vernon exploded, when the butler had withdrawn. "You're blushing like a June rose! Willa, are you holding out on us? Have you a steady you are keeping company with, unbeknownst?"

"Don't be absurd, Vernon!" She dimpled, in spite of herself. "That was only from Mr. Thode. He was going to call this afternoon with his sister, but he can't. He's had a slight motor accident."

"Then Starr must have met a steam-roller!" Vernon stopped, and added in sudden suspicion: "I say, you didn't give me away? You didn't mention——?"

"I?" Willa's eyes widened demurely. "I expressed polite regret, of course. What have I to do with motor accidents?"

"Nothing, I hope, if you go slow," Vernon hesitated. "I don't want to butt in, Willa, but I'd like to give you a hint, if you don't mind. Gray cars are not invisible."

She had paused at the door.

"Just what does that mean?" she demanded. "Of course I know you and Starr Wiley followed me the other day, but how do you know where the car came from?"

"I don't," retorted Vernon quickly. "That's your own affair, Willa, only I thought you ought to know that Art Judson and one or two others spoke of the nifty little car they'd seen you about in, in the last two or three days. I thought I had better tell you before Mason North gets hold of it and asks questions."

"Much obliged, Vernie, but if he does I sha'n't answer them." Willa smiled. "I'll take you out some day if you like. The little car is a wonder and you and Starr Wiley would never in the world have been able to hang on the trail that time if I hadn't meant you to! If anyone asks you about the car, however, you never heard of it. Understand?"

She turned lightly and ran from the room, leaving her cousin chuckling. The simple, formal little note was pressed tightly to her breast as a most passionate avowal might have been, and her eyes were like dew-drenched violets when she reached her room. Thode had come at the moment of her unapprehended need, and he had fought for her once more, asking no guerdon but the unalienable right of man to protect the women of his world and kind from insult and contumely.

And she? She must repay him by thwarting his ambition, dashing his hopes, bringing to defeat his most cherished plan! What would he think of her when he learned the truth and recalled how she had accepted his confidence and given him in return only silence pregnant with deceit?

Her head drooped and burning tears smarted in her eyes, but she held them back grimly. If Willa Murdaugh was a self-pitying weakling, Gentleman Geoff's Billie was not, and she would see the game through! Because of all that the old name had meant she would not be a quitter, though her own happiness be forever lost. What was her happiness? she demanded wrathfully of herself. A side-bet, nothing more! She was out for bigger stakes than mere happiness, and she was playing to win.

Wrapping herself in her fur coat, with a tiny close-fitting cap upon her head, she slipped out of doors and around the corner to where, half-way through the block, Dan Morrissey waited with the gray car.

It was commencing to snow; great, soft, feathery flakes which lighted upon her as softly as thistledown and melted each in a single glistening drop like a tear. The air was coldly still and the sky a sheet of lead.

"Have I kept you waiting long, Dan?" she asked as he tucked the robe about her. "I'm sorry, I hope you've not been cold. It looks as though we were in for a real storm, doesn't it?"

"I wisht it'd come down a regular blizzard, Miss," he responded dourly. "Then maybe we could shake off the boys that have been hangin' on my trail for dear life! It's not cold I've been, sitting here trying to figure out how to stall them, but hot under the collar! Where to, Miss? It don't make any partic'lar difference, they'll be right along behind!"

"Then around the Park, please, Dan. You can tell me about them as we go."

She snuggled down in the soft robes as the car leapt and fled like a lithe gray cat through the storm. Her thoughts were busy with the new problem; these followers were Wiley's men, of course. He had boasted that he would have more able tools to aid him in the future than Vernon had proved. Where had he obtained them?

"Are they professional detectives, do you think, Dan?" she asked.

He needed but the word to start him.

"They are that! I was chauffeur once for a private detective agency, and I know them and their ways, though these fellows seem to have a new wrinkle or two. It started a couple of nights ago when I was waiting in the garage for a call from you, Miss. A fine big, new touring car was edged in beside mine and the chauffeur, a little dark feller, began talkin' to me. I remembered what you'd told me, and keepin' my own mouth shut, I let him rave. In just about ten minutes I knew it was all bunk; he was tellin' too much, tryin' too hard to get thick with me all of a sudden. 'His gentleman was a free-handed sport and what was good enough for him was none too good for his driver; champagne, the fellow wanted me to go out and have with him, and I couldn't tell you what-all, Miss."

"I rather expected that," Willa nodded.

"Then, when I got home to my boardin'-house, there was a new lodger in the room next to mine, a long-legged, sandy-haired galoot. The same thing began again; he came in to borry a match and stayed half the night. I let him down easy, though if I hadn't remembered your instructions I'd be after sendin' him home through his own transom! Everywhere I've been for the last two days, barber shop and all, I've been tailed. It's fun if you look at it in one way, but it gets my goat, too. If you say the word, Miss, I'll sail in and lick the bunch of them!"

"No, Dan; not yet," Willa smiled. "The man behind them is responsible and he's been punished for the time being, anyway. How many men are trailing us? I haven't looked back."

"I made sure of three, but they may be strung out after us like an Irish funeral, for all I know," replied Dan, gloomily. "My chauffeur friend is on a motor cycle now, my red-headed neighbor is in a runabout, and a strange feller in a big car. There's small chance of losing them, I'm thinkin'."

"Then drive straight to that apartment-house from which the two taxicabs followed us the other day. They've spotted me there already, you see, and I've no doubt they've investigated there, so another visit won't do any harm. Wait around the corner for me, as you did the last time."

Willa alighted before the shabby vestibule and without a glance to right or left made her way in and pressed a button marked "Lopez." The front door clicked a prompt response and she ran lightly up two flights of dark and dingy stairs.

A thin, sallow little woman with soft, black eyes awaited her at an opened door and ushered her into the stuffy garish front parlor where she eyed her visitor in palpable nervousness.

"How are my friends?" Willa asked without preamble.

"They are quite comfortable at your mother's house? You have heard from her?"

"Ah, yes!" The woman replied with the slightest trace of a Latin accent. "The young lad has been suffering a little with his back, pobrecito! It is the climate here, no doubt, but my mother rubs him with a remedy of her own making and he is soothed."

"And the Señora?"

The woman hesitated visibly.

"She—she sits all day by her fire and talks but seldom, yet she seems well."

"They understand why I have not been to see them?" Willa eyed her narrowly, for the woman's agitation boded ill.

"Yes. They ask when you will come, but they know it must not be for a time." The Señora Lopez paused, and then added in a swift rush: "My mother bakes for them tortillas and they are pleased together. José begs my mother to tell him of Spain, but the old Señora, she has not the interest. It is always as if she waited, but she is content."

Willa nodded. The description was such as she had anticipated, yet despite the volubility of the other's assurance, the suggestion of something odd and furtive remained.

"Have there been any inquiries for them here?"

The woman smiled in obvious relief, and spread out her hands.

"But yes! You spoke truly, Señorita, when you warned me of those who would seek them. In the evening just after you were here last a gentleman—an Americano—came asking for the Señora Reyes. I knew nothing of her." She drew down her eyelids, significantly. "Next morning, there came a young man of our country. He said that he was from Mexico, but he lied; the speech of the Basque was on his tongue. The Señora Reyes was his aunt, and he came to tell her that he had found her lost son, his cousin. He, too, departed. Yesterday it was a boy. He was an amigo, a compañero of José; he desired to know where he might be found, but he, also, was unsatisfied. We are the Lopez—what have we to do with the Señora Reyes or José?"

Her tone of bland candor was inimitable, but it did not eradicate the consciousness of anxiety and unrest in her bearing at first. Nothing more was to be learned from further parley, and Willa presently departed, leaving behind her a substantial roll of banknotes.

Her mind was far from easy, and as she descended the dark steep stairs she came to an abrupt decision. Something was wrong and despite the hirelings of Starr Wiley she must know.

"Dan," she began when he sprang down to assist her into the car, "I don't know how it is to be done, but we have got to lose those trailers. I don't care how long it takes or how many miles we cover doing it, but we must manage to get to Second Place, Brooklyn, without being followed. Do you think you will be able to make it, or shall I try to give them the slip by taking the subway?"

Dan reflected.

"There's more than one in the big car and you'd be trailed sure, Miss. Better take a chance with me, and I'll get you there safely without them knowing if we ride till morning!"

Then began a strange and devious journey. To Willa,

who, aside from her infrequent visits to the cottage on the Parkway, had seen little of New York and its environs save in the beaten path of the conventional social round, it was a revelation. They tore through crooked teeming side-streets whose squalor was veiled in the falling curtain of snow and shot across broad avenues with gleaming vistas of light stretching interminably in either direction, to dash sharply about a corner and off through a lane of canyon-like factories and sweat-shop hives. Once they skirted huge railroad yards and twice they circled along the river's edge between towering warehouses, with the tang of salt winds swirling the flakes about them and a forest of tall masts looming up ahead.

Dan Morrissey knew the city as only one can who has grown up practically on its streets and he was following a well-defined route in his mind as he wove back and forth through the myriad threads which held together the vast and varied pattern on the loom which was New York, drawing ever nearer the great bridge. The runabout had been left behind, but the larger car still trailed and the sharp exhaust of the motor-cycle reached their ears tauntingly above the subdued rattle of occasional traffic.

All at once Dan commenced to chuckle and Willa could feel his shoulders shake beside hers.

"What is it?" she demanded with a quick glance at him.

"I've just thought of something, Miss. If Delehanty is on his station now, watch us lose the laddy-buck on the motor-cycle!"

They had reached a corner on lower Broadway, whence

the home-going stream of humanity had long since disappeared like ants into the burrow of subway entrances, but where a burly traffic policeman still loomed bulkily in the middle of the thoroughfare.

Dan drew the car up at the curb, leaped out and approached the minion of the law. A short colloquy, and he had returned and the car shot down Broadway.

"You can look back now, Miss," suggested Dan.

Willa turned. The motor-cycle had been halted in mid-pursuit, its rider gesticulating in futile rage and vexation while the obdurate bluecoat held him fast.

"How did you do it, Dan?" Willa asked.

"Delehanty's death on motor-cyclists since one ran him down last summer. I told him this feller was a chauffeur in the same garage as me, and trailing me now on a bet, but that the license on his machine was phony. We'll be there and back before he gets through explaining at the station-house."

Once across the bridge, Dan led the big car far out to a sparsely built-up section of Flatbush and there at last his object was achieved. A loud report echoed behind them and glancing over her shoulder Willa saw the big car swerve and come to an abrupt halt in the ditch.

"Tire burst!" she announced. "Luck is with us, Dan!"

"It was, in the shape of some broken glass!" Her ally retorted grinning. "I said a prayer myself as we went over it. The way is clear now!"

Second Place was a dull row of somber brick dwellings with prim muslin curtains behind each window pane, and an air of bearing its indubitable respectability self-consciously.

The car halted before a house midway the block, and Willa was up the steps in a flash and pealing the bell.

A swarthy middle-aged woman, with a white apron over her ample silk gown, presented herself and stammeringly bade the girl welcome.

"The Señora Reyes and José? I must see them, Señora Rodriquez. I have come from your daughter."

"She did not tell you, then, Señorita?" The woman raised her fat hands in expostulation. "Heaven is my witness, it was not my fault! I did not think to watch her, she did not even glance toward the window! Could I know what she meditated?"

"What is it?" Willa seized the woman's arm and shook it convulsively. "What has happened to Señora Reyes? Tell me!"

All at once a frail, crooked little form catapulted itself down the stairway and fell, sobbing, at the girl's feet.

"Señorita! Señorita Billie! The grandmama has vanished! She rose and went from the house in the dawn, when all were sleeping! She is gone!"

CHAPTER XVI

The Pool of the Lost Souls

WILLA went home at last in a daze of consternation which took no note of the heightened
storm. The unexpected catastrophe was a
death-blow to her long-cherished plan, but even that
faded for the moment before the stern anxiety for Tia
Juana's safety.

The story which Willa succeeded in dragging from the
Rodriguez woman and José was simple on the face of it,
yet many possible complexities presented themselves to
the girl's vivid imagining. Tia Juana had seemed con-
tented enough in her new abode for the first day, taking
a childish pleasure in the novelty of her surroundings,
but later she had become depressed and sunk into a
moody silence save that now and then she muttered
ominously to herself and made strange gestures with her
claw-like hands.

José she had driven from her harshly, only to seize
and draw him close, and on the previous day she had
eaten nothing, but crouched through the long hours
before the glowing coals of her grate. At twilight she
had demanded a large cooking pot which she placed upon
the fire, and with an earthenware jar of liquid and
sundry packets of herbs from the conglomerate heap of
her luggage, she had brewed a concoction that piqued her
landlady's curiosity.

It had not pleased Tia Juana, however, and after glowering darkly into its depths, she had flung it, pot and all, from the window down into the back yard.

She had retired passively enough, but when the Señora Rodriguez came with her morning coffee, the room was empty. There were no signs of a struggle, the silence had remained unbroken throughout the night, and the front door was found to have been unfastened from the inside, although the Señora Rodriguez asserted that she had locked and bolted it before retiring.

This argued that Tia Juana had of her own volition slipped away from the house on some unknown mission, but to Willa such an hypothesis seemed unlikely. In the first place, the old woman was heart and soul in the plan in which Willa herself was the moving spirit, and well content to leave all things to the guidance of her idolized young friend. Then, too, she had the dread of the strange new city of one who had followed a long and open trail and would scarcely in her right mind have ventured forth to brave it on her own initiative. Had some cajoling or threatening message reached her which induced her to play into Wiley's hands, or could it be that Señora Rodriguez had been bribed to aid in her abduction?

Fierce and implacable as Tia Juana's will was, age had taken its toll of her mental strength and resiliency, and Willa shuddered to think of the coercion which might be brought to bear upon her bewildered and shaken sensibilities.

Dan noted his mistress' profound despondency, but ventured no remark until she addressed him just as they reached the bridge once more.

"Dan, you drove a car once for a detective agency, you told me. Did you ever do any detective work yourself? Do you know anything of their methods?"

"I do, Miss!" he responded promptly, a sparkle dawning in his eyes. "Not that I ever did any of it, but I used to watch the other fellers at work and I'm thinking I could go them one better at it. I've seen them make some bonehead plays, in my time, and some wonderful hits, too, I'll admit that."

"Do you want to try a little of it for me?" Willa asked. "An old Spanish woman disappeared early this morning from that house back on Second Place, and I want her found without delay. It's she whom those other men are after; she used to live with her grandson, a hunchback, in that cottage upon the Parkway. There will be double wages in it for you while you're working on it, and a thousand dollars reward if you find her and bring her to me."

She went on to describe Tia Juana, and Dan listened in rapt attention to every detail, fired with instant enthusiasm for the new job.

"You leave it to me, Miss!" he announced confidently when she had finished. "I'll get into that house to-morrow, one way or another, and have a talk with the landlady and the kid. I'll soon find out if they know more than they've told. In the meantime, I'll make the round of the hospitals to-night and have a look-in at headquarters to see if she's turned up missing. Those fellers trailing us this afternoon don't make it look as if they or the man they're workin' for could have got hold of her already and there's a chance that she just wandered off, like, on her own hook. I'll let you know the minute I've got a line on her. Wish I spoke her lingo!"

"Oh, Tia Juana understands English well enough when she wants to, and speaks it, too, but only when necessity compels it. She hates everything American but me. I— I could not bear to think of her wandering about, destitute and dazed and freezing in this storm! Dan, you must find her for me!"

The erstwhile chauffeur promised, with extravagant protestations of assurance, and it was evident that he was in thorough earnest, with illimitable faith in his own powers.

His attitude of mind was infectious and when Willa descended before the Halstead house her own natural buoyancy of thought had reasserted itself, although the mystery remained as black and sinister as ever.

Wiley, still hors de combat from his thrashing at Thode's hands, could scarcely have been a factor himself in this new development and if it proved to be the result of any of his agents' activities, surely Dan would be able to find some trace.

She passed a sleepless night, however, and arose to find a foot of snow glistening on the ground and the air keen and brittle with cold. No word came from Dan, and in the afternoon she threw discretion to the winds and went boldly to the Brooklyn house.

Nothing had developed save that José had worried himself into a fever, and the Señora Rodriguez's lamentations were tinged with a querulous resentment.

The young Señorita was paying handsomely for the hospitality to her friends, and she herself would gladly do anything to aid her country-people, even if they were

but Mexican Spanish and not of the blood. Nevertheless, she was not to blame for the old Señora's departure,
she had not agreed to stand guard over her and surely
the Evil Eye had descended upon her house! She would
nurse the little José as though he were her own, and the
old Señora's room should be kept in readiness for her
return, but she, Conchita Rodriguez, would worry her
own head no longer!

Willa placated the woman's displeasure with promises
of more generous pay, and arranged for extra care and
comforts for José, whom the Señora evidently regarded
with a tenderness born of superstition; to aid a jorobado
brought luck to one's hearth-stone, even as the touch of
his humped shoulders gave promise of good fortune.

Secure at least in the thought of his well-being, Willa
was content to leave José in the hands of his irascible
but kind-hearted landlady, stipulating that daily messages
should be telephoned to her of his condition.

"And if anyone comes to inquire for him, remember
that he is not here, please," she added. "He and the
Señora have both gone; that is, unless a young American named Morrissey should appear. He is a friend of
mine, and trying to help me find the Señora."

"'Morrissey?' I shall not forget." Señora Rodriguez
repeated the name thoughtfully. "No one has been here
to-day but a plumber, who arrived without my order. He
said there was a leak in the cellar next door which came
from my house and he did strange things to my pipes so
that now I can draw no water in my kitchen. Now my
neighbor tells me there was no leak, and I cannot understand. They do singular things, these Americanos."

Willa returned to her home in a more despondent

mood even than before, and a telephone call from Dan late in the evening did not tend to raise her spirits.

"I've canvassed every hospital and institootion in the five boroughs!" he announced. "I even tried the morgue, but there ain't hide nor hair of the old lady. Looks like the earth might have opened and swallowed her up. I take it you don't want me to report her missing at head-quarters, do you?"

"Only as the very last resort," Willa responded. "We must avoid publicity if we can, although of course if she is ill or in any danger I shall have to let every other consideration go."

"You leave it to me, Miss!" The familiar slogan came as cheerfully as ever over the wire. "I don't think the old lady's in bad, wherever she is. Nobody'd dare do anything to her, would they? It ain't a rough-house gang that's after her, from what you told me."

"No, Dan. I am not afraid of any violence to her at their hands. They will only worry and annoy her."

"Well, the chances are, if she just wandered off and lost herself, that somebody's taken her in. I'm doin' fine, so far. I had a grand talk with the dame over in Brook-lyn to-day, and she never once got on to me."

His tone was filled with such honest pride that Willa was loath to disturb it, yet she could not forbear remarking:

"I did, though, Dan, when she told me what had been done to the plumbing! What did you find out from her?"

"Everything she knew and a lot that she threw in for good measure. I didn't have to start her; she was just aching to tell the whole story; how they came to her and all! If them other people get on to the house, she'll spill the beans to them sure, Miss. She don't own that house; she only rents it, and the next time I go I'll have an order from the agent to put in weatherstrips or clean the chimneys and grates. I want a talk with the lad as soon as he is well enough. I'll report to you, Miss, just as quick as anything turns up."

Willa gave him some final instructions and hung up the receiver, to find Angie at her elbow.

"You've been an unconscionable time!" the latter complained, veiling her eyes to conceal their gleam of awakened curiosity and interest. "We're waiting for you to make up a rubber. Who was that message from? Any of the crowd?"

"No," Willa replied directly. "It was from a friend of mine; you do not know him, Angie."

"Oh, I'm sure I didn't mean to intrude.—Dear me! to-morrow's Thanksgiving, and this wretched season is scarcely begun!"

It was a weary holiday for Willa and she sat through the elaborate formal dinner with which the Halsteads celebrated it in an abstraction of mood which gave two of her callow admirers much concern.

The presence of Kearn Thode's sister, however, brought her out of her reverie and later, when Mrs. Beekman sought her out in the drawing-room, Willa left her problem to take care of itself for the hour in her interest in the breezy clear-eyed woman so like Kearn himself.

"I must apologize for not coming yesterday, as I assured my brother I would. An epidemic of something or other has broken out at my kennels and I spent a disheartening and doggy afternoon." She laughed, adding with sudden seriousness: "My brother has told me so many interesting things of you, Miss Murdaugh, that I have wanted to really know you, but I suppose you have been submerged in a sea of festivity with your cousins. I am a gregarious person but not a conventionally social one. I suppose that is why we have not happened to meet since that first dinner; I do not follow the beaten path, as a rule."

"Nor I, except when I am led by the nose!" Willa responded, laughing, too. "But tell me, is Mr. Thode improving?"

Mrs. Beekman gave her a swift, keen glance.

"Oh, yes! He suffered a mere scratch or two; you know what babies men are about such things.—Look at them trailing in now from the dining-room, fed up on the newest stories and the oldest cognac! There's something almost tragic in their boredom, isn't there?"

Willa gasped, a little taken aback by her companion's cynical frankness, and Mrs. Beekman laid an impulsive hand upon her arm.

"Come and lunch with me to-morrow; just we two. We'll have a nice little chat and if Kearn comes bothering around I'll send him away. I want you to tell me about Mexico."

Willa promised with an odd little thrill of warmth at her heart. With the exception of fat, comfortable Sallie Bailey and old Tia Juana, the girl had had no intimates of her own sex, and the competition appeared to be so keen among the members of the set in which she found herself that friendship was eyed askance as a subterfuge to be wary of.

The daily bulletins from Brooklyn were not encouraging, nor was Dan Morrissey gaining ground in the search. Three days had passed since the disappearance of Tia Juana, and Willa decided despairingly that should a week go by without news, she must go to the police and brave the storm of notoriety and questioning from Mason North and the Halsteads, which would mean the end of her cherished secrecy and hem her in with a multitude of complications.

She lunched with Mrs. Beekman as she had promised, in the dingy old-fashioned house on the Square which somehow gave the girl, untutored as she was, an impression of aristocracy that the newer, more ornate piles of stone farther up the Avenue had utterly failed to convey. She was miserably aware that the other woman was making a sympathetic effort to understand her and gain her friendship, yet the thought of Tia Juana drove all else from her mind and she knew she was creating a far from propitious impression.

An unaccountable shyness, too, took possession of her at the possibility of meeting Kearn Thode beneath his sister's discerning eye, and as soon as she could courteously do so, she tore herself away from her disappointed hostess and went over the bridge to José.

The cripple's fever had abated, but he was still very weak. His little hot hands clutched hers nervously and his big eyes seemed to burn into hers as he asked in his own tongue:

"The Señorita has a friend whom she trusts?"

"Yes, José," responded Willa promptly. "Have you seen him?"

"He came this morning, and told me his name. He

said I was to ask it of you, and you would tell me the same."

"Is it 'Dan'?" She watched the thin face brighten.

"That was it! And am I to trust him, too?"

"You can tell him anything as you would me, amiguito, but remember, no word of the Pool!"

"That is written, Señorita Billie, on my heart!—But will the grandmama ever return?"

Willa soothed him as well as she was able, and, after a brief conference with Señorita Rodriguez, took her departure.

A man was standing near the bottom of the steps, lighting a cigarette. Her eyes rested upon him with no flash of recognition until he glanced up and then with a slow smile tossed his cigarette into the gutter. It was Starr Wiley.

His puffed, discolored lips stood out against the pasty whiteness of his face with the grotesque effect of a mask and his eyes gleamed malevolently, but he lifted his hat with the old airy insouciance.

"We meet again, my dear Billie!"

She bowed gravely, and made as if to pass him, but he barred her way.

"Are you in such haste? I've come on purpose to escort you back over the bridge and have a little chat with you. There is something almost comic in the situation, don't you think?"

"If there is, Mr. Wiley, it is discernible only to you." She shrugged. "I will leave you to the enjoyment of it."

"Not yet, my dear! Our bird has flown, I know, but I am curious to learn why you haunt the empty cage."

Willa paused, eying him steadily.

"What is it to you, as long as the Señora Reyes is not here?"

"Because I believe that you will lead me to her more quickly than my agents can!" Wiley's smile became a knowing leer. "Very clever, your conversation over the telephone the other night, designed for Angie's benefit! You knew that she would report it faithfully to me and you counted on it to throw me off the track, but it didn't quite serve its purpose."

Willa's heart gave a leap, and then sank in a sick wave of fear for Tia Juana. She did not realize until that moment how certain she had been that the old woman was in the hands of those whose interest it would be to keep her safe.

Wiley's attitude betrayed the fact that he knew no more than the girl herself where Tia Juana was. What, then, could have happened to her?

"I really must congratulate you once more!" he went on, ironically. "It was a master stroke, a flash of genius, to spirit the old lady away from this latest retreat of hers, and pretend that you, too, were in the dark as to her whereabouts. It was not your fault that the shot fell short of its mark!"

Willa hesitated. Should she tell him the truth? That would, of course, give him equal ground with her and he would move heaven and earth to beat her in the search, but in her hideous new anxiety she would almost rather know that Tia Juana was in antagonistic hands than face the vague but terrible possibilities confronting her.

Starr Wiley accepted her silence as an admission and on the instant his manner changed.

"I have followed you here to tell you that the time is

past for quibbling, and no mere ruse will suffice longer to put me off!" He moved close to her and glared down implacably into her unwavering eyes. "You refused to meet me half way, and now you shall hear my ultimatum: You will produce Tia Juana or take me to her within three days, or I shall tell what I know!"

"Mr. Wiley—" Willa drew herself up very straight and tall—"I have no statement to make about Tia Juana, save that I cannot and will not take you to her. I have listened to your threats and innuendoes until my patience is exhausted and I warn you not to approach me again on this or any other matter. What you know is immaterial to me, you must tell it to whom you please. Will you leave me now, or permit me to depart without a further scene?"

He bowed and stepped back.

"As you desire. Remember you have three days. Think it over well, my dear Billie. It is your present position, the Murdaugh money, a brilliant future and a name, against the Pool of the Lost Souls!"

CHAPTER XVII

ANGIE SCORES

I WAS sorry to have missed you at my sister's, although I do not think you would have welcomed my appearance!" laughed Kearn Thode. "I was striped with plaster like a savage in war paint."

"I had the pleasure of seeing the other victim of that motor accident," Willa remarked demurely. "He was even less prepossessing than usual. I—I knew something of what occurred as I think you could understand from my note. I think that I have again to thank you for your championship."

They were sitting out a dance in the Allardyce's conservatory at their first meeting the night of the Erskine dinner and for some reason speech was difficult to them both. Her eyes, usually so candid, were veiled from him, but Thode swept her with a hungrily wistful gaze.

"You are mistaken. You have nothing to thank me for. I am sorry that any idle gossip reached your ears, but believe me, no other course was open to me. No man could have helped himself—"

"Oh, I understand, of course." Willa blundered helplessly in her haste. "You would have done as much, under the same circumstances, for any other girl, but it is good to feel that there are real men in the world who will protect the name of a friend as though it were that of an own sister."

"It wasn't exactly that, Willa." His voice was very low and his eyes had dropped from her face. "A man would naturally resent any insinuation against a good woman, whether she were his sister or not. There is only one woman in the world for whom a man fights with the primitive blind rage of a human creature for his mate: only, fool that he is, he does not always recognize the feeling which consumes him for what it really is."

He paused, and Willa, too, was silent, but she feared that the very beating of her heart would be audible to his ears. The dreamy waltz had given way to the syncopation of a fox-trot, yet neither was aware of the passing minutes.

"I was blind in Limasito!" he went on. "No woman has come deeply into my life except my sister and I did not know, I did not realize what you had come to mean to me in our few meetings until you were going away into this new existence which was awaiting you, and then I could not speak. I did not follow you then because I had nothing to offer, but I made up my mind to succeed in what I had set out to do, if honest endeavor and the hardest kind of work could achieve it and then, if I were not too late, I meant to come to you and ask you to be my wife."

Willa stirred tremulously, but still her lips were dumb, and Thode misinterpreted her silence.

"Please, don't be afraid!" he assured her, bitterly. "I am not going to ask you that now, for I have failed! I'm not even going to ask you to wait for me, to give me any hope, for I am losing faith in myself; not in my love for you, Willa, but in the success which alone would make it possible for me to approach you. I only wanted you to know that I had awakened to the truth. No girl was ever yet displeased at one more victim bound to her chariot wheels."

"I am not displeased, but I—I am distressed!" Willa stammered through stiffened lips. "You think because I accepted the name and the fortune of the grandfather I never knew, and apparently forgot the old life and all that Dad had done for me, that I am just coldly mercenary! You think I am that sort, ambitious and pushing and soulless! I thought you knew and understood me, I thought that we were friends!"

"That, I hope, we shall always be," he said gently. "It would have been quixotic, absurd for you to refuse the golden opportunity when it came. I did not think of that, nor did I believe you mercenary. I did not mean to whine about my failure, either; it was the chance of fortune and I have lost. You will forgive my having spoken—I had to tell you! I could not keep silent any longer, it was as if you, all unconsciously, were twisting the heart from my breast. You could not help it if you wanted to, you are so sweet, so wonderful! Please, don't be sorry for me, either, it is the greatest thing that ever happened to me and I shall be glad of it, always, even when I have to stand aside and see you turn to a better, bigger man. No matter what happens I shall, all my life through, be at your service."

"Oh, I am not the least bit sorry for you!" Willa cried. "I am exasperated with you! Do you suppose I am the sort of woman to care what a man has, rather than what he is? Am I a painted pampered doll that I must be approached with gifts and sweets and dangled

before the highest bidder? My mother married the man
she loved and starved with him and died working to take
care of his child! Am I less a woman than she?"

"Willa!" He breathed her name in a fervent whisper
and caught her two hands in his. "Willa, look at me!"

She raised her blazing eyes and the flame died to a
soft luminous glow, while the rich color mantled to her
brow.

"Willa, do you mean that you care, really?—Oh, I
vowed I would not ask you until I had proved myself
worthy, and now, when everything is at a standstill, an
impasse, and you yourself have warned me of the impossibility of winning out in my plan for the future, I—I
forget all my resolutions! It is unfair for me to speak
now, it is not playing the game, but will you tell me at
least that you won't be displeased with me if sometime
I come to you, when I have won the right? I will ask
no promise now, I cannot, but if I could know that you
cared ever so little—"

"How can you know if—if you don't ask?" Willa's
downright honesty had gotten the better of her timidity
and with characteristic fearlessness she disclosed all that
was in her own wildly throbbing heart. "I don't know
how a man could prove himself more worthy of any
woman than by taking his life in his hands on a hundred-
to-one chance of saving hers! I don't know what difference the loss or finding of the Pool makes in the happiness of you and me. Go ahead and make a martyr of
yourself over your silly pride if you want to! If I
thought you didn't care, that you were just trying to
carry on the ghastly game they call flirtation up here, I
wouldn't be so angry with you. I'm not Willa Mur-

daugh down inside of me, and you know it!—I'm just Gentleman Geoff's Billie, a waif raised by the greatest-hearted man that ever lived, but I've got some pride myself. I don't want any man who hasn't s-spunk enough to ask me!"

"Willa! Oh, my dearest, will you—!"

"Here comes Winnie Mason!" She drew her hands from his and sprang up with a nervous tinkle of laughter. "That means we've missed three dances, and you were to have had two of them with Angie! You'll be in for a dreadful panning—"

"You wicked little—adorable little—girl o' mine!" he exclaimed softly, as Winnie's mildly inquiring face appeared around a narrow alley between the close-packed flowering plants. "I'm coming to-morrow, before break-fast—"

Willa shook her head, the light waning in her eyes.

"No, not to-morrow, Kearn. There is something that I must do, something I cannot put aside even—even for you."

"In the evening, then? I must see you to-morrow sometime! It's going to be hard enough to live through to-night!"

She nodded, and, not trusting herself to speak again, turned and slipped away to meet Winnie Mason.

That placidly dense young man was mightily pleased with the effusive greeting with which she favored him, and had she vision enough to note it, she might have read in his worshiping eyes a like message to that which she had just heard.

But she was blind, dazed in the light of her own swiftly gained wondrous happiness. The music, the dancers, the little crystal-laden supper-tables, the final romp all passed in a kaleidoscopic dream before her, and only the wintry night wind beating upon her in a frigid blast, as she stepped from the awninged passage-way to the limousine, awakened her to a sense of reality.

Just then, the flash of a street-lamp in at the window fell for a passing moment on Angie's face as she sat half-turned from her cousin and Willa caught her breath to stifle a sudden startled exclamation. She had seen Angie in many fits of temper, sullen and raging, but never had the girl's expression been so fiendish! The doll-like beauty was gone in a distortion of anger, but there was a suggestion of malignant triumph, too, which aroused Willa's apprehension.

She knew that in her heart Angie despised her as an upstart and bitterly resented her small success in the social world, beside blaming her for the episode with Starr Wiley. She remembered, too, how Angie had betrayed her to him. In her maddening anxiety for Tia Juana's safety, Willa had given no thought to the means Wiley must have used to reinstate himself once more in her cousin's willing eyes.

Was this evidence of fury directed against her because she had been the unwitting cause of Kearn Thode's defection in the matter of the two dances, or was something deeper and more significant in the wind?

Willa was not left in doubt for long. She had scarcely finished her preparations for the night and was braiding her long black hair into a massive rope, when a light, brittle tapping came upon her door

Almost before the wondering assent had left her lips, Angie slipped in and stood before her. She was still in her spangled dance frock and her round blue eyes were snapping fire.

"I suppose I have come on a thankless mission, Willa," she began. "Every time I have tried to help you or teach you anything, you have looked on it, in your spiteful way, as mere jealousy on my part, although why I should be jealous of you, heaven only knows!"

"Please, Angelica! We have had all this out before and I am very tired. Would you mind if I asked you to wait until morning?" Willa gave her hair a final twist and turned from the mirror. "I am honestly sorry Kearn Thode missed those dances with you to-night, but it really wasn't my fault—"

"Do you suppose I wanted to dance with him?" Angie interrupted in immense scorn. "I only permitted him to put his name down on my card in ordinary courtesy because of his sister; she has such a caustic tongue that one must keep on the right side of her. If he chose to ignore his dances with me it was because he was playing a game which you, you conceited little simpleton, couldn't see through. Oh, I heard what he said to you in the conservatory—!"

"You listened!" Willa turned on her at last. "Lord, what a miserable specimen of a girl you are, anyhow! I knew you were spying about and listening at my heels here at home to learn what you could and run with it to the man who's making a tool of you and a fool besides, but I didn't think you were so low down as to skulk about and pry into affairs which are no concern of yours! Is nothing sacred to you?"

"I was only doing my duty!" Angie returned loftily. Then her consuming rage got the better of her once more.

"You dare to speak of anyone making a tool of me! It is you who are waiting for anyone's hand! Starr Wiley made a fool of you, and you simpered and purred and thought you were taking him from me, when he was only amusing himself for the moment because he was jealous of me with Art. Judson! Now, in your bursting conceit you think this impecunious fortune-hunter, Thode, is in love with you. I listened because it was my duty to keep any member of the family from throwing herself away and I wanted to see how far he would dare to go. I'm here now to tell you the truth."

"I do not want to hear another word!" Willa cried hotly. "It is no affair of yours and you shall not speak of Kearn Thode as a—a fortune-hunter! He is the only real man in this whole spindling, self-seeking, artificial crowd! If you listened, you know how proud and independent he is!"

"I heard, but that was only his cleverness; he knew how eager you were and he simply led you on to almost propose to him yourself! That was good stuff about not knowing he cared for you down in Mexico until you were leaving. What would you say if I were to tell you that he made a deliberate play for you from the moment he reached that town? Oh, he's serious enough! He'll marry you if he can; that's what he meant to do from the first."

"I think you must be mad!" Willa stared at her cousin in sheer wonder. "Why should he have wanted to marry me? There were lots of other girls in town——"

"Because he knew who you really were all the time! He knew before Mason North ever found you, and he knew, too, what a fortune you were coming into. You needn't look at me like that, I know what I am talking about!"

"I don't think you do," Willa remarked simply. "You must have taken leave of your senses or else Starr Wiley has been making you believe the silliest sort of lies. How could Kearn Thode have known who I was? No one did but—but the man who had made me his own daughter, and he would not tell me because he did not want to hurt me by letting me know what mean, contemptible snobs my people were and how they had served my own father for marrying my brave mother! Kearn Thode knew nothing!"

"What if I were to show you proof? Here is a letter in his own hand, telling all about you and what he meant to do." Angie pulled a crumpled wad of paper from her bodice and held it out, her whole body quivering in triumph. "Read it and then you'll know whether he cares for you or not! Read it, I say!"

"And I say to you that if you don't leave this room at once I will ring and have you put out! Don't you imagine that I can see through a scurvy trick of Starr Wiley's to get back at the man who beat him twice to a mere pulp? I do not want to see the letter, I will not read it. It is all a lie!"

"Then listen!" Angie smoothed the sheet of paper and fairly danced in her excitement. "You shall listen! You shall know what that man is scheming to marry you for! There is only a part of it here, but it ought to be enough to open your eyes, blinded with conceit as you are!"

"I will not——!" Willa began indignantly, but Angie's voice silenced her.

"——'Except for him, of course, no one here knows her real name'," she read, "'and it wouldn't mean anything to them if they did, but I spotted her at once and later events have only proved the truth of my suspicions. She is the undoubted owner of almost boundless wealth and when I have gone after her and won her consent——' "

"Stop!" Willa clapped her hands to her ears. "I will not listen to one more word! It is a lie, I tell you! A lie!"

"There isn't any more," Angie announced with a sly grimace. "That is the bottom of the page, but it ought to be enough for you."

"Kearn Thode never wrote a word of it!" exclaimed Willa passionately. "I would not believe you if you swore it from now till you die! Go, before I make you!"

"Oh, I'm going." Angie shrugged, and the letter fluttered from her fingers to the floor. "I've no desire for a disgraceful brawl, I assure you! Of course, I am not familiar with Kearn Thode's handwriting, but I have proof enough to satisfy me that the letter is his. If you marry him now, you will have bought him with your eyes open and have no one but yourself to blame if you're not pleased with your bargain! I have done my duty anyway, my dear cousin. Good-night."

Her footsteps died away down the hall, and Willa dropped into a low chair before the hearth, covering her face with her hands. It was just a trick of Wiley's, of course! She would not let her gaze stray to that tell-tale sheet of white paper upon the floor, and yet something seemed to draw her eyes to it with an almost physical strength.

Wiley must have written it himself and put it in Angie's hands to work what mischief she might with it. There could be no harm in one glance at it; a glance which would prove instantly its falseness, just as she knew it in her heart to be at best a forgery.

Slowly Willa rose and step by step made her way to where the letter lay. She made no effort to touch it at first, but it had fallen with the written side uppermost and gradually as she stared down at it the scorn in her face gave way to wonder and then despair.

The brief note she had received from Kearn Thode, after he had thrashed Wiley at the club, was engraved deep in her thoughts with every line distinct and the characters on the paper before her eyes were so similar in every detail that it seemed impossible for them not to have been fashioned by the same hand.

With grief and horror surging in her heart, Willa rushed to the little drawer of her dressing-table where the first note had been treasured, and drew it forth. Then, seizing the other paper from the floor, she held them beneath the glow of the lamp with shaking hands and compared them.

The next minute she had crumpled them both fiercely and cast them from her, flinging herself across her bed in a paroxysm of bitter grief and disillusionment.

Kearn Thode had written both letters; there could be no longer doubt. He was like all the rest! Truth and chivalry departed from the world and her shattered dream, and once more Willa found herself alone, but in a depth of solitude she had never known before. Love had gone.

CHAPTER XVIII

Midnight for Cinderella

WHEN the late lowering dawn seeped in at the windows, Willa raised herself wearily and crept to her desk. Her face with the tears dried upon it was ghastly in the morning light, but her eyes held a look of grim determination. Seating herself, she took up her pen and wrote without hesitation:

"My Dear Mr. Thode:
"I beg that you will not call this evening, that I may be spared the painful necessity of having you shown the door. In the light of my present full comprehension of your motives, I no longer wonder that even you hesitated at the moment of your odious proposal. The only possible reparation you can make for the humiliation you have brought upon me in my inmost thoughts is to so arrange that I need never look upon your face again.
"In all sincerity,
"Willa Murdaugh."

The letter finished, she sealed and stamped it; then her worn-out body slumped in the chair and her head bowed upon her folded arms on the desk.

The collapse lasted but a moment, however. The same dogged determination which had forced her weary spirit to the pronouncement of the verdict upon her love, drove her yet indomitably on. As she lifted her head her gaze mechanically fell upon the calendar before her and a slow, infinitely sad smile curled her lips. It was the beginning of the third day since Starr Wiley had issued his ultimatum. He must carry his threat into execution or admit it to have been sheer bluff. Curiously, she looked upon the impending crisis with the impassivity of a bystander. What did it matter now?

Then realization came back in a full tide and she sprang to her feet. The weary plodding search which had taken her half over the city in the past few agonizing days had been fruitless, yet must it still continue until definite news of Tia Juana could be learned. Dan Morrissey had been faithful, but his ardent spirit outran his detective skill and his initiative advanced no farther afield than a daily round of the hospitals and temporary shelters of the city's driftwood, and a hopeless concentration on the neighborhood from which the aged woman had so mysteriously vanished.

Willa herself had no more comprehensive plan; she had advertised discreetly in Spanish in the "personal" column of a morning newspaper and followed every tentative line of investigation which presented itself to her, but messages to each stage of the journey back to Limasito and exhaustive questioning of the few individuals with whom Tia Juana had come in contact in New York were alike unproductive of result.

Hopelessness was stealthily enveloping her spirit, but she resolutely fought it down. She must not give up, she would not until Tia Juana was safe. She had been instrumental in bringing the aged woman to an alien land,

and she was responsible for whatever misfortune might have come upon her. Then, too, there was her purpose still to be achieved; that at least remained to her.

At breakfast Angie addressed her in honeyed tones, scrutinizing her hungrily meanwhile for evidence of the result of her maneuver, but Willa was stonily noncommittal. The meal progressed in a constrained silence which was broken only by the shrill summons of the telephone.

Señora Rodriguez's staccato voice came over the wire in such an outpouring of hysteria that at first Willa could make nothing of it, but at length one phrase smote her ears:

"It is the jorobadito, José, who has disappeared now!"

"What?" Willa faltered. "You mean that José has gone also? It cannot be, Señora Rodriguez! There must be a mistake! He would not go unless he were abducted!"

"No, Señorita; there was no abduction!" the Spanish woman cried. "The little José was all of yesterday most thoughtful. Scarcely could I arouse him to eat, and as his fever abated I allowed him to sit in the sun upon the glass-enclosed back porch and did not urge upon him the medicine he hates. Last night as he went to bed he kissed my hand quite suddenly, a thing he has not done before, though always was he courteous. This morning he was gone as the old Señora went, without warning.— Señorita, I am a poor woman, but I would give half I possess to have the pobrecito back for he is frail and weak to be alone in this great city and he has not a peso with him. Moreover, he brought me luck. What can I do, Señorita, to find him once more?"

Willa cut the woman's protestations short, and, calling up the garage—their prearranged rendez-vous—instructed Dan to meet her at the bridge.

Intent on the new calamity, she gave no heed as to the probability of having been overheard by Angie, but hurriedly departed.

The deeply concerned Dan broke all records and narrowly escaped arrest in getting her to the Rodriguez home, but nothing further could be elicited from its dismayed châtelaine. Her sincerity, however, was self-evident; she could have had no hand in the disappearance of the little hunchback.

The day was spent in a feverishly renewed search which brought no surcease of anxiety and at its end Willa dragged herself with leaden feet to her room. Her head seemed bursting and she shook as with an ague as she dressed for the tedious dinner and the still more tedious game of bridge which was the program of the evening. She dared not absent herself, explanations enough would be demanded of her for the day's broken engagements, but she looked forward to the hours ahead with a dread foreboding which she could not name.

It was merely nerves, she assured herself; she was worn-out mentally and physically with the continued strain and ceaseless effort and she forced her thoughts resolutely away from the false but ecstatic happiness which might have been hers on that evening save for the discovery of Kearn Thode's perfidy.

The arrival of the expected guests commanded her descent to the drawing-room, dinner somehow dragged through its almost interminable length and the bridge-tables were made up, when a diversion occurred.

The door-bell pealed, and Welch obeyed its summons, then came and called Ripley Halstead quietly from his place. No premonition warned Willa, even when her cousin returned visibly perturbed and excused himself for the evening, pleading an unanticipated business conference.

The tables were readjusted and the game went on to its close. Then came supper, and when the last of the guests had departed the hands of the clock were on the stroke of twelve and Willa turned with a sigh of relief to ascend to her room.

Midway the stairs, she was halted by hearing her name called in strange, stunned accents, and, turning, saw Ripley Halstead standing in the library door, regarding her with dazed, half-incredulous eyes, as though she were a changeling.

Instantly the truth came to her, and with head held high and a slight scornful smile upon her lips she descended and approached him.

The long table in the center of the library was strewn with large legal-looking documents, and beside it sat Mason North, his rotund body sagged in the chair, his good-natured face drawn and haggard. Opposite him stood Starr Wiley, his bruised lips twisted into a leer of triumph.

The girl looked gravely from one to the other and then turning to her cousin, waited submissively for him to speak.

"Willa, my dear——" he paused, clearing his throat nervously—"I have something to tell you which will be a painful shock to you. It has utterly unnerved me. I— I would not have dreamed that such an astounding dis-

covery could come to pass and at this late date it is particularly distressing——"

"Better permit me to tell her, Ripley." Mason North
rose heavily to his feet and stood with one pudgy hand
braced upon the table as if for support. "The mistake
was mine in too eagerly grasping the obvious as proof.—
My dear Wil—my dear girl, I am profoundly grieved, but
it has been brought to our attention that—that there are
grave doubts as to your identity! In fact, belated but
seemingly irrefutable documentary evidence appears to
prove that you—you are not Willa Murdaugh!"

The girl stood like a statue, but from behind her Mrs.
Halstead gasped convulsively, and there came a little
squeal in Angie's treble tones.

"Sit down, my dear." Ripley Halstead drew forward
a chair and Willa sank obediently into it, her eyes never
leaving those of the attorney.

The others came in and seated themselves unbidden;
all but Vernon. He took up his stand behind Willa's
chair and for a moment his hand brushed her shoulder
as if to assure her of his presence in case of need.

"It is only just that an immediate and detailed explanation be made to you," North continued. "I am sure
it is unnecessary for me to express my regret and sympathy, but I want you to realize that I am as entirely at
your service in every way as I was prior to this discovery.

"When I found you in Limasito and retraced your history from the time the man known as 'Gentleman Geoff'
adopted you supposedly in Topaz Gulch, I overlooked
one significant phase in his peregrinations. Willa Murdaugh's parentage and the circumstances of her birth

were in every particular as I have told you; Ralph Murdaugh died when the baby was two years old, his wife lost her life in a fire two years later and the child was actually adopted by Gentleman Geoff and taken with him on his wanderings.

"Now it has transpired that the first heavy snow of the following winter caught him midway between two mining camps far up in the Rockies, near Flathead Lake, Montana. Does that name recall any memories to you?"

Willa shook her head, mutely, and the attorney after a moment's pause went on:

"It is scarcely likely that it would, for you yourself could have been no more than five years old at the time. However, Gentleman Geoff and the little Willa were lost in the blizzard, and, after suffering untold horrors, he finally made his way to the cabin of a trapper, named——" he hesitated and glanced down at the papers beneath his hand—"named Frank Hillery. This trapper Hillery's wife had run away with another man some years before, leaving him with a little daughter on his hands, a child of about five years, called Louise."

Again he paused, coughing. The Halsteads, mother and daughter, sat spell-bound, but Willa was outwardly the coolest person in the room. The story in its every detail was stamping itself indelibly upon her mind and for the moment even the presence of Starr Wiley was forgotten.

"When he reached the trapper's cabin, Gentleman Geoff was blinded by the snow, delirious and half frozen. Hillery took him in, unwrapped the fur pack he carried on his back and discovered the body of little Willa. She had died from exposure."

Vernon uttered a sharp exclamation, and the girl seated before him clasped her hands tightly, but no other sign greeted Mason North's announcement. He passed his hand across his brow and drew a deep breath.

"Hillery buried the child and nursed Gentleman Geoff through a long illness. It was well into the following spring when he was able to proceed on his journey, and when he did, he took the trapper's little daughter, Louise, with him, and called her 'Billie' as he had nicknamed the other. His future wanderings never took him back over the same route or to any of the places where the real Willa had been known, consequently the substitution was never discovered until these papers came to light. No one had visited the trapper's lonely cabin during the period of Gentleman Geoff's presence there. Hillery deserted it the following summer and went southward to Arizona where he eventually died six months ago. Undoubtedly, those who had known him and passed the cabin clearing took it for granted that the little grave was that of his daughter, Louise, but these documents, found among Frank Hillery's private papers after his death, bear witness in crude but unmistakable fashion to the agreement between the two men and the adoption of little Louise by Gentleman Geoff."

Mason North seated himself once more with a gesture of relief that the bomb was exploded, and all eyes turned to Willa.

"How is it, then, that I remember the fire in which my mother was destroyed?" She was wholly innocent of an intention to defend her position, but asked her question in the first bewildering shock, unconscious of the fact which her form of speech betrayed, that she could not all at once disassociate herself from the identity she had accepted only a few short weeks before. "Why, I even recall vaguely a song which the woman I supposed must have been my mother used to sing all the time, though I cannot quite bring it back to my mind. I am sure if I heard it once, I should remember!"

The attorney visibly hesitated, and it was Ripley Halstead who replied as gently as possible:

"Often one believes that one can recall experiences of their very early years which they have actually learned from hearsay, from countless repetition in their presence."

"But Dad never spoke of that time in Nevada; he never once referred to it to the very hour of his death! I recall vaguely being lost in the snow and I have often heard Dad speak of Hillery's kindness and care; he used to say that the trapper had saved both our lives. A number of people in Limasito have heard the story from his own lips, Jim Baggott and Henry Bailey and Rufe Terwilliger—but Rufe is dead now, he was killed in El Negrito's raid——"

She paused as if a hand had closed suddenly about her throat, while a tiny patch of color crept into each cheek and her eyes, large and luminous and swiftly keen, sought Starr Wiley's. Her clasped hands tightened, then relaxed and a little smile hovered about her lips once more; a coolly calculating, somewhat grim little smile. The story had engrossed her for the moment to the exclusion of all else, but mention of the raid recalled her sharply to the presence of its instigator.

Wiley's vague threats were plain to her now, his purpose practically achieved. He had kept his word, he had exposed her, but was her early memory indeed tricking her? Was this latest revelation true, and had he actually stumbled upon authentic records, or manufactured them to avenge himself upon her and eliminate her from his path? Willa's mind still groped in a quandary, but every instinct within her arose to combat.

"Why would Dad have mentioned Hillery at all, if he did not intend that I should ever learn the truth?" she asked quietly. "Indeed, why did he adopt the trapper's little daughter and call her by the other's name?"

"Well," Ripley Halstead replied after a swift glance at the attorney as if for help, "probably he had grown fond of the dead child and wanted another to take her place."

"He undoubtedly did!" It was the first time Starr Wiley spoke in the girl's presence and a short ugly laugh accompanied the remark. "Not wholly because he had taken a liking to Willa Murdaugh, however. Why blink the facts, Mr. Halstead? It is plain on the face of it that he must have looked up the real Willa's parentage and connections, and realized that the storm had robbed him of a potential heiress in whose probable inheritance he would sometime have shared——"

"That is a lie." Willa's tones rang out without passion but clarion clear in her absolute certitude. "Anyone who knew Dad ever so slightly would testify to its falseness. Why did he not keep himself informed of my grandfather's changing attitude and come forward and claim the inheritance when the search for me began? Whether I am Willa Murdaugh or not, there can be at least no reason why I should remain to hear the memory of the finest man who ever lived defiled by such a base imputation. If you will excuse me now——"

She half rose from her chair, but Starr Wiley fore-stalled her.

"Your pardon—I will go." He bowed with an under-current of mockery in his suave manner. "Naturally, Miss Billie, you resent my interference in your career and I deplore the fact that the onerous duty should have fallen upon my shoulders. However, it was a duty, no matter how repugnant, and I could do no less than place the facts before Mr. North and Mr. Halstead. I am sure my attitude requires no defense and I trust, when you will have had time to think matters over calmly, you will not blame me too bitterly. Believe me, I would have spared you, gladly, had it been compatible with my sense of the right. It is long past midnight, and I will leave you, if you will permit me, Mr. North."

He turned deferentially to the attorney, but not before Willa had caught the significance with which he men-tioned the hour. Twelve o'clock had struck, indeed, as he had prophesied, for this latter-day Cinderella, and the pumpkin coach had vanished. The story differed only in that there was no fairy prince to find her once again; he had vanished, too, stripped of his splendor, but before the magic hour. Or, rather, he had never existed save in the exalted fancy of the girl back there in Limasito!

Cinderella must pick up her slipper herself, and go forth into the world.

CHAPTER XIX

The Vender of Tomales

AFTER Starr Wiley's departure Mason North placed the documents in Willa's hands, explaining each in turn and she forced herself to a stern concentration on them that she might master every detail. Already she was gathering her forces, although no definite purpose outlined itself in the chaos of her thoughts. Only a blind, as yet unreasoning, repudiation of the story to which she had just listened sprang full-grown to life within her and the very strength of her conviction urged her to examine well the evidence against herself.

It consisted of the marriage-certificate of Frank Hillery and Louise Henson, dated December 12, 1895; the birth-certificate of Louise Francis Hillery, October 3, 1897, several maps of the Flathead Lake territory with trails marked upon them in red ink, the death-certificate of Frank Hillery, dated April 16, 1916, and a huge sheet of foolscap paper scrawled with labored characters in wavering lines. At the bottom two signatures were appended, the first in the same painstaking hand as the body of the document, but at the second Willa's breath caught again in her throat and her eyes blurred.

The letters before her, in the same angular heavily down-stroked writing she knew so well, formed the name of Gentleman Geoff, but a word had been added; one that she had never seen or heard before. Abercrombie! Gentleman Geoff Abercrombie!

Had that been indeed the unmentioned surname of the man who had reared her as his own? Why, then, had he, who had given her all else, not given her, too, the name to bear?

The document set forth in brief that Frank Hillery, being of sound mind and sole guardian of his daughter, Louise Frances, did give her to Geoffrey Abercrombie, known as "Gentleman Geoff," for absolute adoption; the said Gentleman Geoff promising to bring her up in all ways as his own child and to leave her whatever he might die possessed of. It was dated March 12, 1902.

"You will permit me to have photographic copies of each of these papers, Mr. North?" Willa asked, when the last had been laid aside.

"Certainly, my child." The attorney's voice was suspiciously husky. "Allow me to assure you that there will be no hurry, of course. It will take some weeks to verify and substantiate this evidence, and in the meantime——"

"Willa shall remain with us, of course," Ripley Halstead said with deep feeling. "This is a most unwelcome revelation to me, I may say to all of us. We have grown greatly attached to Willa and come to look upon her as quite one of ourselves.—There is no reason, my dear, why you should not stay on indefinitely. I am sure my wife will be glad to second me in this."

"Of course." Mrs. Halstead spoke through tightened lips. "This has been a most regrettable mistake, and one which will entail a hideous amount of notoriety, but that cannot be helped now. It is an almost overwhelming shock, but it explains many things which I have found incomprehensible. After all, this poor young girl is the worst sufferer, and she will be welcome here as long as she cares to stay."

Angie gasped, but made no comment and it was Vernon alone who echoed his mother's assurance in sincere enthusiasm.

"Thank you," Willa said simply. "You are all more than kind, but you realize, of course, that I should feel like an interloper; my place is no longer here."

"But, my dear, it will not do to be too hasty! Suppose that these documents are not—suppose no mistake was made in the original identification——?" The attorney was halted by her steady gaze.

"Mr. North, you are convinced already. Why delay the inevitable?" She rose. "However, we won't discuss it further now, if you don't mind. I—I feel very tired."

"Of course, dear child! We have kept you up till an unconscionable hour!" Mason North approached her with outstretched hand. "Remember that you will always find a friend in me. Come to me at any time."

"Thank you. May I send for the photographic copies of the documents to-morrow?" Willa turned to the others in a grave dignity not without its pathos. "You have all been very good to me; whatever happens I shall never forget that. I wish now that I had been more amenable to your advice and suggestions, but it is too late to think of that. Good-night."

Her head was still high as she walked to the door, but when it had closed behind her, she paused trembling as though suddenly bereft of her strength.

In the silence, Angie's querulous tones rose sharply from the other side of the door.

"I felt all along that something was wrong! I knew that wild uncouth thing couldn't be a Murdaugh, in spite of the common mother——"

Willa put her hands to her ears and fled madly up the stairs to her room where she sank limply upon the couch. Exhausted in mind and body with the storm of emotion which had swayed her and the strain of the protracted effort of self-control, she fell asleep at last with one determination firmly fixed in her mind. The roof which had reluctantly sheltered her should do so no longer.

She awakened in the early morning and lay for a moment in drowsy bewilderment before full realization came. Then she sprang from her bed, dressed hastily in her plainest clothes, and, packing a small bag with necessities, stole softly down the stairs.

She shivered as she let herself out into the cold, bleak morning. As yet no plan had formed in her mind save to find a temporary abode in some quiet neighborhood until the search for Tia Juana was ended in some conclusive fashion. That was still the first of the duties confronting her and the change in her fortunes did not swerve her an iota from the charge she had laid upon herself. Later there would be two points to be achieved; the one which had actuated her from the beginning, and another which was even now beating upon her consciousness.

When Dan Morrissey came whistling into the garage an hour later, he stopped short in amazement at the sight of his employer seated just inside the entrance with her bag at her feet.

"Good-morning, Dan. Is the car in order?"

"Yes, Miss. Good-morning." He stared blankly, and then with a start he recovered himself. "Just a minute, Miss! I'll have her out in no time."

"I will wait for you at the Broadway corner. Bring my bag, please."

Willa had scarcely reached the appointed place, however, when Dan came chugging up behind her and in a moment they were speeding away from the vicinity of the garage.

"I have decided to leave home, Dan," she announced without preamble. "I want to live quietly under cover until we have found Tia Juana and José. It is important that none of the family nor their friends shall know where I have gone. Do you know of any place where I can arrange to board for a time? The more simple it is, the better."

"Well," Dan remarked, reflectively, "you wouldn't be wanting a plain, poor kind of a home after all the grandeur you're used to, or I could take you to my sister, Miss. She's married to a shipping clerk and lives in a little two-family house up on Washington Heights. It's quiet and clean and nobody'd think of looking for you there, but I guess maybe you'd want something a bit more high-toned."

"No, it sounds splendid! Just what I am looking for." Willa paused. "But do you think she will take me in? You see, I can't explain very well."

"Explain nothin'!" Dan reddened swiftly. "Excuse me, Miss. Delia's no more of a hand at askin' questions than me, and she's a good judge of people. She can tell you're a lady in a minute, and she'll make you more than

welcome if you can put up with the plainness of everything. I'll have you there in ten minutes."

Dan was as good as his word, and Willa found that
he had spoken truly. His sister proved to be a thin,
pleasant-faced woman with a humorous curve to her lips
and alert twinkling brown eyes. She was ready and
willing to take Dan's employer as a lodger and the terms
were quickly arranged.

Willa gave Dan his instructions, and then shut herself
in the clean, sunny room which had been allotted to her
and looked the situation collectedly in the face.

The more she thought of the astounding tale of the
previous night and strove in vain to find the slightest
corroboration of it in her memory, the more deep sank
the roots of her conviction of its fallacy. She had not
realized how desperate Wiley's determination was to
oust her from his path, nor dreamed that he would risk
forged testimony, but now at length she had measured
the strength of her adversary and her own courage rose
in a dauntless tide to meet his challenge.

In the beginning the Murdaugh name had meant nothing to her and the inheritance merely a means to an end,
but now with Angie's scornful words heard through the
closed door ringing in her ears, she made up her mind
to fight! Not for the sake of position or name or wealth,
but for the "common" brave-hearted mother whose child
she felt herself to be beyond peradventure of a doubt,
and about whose memory all unconsciously a worshiping
love had sprung in her heart.

Meanwhile, pursuant to instructions, Dan had presented himself at the imposing offices of North, Manning

and Gilchrist, armed with the note which Willa had written hastily in his sister's home.

Mason North looked up after perusing it, and favored the messenger with a keen scrutiny.

"H'm! This letter calls for the delivery to you of certain rather important documents, young man. I should like to be sure of your identification before placing them in your hands."

"Well, Sir, I've my bank-book here, and some letters——"

The attorney waved them aside.

"I don't mean quite that. You have been long in Miss Murdaugh's employ?"

Dan was conscious of a movement in the corner behind him and turned to find a mild, round-faced young man rising from the safe he had been in the act of closing and regarding him with vast interest. Dan returned the compliment respectfully.

"How long have you worked for Miss Murdaugh?" The question was reiterated with a touch of asperity.

"For some time, Sir. Ever since she caught the French maid trying to spy on her under the orders of Mrs. Halstead." Dan repeated carefully but with evident satisfaction the message which had been given him. "Miss Murdaugh told me to tell you, Sir, that I was one of the investments she had made with Gentleman Geoff's money. She said you would understand."

Mason North nipped at his mustache reflectively and turned to the younger man. "Winthrop, I wish you'd go and attend to that Erskine matter for me!"

Winnie departed in obvious reluctance and only when the door had closed behind him did his father resume:

"In what capacity are you employed by Miss Murdaugh?"

"Confidential agent, she said I was to tell you." Dan could scarcely suppress a grin of importance. "She told me to remind you that she asked you particular last night if she might send for the copies of the papers, not call for them herself, and you said 'yes.' And you'll excuse me, Sir, but I'm not to answer any more questions."

The attorney shrugged and turned to the telephone, but Dan interposed quietly:

"Miss Murdaugh ain't at home, Sir. She's waiting for me and she says she'll not set foot in the house until I bring her the copies of the papers."

"Very well." Mason North capitulated, and, opening a drawer in his desk, handed over a rolled package. "Here you are. I shall want a receipt, of course."

He made out one, which Dan signed, and with a nod turned to leave, when the attorney halted him on the threshold.

"Ask Miss Murdaugh if she can find it convenient to call here this afternoon; tell her I would like to talk things over with her and will expect her between four and five o'clock."

"Very good, Sir."

Dan departed, colliding violently as he did so with an elderly gentleman who entered the inner office and banged the door behind him.

"Mason, have you heard from her? Do you know where she has gone?"

"Who?" North rose hurriedly. "What is it, Ripley? What has happened?"

"Willa. She's gone!" Ripley Halstead dropped

despondently into a chair beside the desk. "Here's the note the poor, proud little thing left behind her. Mason, I feel as if, between us, we've given her a beastly, rotten deal."

But the attorney did not heed the final observation. He pressed the button in his desk excitedly and when a wondering clerk appeared he barked:

"That young man who just went out of here! Follow him, stop him!"

"Too late, Sir. He went down in the express elevator as I stepped out of the local."

North seated himself again with a gesture of hopelessness.

"All right; never mind, then. Ripley——" as the door closed once more—"if you'd been five minutes sooner I could have located her. Why under the sun didn't you telephone me?"

"Her absence was only discovered as I was leaving the house and I came straight to you." Halstead stared. "What young man were you speaking of?"

"Her messenger. He came with a note from Willa authorizing him to bring her the photographic copies of those documents, and like a fool I gave them to him! We've lost our chance of tracing her, and heaven only knows what difficulties that headstrong wilful child will get into by herself," groaned North. "I took her away from her home and friends in Mexico on this mistaken matter of her inheritance and I feel responsible for her. I'm fond of the child, too; I like her independent spirit even if it did raise the deuce with us, and if any harm comes to her——"

"I won't let myself think of that!" Ripley Halstead's

kind face had grown suddenly haggard. "I have a good deal of respect for her clear-headed ability to take care of herself; nevertheless, I sha'n't feel easy until she is found. I've taken more comfort in her than in my own daughter, Mason. My wife doesn't need Willa's share of the Murdaugh money and I wish young Wiley had never unearthed the truth!"

The attorney had picked up the little note.

"'My dear Mrs. Halstead,' he read.

"'I hope you will forgive me for leaving you so unceremoniously. I do not mean to be rude or seem ungrateful, but I am afraid that in your hospitality you would urge me to remain until the documents are verified at least, and I really cannot do so. If I have been an impostor, it was an unconscious one. Nevertheless, I could not endure a false position. Will you permit me once more to thank you and your family for all your kindness to me, and believe me to be,

"'Ever gratefully yours,
"'BILLIE ABERCROMBIE.'"

"——Poor little girl! I say, where did she get that 'Abercrombie' from?"

"Don't you see?" Ripley Halstead bent forward. "That's the name on that document; the name of the man who adopted her, 'Gentleman Geoff.' She won't claim 'Murdaugh' and doesn't accept 'Hillery,' so she's chosen the one name she's sure of. Do you suppose that means she is going to contest the validity of this new claim?"

"Possibly." North shook his head. "It would be a losing fight for her, though, Ripley. There isn't a chance in the world that Wiley's discovery could be anything but authentic. No one profits by the affair except your own family and no one could have any possible incentive for faking the story. It's too bad the truth didn't come out before, and I'll always blame myself for my negligence, but as long as a mistake was made, it is lucky for us that Wiley stumbled on those records now instead of later, when the fortune was in her hands."

His mission accomplished, Dan was returning to the garage to put the car up and proceed on foot to his daily round of the hospitals and bureaus of inquiry, when half-way down the block a shrill voice piped at him.

"Hot tomales! Very fine hot tomales. Try one, Mister!"

Idly he glanced toward the curb. A diminutive, ragged vender crouched there beside a bright, new hand-cart which contained a huge pot simmering above a charcoal fire, and bore a sign with the legend "Hot Tomales, 5 cents," in obviously home-made lettering.

His mind intent on his errand of the morning, Dan gave it but passing heed and drove on into the garage, yet as he busied himself about the car, the incident kept recurring to his mind. Hot tomales were a queer commodity for a street-seller to deal in; Dan didn't know exactly what they were, but he believed them to be some sort of Spanish or Mexican concoction——

At this point in his cogitations he stopped work abruptly and stood staring into vacancy.

There had been something appealingly familiar even in that fleeting glimpse of the tattered crouched figure, and could it be that it had been hunchbacked?

With an excited cry he dropped the wrench from his

hand and sprang out into the street. Cart and vender were gone, but in the gutter lay a crushed, greasy mess which had been a tomale. It was still smoking and as Dan stirred it with his foot, he saw that a wisp of sodden paper clung to it.

Seizing it, he smoothed it out and read the two jerkily penciled words:

"Mañana.   José."

CHAPTER XX

Winnie Mason Stands By

"I SAY, hello there! Wait a minute, Kearn!" Winnie Mason called as he brought his roadster to a halt with a sudden grinding of brakes. It was two days later and a cutting east wind skirled about the driveway of the Park, rattling the naked branches of the trees like the fleshless arms of a legion of skeletons.

The tall figure on the path waited, but his face was averted and there was a listless, dispirited droop to his whole form which was not lost upon the quick, sympathetic gaze of his friend.

"I'll back her up. . . Now get in, old man, and we'll take a little spin. Jolly glad I ran across you, but what brings you out on a blustering rotten afternoon like this? You're not very fit yet, you know, after that bout of fever you had in Mexico, in spite of the lacing you managed to give Starr Wiley."

"I came to try and walk off a brace of blue devils that have been camping on my trail," Thode explained, climbing into the car with manifest reluctance. "You won't find me very good company, Win, but you've brought it on yourself."

"What's the matter, anyhow?" the other demanded. "It's not like you to load up with a grouch. Has one of those blasted oil wells sprung a leak?"

Thode shrugged.

"I wouldn't care if every gusher in Mexico went up in smoke!" he affirmed, drearily. "I've had a nasty stab in the back, the kind of thing a man doesn't get over in a hurry, that's all. Don't let's talk about it."

"You're not the only one. I say, you'll keep this to yourself, of course, but I've got to tell some one, and you were her friend down there. She told me about that magnificent ride of yours for the troops at the time of the raid, and she just about thought you were ace high. She's such a plucky little thing herself, confound it! That's what makes it so devilish hard, now."

"What are you talking about?" Thode looked up with the first gleam of interest he had shown. "Not Miss Murdaugh?"

Winnie nodded.

"Only she isn't Miss Murdaugh at all, according to Starr Wiley. He's dug up proof that the real Willa Murdaugh died and she is just a trapper's daughter from the wilds somewhere, whom that gambler adopted in order to bilk the estate later. The governor told me all about it, he was so wrought up he couldn't keep it to himself."

"Not Willa Murdaugh!" repeated Thode in stunned accents. "And Starr Wiley brought forward the proof? You'd better tell me all about it, Win, now that you've started."

Nothing loth, Winnie complied and the other heard him through in silence, until he told of Willa's disappearance the morning after the revelation, and the little note she had left behind her.

"I swear I thought the governor would spill over when

he read it to me," Winnie concluded. "It was sort of fine for her to go away like that. I don't care who she really is, she's the most wonderful girl I know. She wouldn't even sign herself 'Murdaugh' after they questioned her right; she used the name of the gambler chap who'd been so good to her."

"How did she learn it?" Thode asked quickly. "He was known only as 'Gentleman Geoff' in Limasito. I'm certain she herself never heard the name there."

"It was signed to the adoption agreement he and the trapper, Hillery, made out when he took her in place of the real Willa. The governor showed me the paper and there it was in black and white: Geoff Abercrombie."

"Abercrombie!" Kearn Thode seized the other's arm in a convulsive grip which made the steering-wheel jerk. "You're sure—you're sure of the name, Win?"

"Dead sure! I'll get the governor to show you the document if you like. But why the excitement? You nearly landed us up against that rock, then."

"Never mind the rock!" exclaimed Thode. "I'm going to take you up on that; I'd give a good bit to see that paper and the signature."

"I'll fix it." Winnie shot a quick glance at his companion. "I say, you don't think it's phony, do you? The governor says it is absolutely the straight goods."

"It isn't that," Thode hastened to explain cautiously. "But I knew Gentleman Geoff personally, you know. It isn't etiquette to ask a man for more of a name than he chooses to give below the border, but I had a hazy idea of Gentleman Geoff's identity and the name in my mind was not Abercrombie. It was just a suspicion of my own and I had nothing to substantiate it, but the old chap interested me and I've always been curious about him. I wonder if he could possibly have been related to the Abercrombies of the Coast?"

"Whoever he was, he must have been rather a fine old codger himself for he brought Will—his adopted daughter up splendidly," Winnie observed with enthusiasm. "There isn't a girl in our set that can come anywhere near her, and I think it is a dashed shame that she's thrown out on her own. She took the whole business like a thoroughbred, walking calmly out like that and leaving them to haggle over the details."

"And she has utterly disappeared?" asked Thode. "No one knows where she is?"

"Nobody but your Uncle Sherlock!" Winnie grinned, and thumped himself upon the chest. "I did a little detecting on my own and I found her all right. She doesn't know yet that anyone has discovered her whereabouts and I don't mean to pass it on to the Halsteads or the governor, either. She's her own mistress now and if she wants to go away by herself, it's no one's concern but hers."

"I can't imagine you in the rôle of a gumshoe!" The other laughed outright, and it was Winnie's turn to gape in amazement.

The change which had come over his companion was too marked to go unnoted; the listless, disheartened mood was gone and in its place the old eager alertness manifested itself, intensified by a sort of half-suppressed excitement.

"I turned the trick, anyway," Winnie remarked complacently after a pause. "You see, old man, I'd heard about the way she'd held on to the money Gentleman

Geoff left her and I've caught glimpses of her more than once riding around town in a speedy gray car with a nifty chauffeur. I knew the Halstead bunch didn't know anything about it so I kept quiet. I recognized the chauffeur in the chap she sent to the governor's office for photographic copies of the documents Wiley dug up, but the governor sent me away just when things promised to be interesting.

"I scouted around outside the building and there, sure enough, drawn up at the curb across the way, was the gray car. I slipped over and took its number. Later, when we heard about her going away, I didn't say anything, but I looked up the record of the car. The license had been taken out under a man's name; the chauffeur's, maybe, but I traced it to a garage up on the West Side. I took this car up there two days ago, and whenever he took his own out I was right on the job after him.

"He found out that I was shadowing him, of course, and he tried like blazes to shake me off, but I was foxy and beat him at his own game yesterday. He drove up to a certain house and she came out herself, as if she'd been waiting for him. I jotted down the address, and beat it as hard as I could. It's lucky I found her when I did, because the car was moved to another garage this morning and I lost its trail."

"What are you going to do?" inquired the other. "Call on her to extend your sympathy? That's about the last thing on earth that Gentleman Geoff's Billie wants, under any circumstances."

He uttered the name with an unconscious note of tenderness in his voice which would have been illuminating to Winnie North, but that young man was busied at the moment with embarrassing thoughts of his own. His face at the other's abrupt question had turned a bright pink, but he replied steadily:

"I don't want to intrude upon her, but I'd like to tell her that I'm standing by in case of need.—I'll tell you what I'll do; I'll drop her a line and ask her if I may bring you up to call, shall I? She can tell you all about this thing better than I——"

Thode shook his head decisively.

"No. I am an old friend, as you say, and if she should want to see me she knows how to reach me. I'm going away in a few days, at any rate."

"Away?" Winnie said impulsively. "Why, old man, you're not returning to Mexico, are you? I thought you were going to stay around town for a month or two."

"No!" There was a determined ring, not without a touch of grimness, in his tones. "I'm going to take Horace Greeley's advice once more: 'Young man, go West.' I'll hit the trail for the setting sun——"

"And find your pot of gold, like the old fairy tale of the rainbow's end? By Jove, but you fellows are dreamers!" Winnie laughed, then touched his friend's shoulder persuasively. "Why don't you stay on here where the money is and work this end of the game for a change? You engineer chaps get out and do all the hard work, and the smug brokers who sit tight in their offices down on the Street reap all the profits. Get in on the ground floor, old man, and let the other fellow do the prospecting."

Thode laughed also.

"Without a working capital? Besides, I know nothing and care less about the manipulations of the financial end of it; the prospecting is all I'm cut out for and it's more fascinating than the market game could possibly be! However, I'm not going West for the elusive pot of gold this trip; I'm going for something far more important, on a little private hunch of my own. You'll wish me luck, I know, old man?"

"I will indeed, whatever your hunch is," Winnie responded heartily. "That stab in the back hasn't downed you, after all. I knew it wouldn't, after you got your second wind! You look like a different chap than you were an hour ago——"

"I feel it!" laughed the other, but again that undernote of grimness rang in his tone. "It's done me a lot of good, this little talk with you, Win. You'll never realize just how you've bucked me up."

Winnie puzzled over the significance of the last remark after he had dropped his friend at the Park entrance and turned north again. Could the stab in the back to which Thode referred have come from Starr Wiley, and had their conversation given Thode a clue to a way of striking back at his enemy? Not through Willa and the lost inheritance, of course; that was a bona-fide discovery, even if Wiley had been the instrument in bringing it to light. However, the fact that Wiley had stumbled upon the documents while in Arizona might have given Thode a lead on some ulterior project out there in which Wiley was trying to cut the ground out from under his feet.

In going over their conversation in retrospect, an idea came which Winnie determined impulsively to act upon. Willa's car had been removed from the garage to which he had traced it, but that did not necessarily mean that it had been taken to another. What if she had sold the car, in preparation for a return to Mexico? He felt that she must not go before he had seen her. Heretofore he had not, as he said, intruded upon her retreat, but he could not bear the thought of her departure without at least her knowing what he had to tell her.

He would go to her now, without giving her an opportunity to refuse to see him! She might be angry, and Willa's anger was something to be reckoned with, but he would make her hear him out!

Darkness had already fallen as he drew up before the neat little house with its twin front doors. He rang the bell of the one to the right and when the tall pleasant-faced woman appeared in answer to his summons, he asked without hesitation for Miss Abercrombie.

The woman eyed him somewhat doubtfully, but ushered him into a tiny immaculate parlor.

"Please, tell her it is Mr. Winthrop North. I haven't a card with me, but be sure about the first name. Say that I have an important message for her and no one knows that I have come."

"Yes, Sir." The woman hesitated. "I'm thinking you've made a mistake and got hold of the wrong Miss Abercrombie, but I'll find out."

In a moment, however, there was a rustle of silk on the narrow stairs and Willa entered. Her eyes sought his in a defensive, questioning stare as she held out her hand.

"Your visit is a surprise, Winnie. I thought—I was not aware that any of my friends knew where I was."

"No one does but me. I followed your chauffeur. Please, don't be angry! I was so afraid I should lose you; that you would return to Limasito before I had an opportunity to see you, that I was desperate."

"Why should you want to see me?" Willa demanded, frankly. "I don't mean to be ungracious, Winnie, we've grown to be awfully good friends in these two months, but I've been through so much just lately that the Willa Murdaugh episode seems far away, and all the people I knew then are like dream people. I—I'm starting in all over again, you see, and I meant to do it with a clean, blank sheet."

"But surely you don't mean to put us all behind you? Our friendship, our admiration, all the happy times we've had together—oh, Willa, you can't drop it all like this!" he stammered. "You can't go back now, you belong to us!"

She smiled.

"You're very good to say so, Winnie, but remember I'm not Willa any more! My place is gone, or rather it never was mine. I do believe in your friendship, but how many of the rest bothered with me because of myself alone? It was the Murdaugh position they accepted, the Murdaugh interests. I'm not cynical, but I try to look things squarely in the face. How many would admit within their circle the waif adopted by a gambler?"

Winnie drew a deep breath.

"Then why not make a place for yourself, or rather step into one which is waiting for you? It doesn't carry the prestige of the Murdaugh name or money, but it's solid and substantial and assured, and all that love can bring to make for happiness goes with it, too. Why don't you marry me, dear?"

Willa started up in unutterable amazement. The mild

round face of the boy before her seemed all at once to have taken on a deeper, more mature expression, strengthening and ennobling it, and a wistful light which there was no mistaking glowed in his eyes.

"Winnie!"

"Oh, I know it sounds silly and presumptuous of me! You've known real men in your life, men who have fought and accomplished things and I've been just an idler. You couldn't care for me now, but if you'll give me half a chance I'll prove myself! I know I could do big things, too, if I had you with me, and I—I love you most tremendously, dear! I've cared ever since that very first night when you broke into Vernon's game in that splendid fearless way and drove Cal Shirley out as a cheat. I never saw a girl with such spirit and I've worshiped you more and more! Willa, won't you let me go to my father and tell him it's all right, that you will stay? He may not have found the Murdaugh heiress in Limasito, but I'd like to tell him that he found my wife!"

Willa's eyes blurred and a rich color dyed her cheeks as she replied softly:

"Dear Winnie! I'll always love you for this, and respect you, too, even though what you suggest is impossible.—'Presumptuous'? You don't know what a big, fine thing you just proved yourself capable of!" Her voice was not quite steady. "Willa Murdaugh was eligible, even a catch, I suppose, but now, when I am stripped of everything that counts in your world and nothing is left me but a past which would bar me from polite society if I tried to batter down its prejudices alone, you offer to brave its opinion, to give me the greatest thing a man can give to a woman. It's splendid of you! I—I can't tell you how wonderful it seems to feel that there are still men like you in the world. But, Winnie, I couldn't marry you! I'm awfully fond of you, but not in that way and one of the things I couldn't accept in the creed of your world would be to marry a man I didn't love. Even if I did care, I don't believe that I could bring myself to accept your sacrifice, but I shall never forget your generosity."

"Don't, please!" Winnie thrust out his hand in a passionate gesture of negation. "The generosity would have been on your part and the sacrifice, too! What does it matter who your own people were? You are yourself, the bravest, finest, truest girl in all the world! I knew you couldn't care, but, oh, I hoped that if there was no one else you would try to like me enough to give me an opportunity of proving to you that I could make you happy anyway. I would be so awfully good to you, and so proud! It is you who would be giving all, not me, and I should try all the rest of my life to be worthy of you. Willa, dearest, won't you think it over, and let me come again?"

She shook her head with a sad little smile.

"I am leaving to-night, Winnie, and going far away. I may return sometime, quien sabe?—but I have played a lone hand ever since Dad was killed and I've got to go on to the end. You're wonderfully kind, wonderfully dear, but I have a long trail to follow and I must travel it alone."

"You're leaving to-night!" He turned and walked to the window where he stood for some minutes gazing out at the blank darkness before him in silence. When he broke it at length and turned again, his face was very pale but composed.

"You will write and let me know where you are and that all is well with you?"

"Perhaps," Willa said gently. "At any rate you will know that I shall think of you always and value your friendship as the one worth-while thing in all this experience. I wish I could have cared for you, Winnie, in that way, but it couldn't be."

"I understand." His voice was very low. "Remember that I am your friend, if I can be nothing more, and I shall be waiting. If you ever want me, or need me, you will have only to send me a word and I shall come if it is half across the world.—I'm going, now. Don't be afraid that I shall tell anyone where I found you. I can't bear to say it, but it is 'good-bye', Willa. I—I hope, wherever you are, that nothing but happiness will come to you. Good-bye, best and sweetest and dearest——"

His voice broke, and Willa held out both her hands.

"Good-bye, Winnie. You're going to be happy, too, some day. I'll always be proud of your friendship and what you have offered me. Our trails may cross again some day, and if they do I shall be glad, indeed. Till then, good luck and every wish of my heart to you, my pal!"

Winnie pressed her hands, then dropped them and stumbled from the room. In the machine, he turned and waved. Willa stood in the window, her slender form outlined against the light behind her, her small head proudly erect, and it seemed to the boy's blurred, exalted gaze as if an aura of golden haze like a halo surrounded it. A passing glance and he was swept along into the darkness ahead, the vision and the memory of her all that remained to him.

CHAPTER XXI

THE RETURN OF TIA JUANA

"I TELL you, Starr, it's all very well to play a waiting game, but we've got to start something and start it soon, or we'll be up against the worst fix we've ever struck in our lives, and that will be going some!" Harrington Chase paused in his restless pacing of the private office to regard his partner with troubled eyes. "We've got to make a big killing or we're due to go under, and you know what that'll mean."

Wiley flung himself around in his chair to face the other.

"I've moved heaven and earth to find that old she-devil!" he exclaimed. "The biggest obstacle is out of our path now, as you very well know, and if Tia Juana would only turn up, we could put it all over her. Gentleman Geoff's Billie is no longer in a position to interfere if she wanted to, thanks to my fortunate discovery of the adoption papers in Arizona, and when I get my hands on the old woman——"

"You've been saying that for the last month," Chase observed, adding with a sly smile: "I'm not undervaluing the lucky chance that put those documents in your way, my dear fellow! What has happened, anyway, in regard to that affair? Until the Halsteads and North have proved the validity of the papers they won't make any premature announcement, of course, and I'm only supposed to share the knowledge, common in their circle, that Willa Murdaugh has gone to spend the winter in the South."

"Oh, they'll spring the news about the beginning of Lent, I imagine, when the social calendar is clear and they won't have so many explanations to make," Wiley responded carelessly. "It's bound to be a nine-days' wonder, but things move rapidly in this town and she'll be almost forgotten by Easter."

"What's become of the girl herself?" asked Chase. "Where did she go when she took herself off in that high-handed fashion?"

"Search me!" Wiley shrugged. "She's eliminated, anyway, from the scene."

"Not if we happen to shift the scene to Mexico!" retorted the other. "What if she has gone back to Limasito?"

"Well, she hasn't." Wiley announced briefly. "Our men down there have their instructions to keep a lookout and let us know the minute she appears, but there hasn't been a sign of her. Personally, I didn't expect it."

"Why not? Where else would she go?"

"My dear Harrington, if you had made as close a study of feminine psychology as I have, you would know that she would rather go anywhere else in the world than return to Limasito in defeat. With her pride it would be intolerable after the eclat of her departure as an heiress to slink back as merely Gentleman Geoff's Billie once more."

"That's some satisfaction," Chase muttered, resuming

his nervous tread. "But granted that she is finally eliminated, what good will it do us as long as Tia Juana remains under cover? Do you understand the situation? We're overcapitalized right now to the limit; we've watered the stock until it would float a fleet of battle-ships and we're dangerously near the line——"

"Well, what can I do?" Wiley ran his hands through his hair. "I've banked everything on this Lost Souls venture, and God knows I've gone the limit to put it through!"

"Have you?" Chase turned at the window. "Just what did you mean to do, if you had succeeded in locating Tia Juana?"

"I should think that would be obvious." Wiley laughed shortly. "We've threshed that all out; I'd get her signature to a bill of sale of the Trevino hacienda where the Lost Souls' Pool is situated, record the deed with the Notary Public at Victoria, and then proceed to develop and advertise the well. What on earth are you driving at, Harrington?"

"Just this!" His partner strode quickly to the desk and bent down, staring significantly into Wiley's eyes. "That's your program, is it? Well, go ahead and carry it out!"

"Sounds good!" Wiley chuckled, sneeringly. "Perhaps you'll be good enough to produce Tia Juana, so that I can start the ball rolling!"

"I will," Harrington Chase responded quietly.

It was Wiley's turn to stare.

"Hope you'll have better luck than I have had, that's all," he said at last, shrugging. "When you find her——"

Chase interrupted him with a gesture.

"I *have* found her!"

"What!" Wiley sprang from his chair. "When? Where? Good Lord, why didn't you tell me before? How did you find her?"

"Wait——!"

Chase straightened and tiptoed to the door leading into the outer office. The next instant he had flung it wide, but no eavesdropper was in sight and the whole suite appeared deserted. He closed the door once more and thereafter ensued an earnest and protracted conference.

As a result, Starr Wiley failed to put in an appearance that night at a dinner to which he had been invited and his excuse pleaded a sudden business trip. Days lengthened into weeks, and when he did not return there was a ripple of surprise and conjecture at his abrupt evanescence, but the varied festivities of the approaching holiday season ousted him from his rather negligible place in the thoughts of his acquaintances.

Christmas came and passed, and the New Year was nearing the end of its first month when he reappeared in the city, and simultaneously a sensational rumor spread like wildfire through the financial circles. It concerned a marvelous new oil well, the "Almas Perderse," which had just been discovered in the richest part of the Mexican petroleum fields, and which was reputed to be the greatest potential producer since the famous "Dos Bocas" itself.

Excitement ran high and the offices of Chase and Company were besieged by the curious and speculative among the smaller fry, but the moneyed interests still held aloof in spite of the artfully conservative bait dangled before them, and for a time developments were at a standstill.

It was during this period that one day Winnie North and Vernon Halstead found themselves compulsory room-mates at an overcrowded stag house-party in West-chester. The events of the preceding autumn had chastened and matured both of the genially irresponsible young men and the resultant change edified their imme-diate relatives even while it caused them to exhibit unflattering astonishment.

Winnie was making a determined effort to learn the intricacies of the brokerage game and Vernon had en-rolled himself at the university on the Heights for a post-graduate course in mining and petroleum engineer-ing. It was natural, therefore, that the subject which arose for discussion between them over a night-cap and cigarette was that of the Almas Perderse well.

"It sounds mighty good, I admit," Vernon remarked. "If anybody but Starr Wiley stood sponsor for it I should have more faith in its possibilities, I suppose, but somehow I can't figure him in a bona-fide deal."

"The governor doesn't share your prejudice, nor does your own father," Winnie remarked. "I've heard them talking and I've a hunch that they're both going to invest pretty heavily in the Almas Perderse stock when it is issued. They have faith in Wiley's knowledge of a good thing when he sees it, and I fancy it's sound, at that. He's been more than ordinarily successful in the past with other propositions, you know, and whatever your opinions of him personally, you'll have to admit that Wiley's reputation on the Exchange is second to none as far as judgment and efficiency and a thorough comprehension of the oil game are concerned."

"Yet the big investors are holding off, I understand," Vernon observed thoughtfully. "I wish my father wouldn't monkey with it. What's the game, Winnie? What are Chase and Wiley doing to launch the Almas Perderse?"

"Well, they've recently increased their capitalization to twenty-five million and they told the governor they want to raise ten million more at once. They're offering a million shares at ten dollars, par value, and they claim a jump to one hundred or better is inevitable within a few months, as soon as the development starts. The governor thinks he's being let in on the ground floor."

"It would look like it, if the thing is on the level." Vernon shook his head. "They're liable to bring in a gusher that'll send the price soaring."

"Whatever that means!" Winnie laughed. "You'll be some little petroleum engineer yourself one of these days! I don't know anything about it myself, but it seems to me the figures that Wiley stated to the governor as the initial cost of development were pretty steep; twenty-five million, including an eight-inch pipe line to Limasito and tankage equipment there."

"No, that's not excessive," demurred Vernon. "The pumping stations every ten miles will average fifty thousand alone, and every foot of the pipe must be transported by peons—laborers, you know—on their shoulders through the swamps. Moreover, now that it seems inevitable that we shall get in the war ourselves, it's going to be next to impossible to get tankers at any price to bring the oil up from Mexico.—But I'm only a tyro yet; Kearn

Thode can give you the details far better than I can. What's become of him, by the way?"

"He's out West, somewhere." Winnie ground out the stub of his cigarette. "He went soon after your cousin——er——"

"By Jove!" Vernon rose. "I'd give anything to see Willa again! Wasn't she the most wonderful little thoroughbred that ever lived!"

"She was," Winnie responded, his voice very low. "We'll never know a girl just like her, Verne. There's not another in the world."

Vernon glanced with unusual keenness at his friend and when he spoke his tone was roughly sympathetic.

"Hard hit, Winnie? Well, so was I, for that matter. Not that she would ever have looked at me, of course, but if she'd stayed another day I meant to ask her to stay always. She put me on the road to making a man of myself; some day I'll tell you how, maybe. It has a good deal to do with my distrust of Starr and his 'Almas Perderse'."

At an ungodly hour the next morning Winnie North was summoned to the telephone.

"Hello! What the deuce is it?" he demanded sleepily, but the voice which came to him over the wire speedily dispelled his somnolence.

"That you, Win? This is Kearn Thode."

"What! Gad, old man, it's good to hear your voice!" Winnie exclaimed. "When did you get in?"

"Just last night. I tried to get hold of you, but your father told me you were up there at Stoney Crest——"

"Come on out! Jim would have asked you if he'd known where you were. I'll tell him——"

"No," Thode interrupted tersely. "Sorry, but I can't waste a day! I've got to see you at once, this morning if possible."

"All right," Winnie responded. "Tell you what I'll do; I'll grab Jim's speedster and meet you at the Bumble Bee Inn. I can make it in an hour and so can you, as it's about half way out. Nobody'll be around in the morning and it's deserted anyway this time of the year, so we can have it to ourselves. I say, what's the racket, Kearn?"

"Tell you when I see you. Don't fail me, Win. Good-bye."

When Winnie drove up to the road-house an hour later, a lone taxi' stood outside and a familiar figure was seated at one of the tables in the otherwise empty restaurant. As it rose he saw that the two months had brought Kearn Thode back to what he had been before the fever laid him low in Mexico. He glowed with the old health and strength, and in his eyes was the triumphant fire of achievement.

"Hello, old man! You're looking wonderfully fit again, thank the Lord! Did you find that important something or other that was worth more than the pot of gold?"

Thode smiled as they shook hands.

"I found what I went after," he replied quietly. "And you? I hear you're settling into the harness in great shape."

Winnie flushed.

"The governor would boast, I suppose, as long as I succeeded in keeping out of jail," he observed. "It's a horrible responsibility to be an only son! But what's the

big idea? You didn't chivvie me out of bed in the cold
gray dawn for nothing!"

Thode beckoned to the solitary waiter, hovering in the
pantry doorway, before responding.

"We'd better have some coffee and a bite first. Then
I want the news; remember I've been out in the wild and
woolly since before the holidays."

When their order had been given, Winnie observed:

"I suppose you've heard about Wiley. He's been down
in Mexico and grabbed off a new oil well, the Almas
Perderse——"

"The Lost Souls!" Thode's hands clenched, and he
drew a deep breath between set teeth. "So he pulled it
off, did he? By Jove, I wonder——"

"What?" asked the other after a pause. "Did you
know about the well, too?"

Kearn Thode laughed.

"I'd heard of it," he acknowledged. "I wish him joy
of his discovery! Is he making headway while the going
is good?"

"Rather! I say, it isn't bunk, is it? I mean, this Almas
Perderse is the real thing, a good financial proposition?"

"If it is really the Almas Perderse and he holds a
clear title, it's the greatest prize in the oil fields to-day."
Thode's face sobered. "Why do you ask?"

"Because the governor and Ripley Halstead are going
into it heavily," explained Winnie. "I don't know how
much stock Halstead's subscribed for, but the governor
is going to take about fifty thousand shares at par, ten
dollars. He's bugs about it; thinks he's going to make
his everlasting fortune."

"Win, tell him to drop it!" Thode said earnestly. "I

can't explain now for there's more at stake than the Lost Souls, but I know what I'm talking about. He might as profitably sink his money in a bottomless pit as in that oil well!"

"Look here, I don't understand!" Winnie's voice shook. "You said just now it was the greatest prize in the oil fields to-day. What's wrong with it?"

"I told you I couldn't explain," Thode responded doggedly. "You've simply got to take my word for it, that's all. I'm not sure enough of my ground to make a definite statement yet or I would warn your father myself, but I'm so far convinced of coming trouble that I wouldn't see a friend of mine put a dollar in it if I could persuade him not to. I don't mind admitting that my own trip to Mexico last fall was made in the hope of locating that well myself, but it isn't sour grapes now with me. I give you my word of honor, Win, that whatever your father invests in the Almas Perderse well under the present conditions will be irretrievably lost."

"I wish to the Lord you would go to the governor yourself!" exploded Winnie. "He wouldn't listen to me in a million years, and even you would have to show him! He has looked thoroughly into the proposition according to his judgment and he has the utmost faith in it or he wouldn't plan to back it at all. Are you sure, Kearn?"

"Which means that you are not; I haven't succeeded in convincing you." Thode shrugged. "What chance would I have of convincing your father? I'm warning you, Win, I can't do any more. It's up to you now; remember that I am as earnest in this as I have ever been in my life, and it is only because of our old friendship that I have dropped you a hint. Whether your father acts upon it or not, beg him to respect my confidence, at any rate for the time being. I asked you to meet me to-day——"

"Yes?" Winnie's tone was absent, his mind still grappling with the quandary into which the other's warning had plunged him. "What is it, Kearn?"

"Do you remember our last meeting before I went away, when you picked me up in the Park?" Thode pushed his cup aside and leaned forward over the table. "You told me you knew where Miss Murdaugh went when she left the Halsteads. I want you to take me to her at once, without delay."

Winnie shook his head.

"Sorry, old man. I saw her within an hour after dropping you at the Park entrance and found her on the eve of departure. She told me she was leaving New York that night, but she wouldn't tell me her destination. I called again the next day and found she had gone; I haven't heard anything of her since."

"That's a facer!" Thode groaned. "I had counted on finding her here. Could she have returned to Limasito?"

"No, I've made inquiries. You see," Winnie explained hastily, "we'd grown to be pretty-good friends and naturally the governor felt responsible for her, in a way. He's been in constant communication with Jim Baggott down there—the man who runs the hotel——"

"I remember."

"The governor located her first through him, you know, and he seems to have been the one she trusted most after her foster father died, but even he has heard nothing from her, or pretends he hasn't." Winnie paused. "The governor has done everything possible to find her and satisfy himself that she was all right, but she has dropped completely from sight. He has aged over the whole thing, I can tell you! I think he would give half he possesses to know that all was well with her."

Thode beckoned once more to the waiter, and, throwing a bill upon the table, rose.

"If Miss Murdaugh has gone, I'm off to-night," he announced. "It was to see her that I returned to New York, but since there's no chance of that now I must take the trail again."

"I say, you haven't stumbled upon anything that would be to her advantage, have you?" Winnie demanded suddenly as he followed his friend to the door. "Anything about the past, I mean——?"

"No, Win." Thode spoke without turning. "It was just a—a little private matter."

"And you're really off to-night? When are we going to see you again, old man?"

"I don't know." He wheeled about swiftly, then held out his hand. "Don't forget to repeat what I have told you to your father and make it as strong as you can. I'm playing a game of my own, and when we meet again it will be cards on the table. Good-bye, Win."

"Good luck!" The other hesitated wistfully. "If—if you should happen by any chance to run across Willa in your wanderings, will you tell her for me that I'm still waiting, as I said I should be; that I am still, as always, at her service?"

CHAPTER XXII

Where Trails Meet

A LONG, narrow valley between snow-capped mountains glistening under the January sun; a cluster of ramshackle, weather-beaten wooden houses elbowing each other on either side of a single straggling street, with here and there a newer concrete building planted firmly like respectable citizens in a disreputable mob. Stray dogs sniffing at heaps of refuse, a group of tethered horses shivering under thin blankets in the hotel shed, a battered jitney or two stalled before shop and saloon. A Chinaman with a huge bundle upon his head, a slatternly woman brushing the dry, powdered snow from the path, a tawdry one pattering along, her rouged face pitiful in the clear merciless light; red-shirted miners crawling like ants to the yawning shaft-mouths half way up the mountainside.—This was Topaz Gulch on a certain wintry morning.

In the office of the Palace Hotel, the proprietor tossed aside his week-old Chicago newspaper and rose with alacrity as a slender, girlish figure, clad in a great fur coat, came lightly down the stairs.

"Everything all right, Ma'am? Did the missus make you comfortable?"

"Yes, thank you." The girl nodded, smiling. Then her face sobered. "I wonder if you could tell me—may I ask how long you have been here in Topaz Gulch?"

"Five years, Ma'am," he returned promptly. "For a boom town that didn't grow as was expected, nor yet peter out entirely, Topaz is holding her own and business ain't so bad; besides, the air is good for the missus. That's why we come in the first place."

The girl had paused at the window, gazing up the western slope.

"That is the Yellow Streak?"

"Yes'm, that's the mine. Folks thought at first that she was going to pan out another bonanza, I guess, but now she's just about profitable enough to make it worth while to keep her going. Great town, this must have been when she was first opened up."

The girl scarcely heard. She was thinking of the weary, consumptive young time-keeper who had struggled up that gray slope with daily weakening tread and of the girl who, with her baby in her arms, watched him perhaps from the door of one of those dilapidated, weather-worn shacks upon which she herself now gazed. With blurred eyes, the erstwhile Willa Murdaugh turned to her informant.

"Have there been many changes since you came?" she asked.

"Well, no," he considered. "Once in a while some hustler from the Coast lands here and runs up a concrete store, but usually he don't stay long; there ain't enough doing. The population's always shifting; there's been a whole new outfit up at the mine since we come, but everything seems to go on just the same, so you couldn't rightly call it much of a change. The moving-picture houses are about all that's marked any difference in things here, I guess."

"I wonder if there is anyone left in the town who was here fifteen years ago." Willa spoke with ill-concealed eagerness. "Who is the oldest inhabitant you know of?"

The proprietor looked his surprise.

"Well," he began at last, "there's Bill Ryder; he come in with the first rush, they tell me, and he still runs the Red Dog Café. Then there's Pete Haines, a half-witted old cuss—begging your pardon, Ma'am!—that's got enough dust cached somewhere to keep himself drunk perpetual; and the Widow Atkinson, and Big Olaf, and —and Klondike Kate."

He hesitated at the last name, and a brick-red flush suffused his stolid face, but Willa paid no heed.

"Who are they?"

"The Widow Atkinson runs the eating-house for miners at the end of the street; hard-shell temperance, she is, and they say Atkinson used to wait on table with her apron tied round him and dassent even smoke indoors." He paused. "Big Olaf is a Swede who got hurt in the mine years ago and the company gives him an annuity. Kind of cracked he is, too, but harmless. You see, Ma'am, when the big boom died down gradual and the town settled into a one-horse gait, the young folks naturally pushed on to the next strike that promised a fortune, and the old ones drifted back to where they come from."

"And Klondike Kate; who is she?" Willa persisted.

Her host shifted from one foot to the other in an agony of embarrassment.

"She—she's just a woman that stays on here because there ain't any other place for her to go, Ma'am. She does odd jobs when she can find any to do and the missus helps her out now and then, but she ain't the kind you'd want anything to do with. The missus'll tell you if you ask her."

"I understand," said Willa quickly. "Is that the Red Dog over there, where the man is sweeping sawdust out to the road?"

She had crossed to the door and opened it, and her host approached, peering over her shoulder.

"Yes'm, that's Bill Ryder himself."

"I would like to talk to him," Willa announced. "I want to ask him some questions about the early days here."

"I'll fetch him for you!" her host offered, recovering hastily from his astonishment. "You just wait here, he'll be right pleased to come——"

"No, thank you. I will go over, myself." Willa fastened her cloak with a decisive air. "He came with the first rush, you tell me? Then he should be able to remember what I want to learn."

She picked her way across the hummocks of frozen mud powdered with snow in the road, and approached the rotund, jovial-faced little man who was swinging his worn broom energetically in a cloud of sawdust.

He paused as she neared him, his jaw sagging at the apparition of a dainty, richly dressed, strange female alone on the street of Topaz.

"Good-morning. You're Mr. Ryder, aren't you?" she smiled.

"That's me, Ma'am." He pulled off his soft-brimmed hat, revealing a wide expanse of shining pink scalp, fringed with a scanty growth of grizzled hair.

"The proprietor of the Palace Hotel tells me that you

are one of the oldest inhabitants left, Mr. Ryder, and I wonder if you would mind telling me something of the people who used to live in Topaz Gulch years ago. I am trying to locate some lost relatives."

"I'll be glad to tell you anything I can, Ma'am." His round face quickened with interest. "I keep bachelor house, but if you don't object to walking through the bar—it's empty now—there's a room back where we can talk."

He led the way and Willa followed him. Bare and ramshackle as it was, the sight of the bar and the little tables fronting it brought acutely to her memory a like room, larger and more resplendent, with baize-covered tables and flaring oil lamps; a tall, spare figure inexpressibly dear to her memory replaced for a moment the rotund one before her and the veil of the past seemed lifted. She was back once more in the Blue Chip.

The vision was dispelled, however, when she found herself in the little back room, scarcely more than a closet, with room enough only for the rusty stove, table and chairs.

"Private poker-room," Mr. Ryder announced with pride. "Enough coin's changed hands here to buy the greatest gold-mine in Nevada! Make yourself comfortable, Ma'am. Now, who was it you was looking for?"

"Do you recall Jake's place, the dance-hall that was burned down?" Willa began.

"Like as if it was yesterday!" The little man seated himself in the chair opposite and put his hat on the floor beside him. "Topaz was a roaring gehenna in them days and one night Red-Eye Pete started in to shoot out the lamps at Jake's. One of 'em exploded and it was all over

in no time. Red-Eye himself and Ray Clancy, the pian-
ner-player, and two o' the girls was lost. I got a busted
arm and most o' my hair singed off going in after 'em,
but 'twarn't no use."

"You knew the—the girls?" Willa had difficulty in
controlling her voice.

"Sure I did! Blonde Annie and Miss Violet. Annie
was just a—a girl like you'd expect, Ma'am, but Miss
Violet, she was a regular lady. Young widder with a
toddling baby and a voice like an angel.—Say, that's
funny!" He broke off, staring at her. "It ain't about
her that you've come, is it?"

Willa nodded, not trusting herself to speak.

"Well, don't that beat—beat everything!" Mr. Ryder
recovered himself in some confusion. "Two or three
years ago a lawyer shark from New York City—a man
named North, I remember—come here asking an all-fired
lot o' questions, and only last fall another feller turned
up on the same game. I told 'em all I knew, which
warn't much. They called themselves Murphy, Miss Vi
and her husband did, but I guess that warn't their right
name. Nice young feller he was, but quiet and sickly.
When he died we wanted to pass round the hat for the
widder, like we always do, but she wouldn't have it; she
got work instead at Jake's, singing and dancing, but she
kept everyone in their place and there warn't a man here
that wouldn't have stood up for her till the last gun
fired."

"And the baby—do you remember it at all?"

"Little Billie?" Mr. Ryder laughed. "There ain't
enough babies around a mining camp to make you forget
any one of 'em, and you couldn't rightly forget Billie if

you tried. Fat and curly-headed she was, and the spunk-
iest little critter you ever see, always falling down hard
and scrambling up again by herself and laughing to beat
four of a kind. Her ma tried to keep her home, but
there warn't a chance; she went wherever her little legs
would carry her, and the whole town looked out for her.
She must be a woman grown, now."

"I don't suppose you would recognize her if you
should see her," Willa observed wistfully.

"Me? Lord, no!" he exclaimed. "Babies grow up
into most anything, as far as looks go! She was about
four when her ma was burned, and Gentleman Geoff,
the gambler, adopted her and took her away. The whole
town wanted to keep her, but in them days Topaz was
no place for a girl to grow up in and there wasn't a
woman here of her mother's kind."

"It is possible that a woman might remember her
where a man wouldn't." Willa was following her own
train of thought. "The proprietor of the Palace spoke
of two women left who were here at that time; a Mrs.
Atkinson and Klondike Kate. Would they be able to tell
me anything more, do you think?"

"Not the widder!" Mr. Ryder responded with emphasis. "She put Miss Vi to work in her hash-house
for a week when young Murphy died; starved her,
slammed the kid around and drove her till she fainted.
She warn't used to hard work, Miss Vi warn't, and the
Widder Atkinson would have killed a horse. When Miss
Vi took to doing turns at Jake's instead, the Widder
'lowed she was no better than she'd ought to've been,
and near got lynched in consequence. You've only got
to mention Miss Vi to her even now to have her r'ar

right up on her hind legs. She wouldn't tell you nothing if she could."

"The other one, Klondike Kate. Did she know this Miss Violet?"

"Sure. She was one o' the girls at Jake's, like Blonde Annie and the rest. I guess you ain't ever come in contact with that kind, Ma'am, but it wouldn't hurt you to talk to her once and if anyone could help you maybe she could. That kind don't get much forbearance from other women, but Miss Vi was good to her and nursed her through a spell o' sickness and Klondike Kate just about worshiped her and the baby. 'Twas Kate saved little Billie when Jake's burned. She was the first after poor Miss Violet to remember the baby and she turned back and got her."

"She—she saved the child!" Willa's voice trembled, and she rose quickly. "Where can I find her? It is good of you to have told me what you could, Mr. Ryder. You don't remember anything else about this Miss Violet and her baby; she left no papers with anyone?"

"No, not that I know of. The lawyer asked me that, too, and the young feller who came last fall. Riley, his name was, or something like that."

"Starr Wiley?" Willa smiled. "Did he ask you anything else, Mr. Ryder?"

"He was trying most particular to find out Gentleman Geoff's last name, but nobody ever heard it here. You'll find Klondike Kate living in the last shack on the west side o' the street before you come to the coal-yard. She ain't a pleasant sight to look at, poor old Kate! The fire caught her, too, when she rescued the baby, and though she was a fine-appearing girl before then, her own mother wouldn't know her now, or want to, I guess, for that matter. She's square, I'll say that for her; whatever she tells you, you can bank on."

Willa took leave of Mr. Ryder and departed upon her quest. He followed to the café door and stood looking perplexedly after her as she made her way down the rambling street. He was trying to fix in his mind the vagrant, subtle sensation of familiarity which possessed him when he had first caught sight of her face. Stolid and slow of wit as he was, the conviction grew that she or someone very like her had crossed his path before. Then the face of the song-and-dance artiste at Jake's flashed across his memory and the next minute he was pounding heavily after the girl.

"Hey, Ma'am! Wait a second!" he panted.

Willa turned.

"Excuse me, Ma'am, but it come to me that you might be little Billie, yourself! Are you? I'd like powerful well to see her again!"

"Look at me!" commanded Willa. "Could you swear, Mr. Ryder, that I was the child you call 'Billie'? Could you take your oath on it?"

He looked long and searchingly while she waited in breathless suspense. At last he drew back, shaking his head.

"No'm, I couldn't. Meaning no disrespect, there's a look about you of Miss Vi, but fifteen or sixteen years is a long time to trust your memory and I couldn't swear to nothing."

Willa sighed and turned away.

"My name is Abercrombie," she said. "You are right, Mr. Ryder. Fifteen years are a very long time."

The shack next the coal-yard was more forlorn even than the others, though the sagging porch was swept clean, and ineffectual attempts had been made to mend the breaks in roof and walls with fresher slabs of unpainted wood which stood out against the gray weathered boards like patches on an old coat.

There was no bell, but Willa knocked patiently on the panel until there came a slow tread within and the door opened. A thin, angular woman stood there, her dark hair streaked with gray, and Willa glanced at her, then swiftly averted her gaze in pity. The face before her was drawn and scarred as if the hot hand of wrath had clawed it, searing and distorting it to the hideous, grinning semblance of a mask.

"I beg your pardon." Willa's voice was very gentle. "I am looking for someone known as Klondike Kate. If you are she, I have a great favor to ask of you."

She had sounded the right note; the woman, who for so long had been the recipient of grudging, half-contemptuous favor herself, gasped and flung wide the door.

"Come in, Miss. I'm Kate, right enough. Sit down close to the stove; I ain't got much of a fire." The voice was singularly clear and sweet.

Willa glanced about her and then back at the woman who had dropped into a low rocker beside a table heaped with red flannels, which she had evidently been mending. The room was tiny and pitifully bare, but scrubbed clean, and pathetic bows of faded ribbon strove to conceal the worn spots on the coarse snowy curtains. A small pot bubbled on the stove and two cold potatoes and half a stale loaf on the shelf betrayed the meagerness of the larder.

The woman had given an impression of age at first, but Willa saw now that she could be scarcely more than forty and her eyes were rather fine despite their hint of tragedy.

"I'm looking for someone who can tell me about Violet, the girl who used to dance at Jake's." Willa chose her words deliberately. "Mr. Ryder says you were a friend of hers, years ago."

"Bill Ryder said that?" Klondike Kate drew a deep breath. "A friend? She was the best friend a body could ever have! But you could hardly have known her; she died fifteen years past."

"I know. I was wondering if you knew her story; if she left any papers with you?"

"Who are you?" the woman asked suddenly, bending forward. "If I knew Vi's story, would I repay her for all her kindness by telling it to a stranger? Why should I show you her papers if she did leave any with me, when that lawyer could get nothing out of me two years ago, for all his blustering?"

"Would you do it if you could help her baby to claim what is her own?" Willa asked earnestly. "My name is Abercrombie, but I happen to know that the girl your friend left behind her is trying to prove her identity. I thought that you would want to help."

"Oh, if I could!" Klondike Kate clasped her toil-worn hands. "Vi told me about the rich father-in-law who hadn't ever forgiven her. Where is Billie, Miss Abercrombie? Is she well and happy? She was such a pretty thing!"

"She is well," Willa responded slowly. "She never knew that it was you who saved her from the fire."

The scarred face flushed.

"I forgot her first, that was the awful part. She'd been ailing and her mother couldn't leave her home, so while she did her turn I sat in her dressing-room, mending my skirt and talking to the kid. When I heard the shots and the lamp exploded and the blaze flared up, I just made a jump for the door. Then I remembered Billie and went back, and the flames caught us both."

"But—but she isn't scarred!" Willa cried.

"No. I—I tore off my skirt and wrapped her in it. Only her little bare feet stuck out and one of them got burned real bad."

"One—of—her—feet!" repeated Willa breathlessly. "Did it leave a scar? Oh, think—think!"

"Why, I guess it must have, Miss Abercrombie." The woman stared at her. "The right foot it was, and there was a bad burn on the inside of the ankle right up from the heel, like a tongue of flame had licked it. It wasn't hardly well when Gentleman Geoff took her away."

For a moment Willa sat as if stunned, then she bent swiftly, and, whipping off her shoe and stocking, thrust out a slender pink foot. The inner side was seared with a tiny forked red line, slight but unmistakable.

"You!" Klondike Kate rose slowly. "You are Billie!"

With a little sob Willa went to meet her, and in an instant the two were crying in each other's arms.

The older woman was the first to recover herself.

"Oh, my dear, to think that I didn't know you! I ought to have seen from the first—your mother's hair and eyes——"

"But you know me now!" Willa smiled through her tears. "You could swear to me by that scar, couldn't you? You see, there is someone trying to claim I'm not the girl you knew as Billie, and I have no other proof. I never fancied that little scar meant anything; I haven't thought of it in years. You saved my life once, at the risk of your own—will you help me now?"

"Will I?" Klondike Kate wiped her eyes. "I'll go to the last ditch for you! I've lived right for fifteen years, and I guess my word is as good as the next one's. You just take me to whoever says you're not little Billie and I'll prove their lie before any court on earth.—That reminds me; I have something for you. It won't help make good your claim, for they might say an impostor got it from me, but it's yours and you ought to have it."

She mounted the rickety stairs to the loft, and in her absence Willa slowly put on her stocking and shoe once more. Her own inner conviction had been justified and an elation almost solemn in its intensity filled her heart. She was Willa Murdaugh! She could prove her right to the name which had been wrested from her!

When Klondike Kate descended she bore in her hands a folded paper, yellowed and worn, and a tarnished locket on a bit of faded, scorched blue ribbon.

"I was sick when Gentleman Geoff left town with you or I'd have tied the locket on you myself," she said. "It's got both their pictures in it, mother and father. See!"

She opened the case, and Willa gazed through renewed tears at the two young faces vibrant with life which smiled back at her: the man's thin and intellectual with the eyes of a dreamer and the chiseled lips of a poet; the woman's stronger and more practical, her gaze sweet and level, her dark hair in a soft cloud about her low, broad forehead.

Willa pressed the locket convulsively to her breast in

the first overwhelming tide of possession which had ever swept over her. These were her own people, flesh of her flesh! They had dared to love against insuperable odds, and, succumbing at last, had left her as the pledge of that love! She would prove worthy of them!

"It was taken from her neck when they found her after the fire," Klondike Kate said softly. "Jake gave it to me to keep for you.—Here's what she prized most of anything she had; she put it in my hands herself to keep for her."

The yellowed paper, unfolded, proved to be the certificate of marriage of Violet Ashton and Ralph Murdaugh, dated January 2, 1896.

The two talked long within the little shack, and when Willa emerged at last the sun had disappeared behind a bank of level, leaden cloud and the still cold which precedes a snowfall had settled down upon the valley.

Since her arrival the night before Willa had fought resolutely against the vague memories which seemed to assail her at every turn, fearing the snare of mental suggestion, but now she strove wistfully to foster a sense of nearness and familiarity with the dreary scene.

The reaction from her triumphant hour had come, and with it a forlorn hopelessness of spirit. What did it matter, after all? Outcast or reinstated in the empty pomp and circumstance of society, no one had really cared save Winnie, and he had not counted.

The tragedy of utter isolation from all human ties descended upon her and in the depths of her desolation she was oblivious to the sound of footsteps approaching on the frosty, hard-packed road. It was only when they halted that she glanced up—and found herself looking into the eyes of Kearn Thode.

CHAPTER XXIII

THE SLIPPER OF CINDERELLA

FORGETTING for a moment all else but the joy of his presence, she held out both hands with a glad little cry.

"Kearn!"

He took her hands in his, but released them after the merest touch, and in the hungry wistfulness of his gaze there was no answering gladness.

"Miss Murdaugh, I have an explanation to make for my disobedience of your injunction," he said stiffly. "I have deliberately followed you here, but it is only that I may put you in possession of certain facts which are of moment to you. Will you forgive me if I intrude upon you for an hour?"

The brightness faded, and she bowed her head in silence. She had forgotten his duplicity and the cold-blooded mercenary game he had played, but the memory of it returned with his first words. Passionately she wished that she might never have learned the truth! He would have played the game to the last round, he would have been kind at least, and she might have lived on in her fool's paradise. Then a wave of contempt swept over her for her own cowardice and she straightened.

"I am very glad to see you." Her tones were gravely conventional. "If you have followed me out here, as you say, to render me a service it must be one for which I shall be deeply grateful, Mr. Thode. I am staying at the Palace Hotel and if you will walk there with me we can talk, secure from intrusion. How did you know I was here?"

"Winthrop North told me of the sudden change in your plans for the future, and that he knew where you had gone when you left the Halsteads. I made a hurried trip West and there discovered what I have now to tell you." He spoke slowly as if weighing each word. "I went back to New York to see you, but could only learn that you had disappeared. However, since you had not gone to Limasito, it occurred to me that you must be here, in an attempt possibly to prove your identity."

"And what you have to tell me bears on that?" Willa asked.

"It does, most conclusively. Starr Wiley must have had a very vital motive in getting you out of the way, for his story was a lie from start to finish; his papers a deliberate forgery!"

"If you have proof of that, Mr. Thode, you have indeed rendered me a service I can never repay!" she cried. "Once more I am in your debt!"

"My news does not surprise you?" he asked, with a quick glance at her face.

"No. I have suspected it from the moment Starr Wiley announced his discovery, for he had threatened me with it in advance; had tried to bargain with me, in fact." Willa paused. "I had intended to go on from here to the Flathead Lake country in Montana and then to Arizona in an effort to establish what you have discovered. I am anxious to know how you stumbled upon the truth."

It was only when they had reached the little hotel sitting-room and established themselves before the replenished stove that Kearn Thode enlightened her.

"You may remember, Miss Murdaugh, that I knew Starr Wiley before I met him again in Limasito, and that knowledge alone would have impelled me to distrust at sight any claims which she might produce, no matter what their nature," he began. "When Winthrop North told me that our friend had been the means of proving you were not the granddaughter of Giles Murdaugh, I doubted, and when I learned the name which Gentleman Geoff was supposed to have signed to the adoption papers with the trapper, I knew the whole thing was a frame-up. Gentleman Geoff's name was not Abercrombie."

"How do you know that?" Willa asked, amazed.

"He told me the truth himself, just a little while before he died," Thode responded. "I gave him my word to keep his confidence, but now in your interest I know that he would have me speak. He was Geoffrey Rendell, of a fine old family, university bred and with a brilliant future before him, if he had so chosen. I have traced as much of his career as anyone can ever know now and I will never betray the reason for his ultimate choice, but you may rest assured that his nickname was no label of chance or whim. He was a gentleman always in the truest, finest sense of the word."

"Nothing could ever make me doubt that for an instant," Willa said with glowing eyes. "There could have been nothing discreditable in his past and he was a clean sportsman in the life he chose, square and philosophical; a game loser, a generous winner! Poor Dad! Mr. Thode, tell me how you succeeded in learning the truth."

"When I was convinced that trickery was at work I persuaded Winthrop to let me see and photograph the adoption agreement. With that as a basis I went straight to Pima, in Graham County, Arizona, where Frank Hillery, the trapper, had died and Wiley professed to have run across his papers. Hillery died only seven or eight months ago, you know, and it wasn't difficult to find out all about him.

"He landed there in the spring of nineteen four, and opened a little store with general merchandise. He was still keeping it when he was stricken with typhoid last year and died. I readily found the widow who had kept house for him all those years and interviewed his friends. His long sojourn in the wilds evidently had their reaction when he settled down in civilization once more, for he became exceedingly garrulous, and his friends were familiar with every detail of his past life. His favorite narrative was of the coming of Gentleman Geoff with you to his cabin; of the death of his own little daughter and of Gentleman Geoff's long illness and subsequent gratitude and generosity to him. Your foster father, in recognition of his hospitality and care, had given him sufficient money to start in business, and Hillery never forgot it. When he died he left no papers except a brief will, and his old trunks and boxes remained undisturbed in the attic, until about three months ago when a strange young man appeared in Pima."

Thode paused and Willa caught her breath. She had momentarily forgotten the narrator himself in her interest in his story, and the quick color came and went in her cheeks. It seemed to the young engineer that she bloomed like a splendid rose in the homely, bare little room and the wistfulness deepened in his eyes, but he went on in a sternly impersonal voice:

"The man was Wiley, under an assumed name, of course. He posed as a nephew of the dead man, and when the beneficiaries found he had no intention of attempting to dispute the will, being wealthy himself, they gladly made friends with him and told him all they knew of his late uncle.

"Wiley went to board with the widow, and it seemed only natural that he should want to go through his uncle's effects. The widow gave him free access to the attic, and it was there, in one of those boxes, that he professed to find the packet of papers which he afterward produced. Undoubtedly the marriage-certificate and the maps were genuine; only the article of adoption had been added. He left soon after, and nothing further was known of him there.

"When I learned that much, I, too, went to board with the widow and learned every detail of Wiley's stay. One of Hillery's oldest friends had a son who had gone to the bad and was serving a term for highway robbery in a prison near Phoenix. I found that Wiley had taken a great interest in the lad and paid him more than one visit, promising to use his influence to have him pardoned. I went to Phoenix, talked with this prisoner and a few others, and incidentally looked over the records.

"I discovered that Wiley had interested himself particularly in an ex-forger whose term had expired at about that period, and it was understood that Wiley had provided him with a new start in life. I hunted up this man—it wasn't hard for he had bought a ranch and was trying to go straight—and under threat of arrest obtained his written confession.

"The money for the fresh start was the price Wiley had paid for the execution of the false document. I have the confession here in my bag, and I will show it to you later. It is absolutely conclusive proof. Miss Murdaugh, I may be an accessory after the fact, but I felt sure you would not want the forger punished, and I gave him time to sell out his ranch and disappear. I am under the impression that he has gone to Canada to enlist, and if so——"

Willa shook her head.

"No. I don't believe he had any idea of the purpose to which the document would be put, or its far-reaching effects, and if he has gone to war, his punishment is on the knees of the gods."

"Exactly. He did not know. The name of Murdaugh wasn't mentioned in it if you remember, only those of Hillery and the supposed Abercrombie."

" 'Abercrombie!' " repeated Willa meditatively. "I wonder how Wiley came to add that?"

"I finally solved that. Wiley wanted to add clinching verisimilitude to the document and took a long shot. Like many another amateur criminal, he overreached himself, and that one fact, you see, led to the whole discovery. He must have followed Gentleman Geoff's trail through his wanderings from Topaz Gulch, seeking a loop-hole to prove you were not the baby originally adopted, and when he came upon the story which was told to him in Missoula, Montana. of Gentleman Geoff's illness in the

trapper's cabin on Flathead Lake, one can easily see how
the whole scheme popped into his head. There were the
two men and two little girls of the same age, isolated far
from civilization for a long winter. One child dies, the
other departs with Gentleman Geoff. What more simple
than to arrange for a plausible substitution of the children? Gentleman Geoff being dead, the only possible
obstacle could be in the person of the other member of
that lonely quartette, Frank Hillery, the trapper. We
know now how Wiley traced him and overcame that difficulty.

"Wiley's efforts culminated in Arizona, but mine only
began there. I traced him back step by step on the trail
he had come, following Hillery, and in Missoula I
learned more of Gentleman Geoff. Wiley must have
learned there what I did, that Gentleman Geoff's last
name was known to be Abercrombie, but Wiley didn't
investigate deeply enough.

"I did. I found that Gentleman Geoff Abercrombie
had a most unsavory name there as a crooked gambler
and card-sharp—— No, Miss Murdaugh, please don't
protest!"

Willa had turned upon him with flashing eyes.

"He had operated several gambling-casinos for brief,
abruptly terminated periods in Idaho and Montana,
keeping about two jumps ahead of a lynching posse most
of the time and was last heard of in New Mexico five
years ago, when the Blue Chip was in full blast in Limasito. In other words, there were two Gentleman Geoffs!
The second must have been a cheap swindler and card-
sharp, who learned of your foster father's fame as a
square gambler throughout the West and sought to profit

by it. His operations were on such a small, petty scale,
however, that it is no wonder the story of his exploits
never reached the ears of the real Gentleman Geoff.
Your title to your name is assured now, Miss Murdaugh."

"And you have done all this for me!" Willa mused,
then turned her level direct gaze upon him. "Why, Mr.
Thode?"

"Because I promised the man who brought you up and
cared for you always that I would do what I could to
further the duty he had assumed and so splendidly carried on," Thode responded simply. "When he lay dying,
he told me that, although you yourself did not know it,
you were of different blood and caste from your associates in Limasito. His own words were that you were
born a lady and must go back to your own."

"Dad said that?" Willa's lips quivered. "I learned
to-day that he was in love with my mother always, and
she had told him her whole story. I have found a friend
here, too, Mr. Thode, a poor woman who is frightfully
maimed from saving my life in the fire which killed my
mother. I—I have a scar from it which she recognized
and so there is another witness to my identity, but without the valuable proof you have brought me I would still
have found it almost impossible to offset the evidence of
that false document. I cannot thank you for all that you
have done and I still cannot quite understand——"

"It was for Gentleman Geoff," he reminded her courteously but coldly. "I had given him my word and I
meant to keep it to the utmost of my ability. My task, I
think, is almost completed."

Willa drew back, in wretched indecision. If only it

had not been for that hideously betraying letter which Angie had put in her hands how clear the way would be before her! If the testimony offered of his mercenary motives in making love to her had been verbal she would have scorned it, no matter who swore to its truth, but his intent was made plain in his own writing and could not be gainsaid.

"You will not let me offer you my thanks," she murmured. "But I am indeed grateful. Can we not at least be friends, Mr. Thode? I—I regret that bitter, angry letter I sent to you, but I had learned something which hurt me deeply. Won't you be magnanimous enough to forget it and let us go on as if nothing had occurred?"

"I shall be glad to be your friend and serve you in any way that I can, Miss Murdaugh," he responded dryly. "I have something further to tell you which I think concerns you closely. Are you aware that Starr Wiley and his partner, Harrington Chase, have purchased from Tia Juana Reyes the property known as the Lost Souls lease and are already issuing stock and developing the well?"

Willa rose slowly to her feet, staring at him as if she could not believe the evidence of her own ears.

"You—you cannot mean it!" she gasped. "It cannot be true; there is a mistake somewhere! Please, say that again, Mr. Thode!"

He told her all that he had learned in New York, and she listened breathlessly, her varying color concentrated in two vivid burning spots upon her cheeks. A steady light deepened, too, in her eyes, and when he had finished his story he looked at her in unconcealed amazement. Far from being down-cast and distressed, she seemed to his half-incredulous gaze to be triumphant, but she only remarked quietly:

"This is news indeed, Mr. Thode, but it simplifies everything. The stakes I have played for since I left Limasito are in my hands at last. I cannot explain now, but you will learn the whole truth very soon. Starr Wiley and his partner are still in New York?"

"No. They have both gone down to Limasito, to inspect developments on the well. In the society column of a belated newspaper which reached me yesterday, I read that two of the principal stock-holders, Mason North and your cousin, Ripley Halstead, together with their families, had gone also in a private car to Mexico. You will return to New York now, will you not?"

Willa's eyes sparkled dangerously and she clenched her little hands.

"I—I have some arrangements to make here; I must provide for Klondike Kate's future, and obtain her deposition. She was my mother's friend, who recognized me. Then, Mr. Thode, I shall leave, but not for New York. I, too, am going to Mexico! I want to see the Lost Souls well and learn from Tia Juana's own lips the story of its transfer."

"I shall be down there myself," Thode announced, rising. "If you recall our conversation when we met again in New York you will remember that I told you of my own ambition to find Tia Juana and try to obtain possession of the Lost Souls lease. You know how the map was stolen from me in the beginning, but I am not sure yet that I have been beaten?"

"What do you mean?" Willa asked. "And why do you

think that your news about the sale of the well concerns me closely?"

"I have only one answer to both questions," rejoined Thode. "Knowing Starr Wiley, I believe that trickery and fraud are at the bottom of his acquisition of the well, and it concerns you because your cousin, Ripley Halstead, has invested a large part of your inheritance in it. If fraud is connected with the transaction by which Wiley gained possession of it, I mean to expose him on this count as well as his conspiracy against you. I had set my heart on the Lost Souls venture, like an over-confident young fool! I even wrote to my employer after you had gone and I discovered that Tia Juana was Juana Reyes, the owner of the Pool, that I had only to find her to win her consent——"

"You wrote——what?" Willa rose slowly to her feet, her rich color ebbing.

"I wrote that except for Trevino, the Mexican who sold her the lease, no one there knew her real name, and it wouldn't matter to them if they did.—They wouldn't have connected old Tia Juana, of that tumble-down shack in the zapote grove, with the Juana Reyes who could afford to buy the Trevino hacienda, you see. I also said, if I remember, that she was the undoubted owner of almost boundless wealth and when I had gone after her and won her consent to selling a half-interest in the Pool itself——"

"Oh!" Willa cried, wincing as if he had struck her a blow. "You wrote that about *Tia Juana!* And I—I—oh, how blind I was! How wickedly, cruelly blind!"

"Now it is I who do not understand." He shrugged. "What does it matter, anyway? I never succeeded in

finding Tia Juana or in something else which was of
even more moment to me. Gentleman Geoff trusted me,
however, and I have fulfilled that trust. Now I am free
to take up my own fight again."

Willa held out her hand timidly.

"You will allow me to wish you luck, even if I may
not thank you?" she asked. "I—I have much to explain
and you much to forgive, but we shall meet again in
Mexico."

He bowed formally.

"It appears to be inevitable. Fate seems to compel me
to ignore your request that I obliterate myself from the
scene," he added whimsically. "I will try not to intrude
upon you more than I must, however, Miss Murdaugh."

"Yes!" she responded softly. "In spite of my blind-
ness and your pride, fate seems to have appointed you
to the permanent job of knight-errant to the maiden in
distress, hasn't it, Mr. Duenna?"

When the door had closed behind him, she stood quite
still in the middle of the floor where he had left her.
That letter, that portentous letter which Angie had spite-
fully put into her willing, credulous hands had referred
to Tia Juana, not to herself. How plain it all was, now,
and how ruthlessly, unjustly she had driven him from
her! And he? He had repaid her flouting of him by
tireless devotion and a measureless service! Ah, but she
would make amends!

Then a whimsical, tender light flooded her face. Cinderella had come into her own again; the prince had
found her and fitted on the slipper just when she had
been most sure that he had gone from her forever! He
was a very haughty and hurt and angry prince, to be

sure, but there had been that in his eyes which told her that she might win him back despite the bitter misunderstanding. The old fairy tale was coming true, after all!

CHAPTER XXIV

The Lost Souls' Treasure

ON a certain bright February morning Ben Hallock puffed up the Calle Rivera and across the plaza of Limasito as fast as his battered jitney could carry him and rushed into Baggott's hotel with an anticipatory gleam in his heavy eyes.

"Hey, Jim! I got your message and I come a-hummin'!" he announced. "What is it? Vigilance Committee?"

"Sort of!" Jim Baggott fairly pranced from behind the bar, his round face shining with excitement. "Here's a gentleman from New York, old friend of yours."

Ben Hallock turned to find himself facing an elderly personage with an impressively pointed gray beard and keen eyes behind gold-rimmed pince-nez.

"Jumping Jehosaphet! If it ain't Perry Larkin!" Ben pumped the stranger's hand energetically. "Mighty glad to see you, Sir! Your engineer, Kearn Thode, called on me last fall; fine young feller he is, too! You heard about what he did when El Negrito came?"

"Yes, Hallock, but I'm even more proud of him to-day!" The keen eyes sparkled. "I want you to meet a—er—a confrère of mine, Mr. Morrissey."

Honest Dan, late taxi'-driver and amateur detective, purpled with embarrassment as he rose and shook hands, but his eyes, too, were dancing.

Ben nodded to Henry Bailey, his ranch neighbor and the only other occupant of the bar, and then turned again to Jim Baggott.

"Now perhaps you'll tell me what in thunder the racket is about! I'd have come to meet Mr. Larkin without you hinting at a lynchin' party!"

"Just you say what you'll have and hold your horses!" Jim chuckled. "I'm acting under instructions, the same that brought Mr. Larkin and this-here young man down from New York, and Hen Bailey in from his hacienda; the orders of Gentleman Geoff's Billie, by God!"

"Billie! She ain't—you don't mean she's comin' back?" Ben cried joyfully. "I told you she wasn't the kind to forget her old friends in spite of the grand life she's walked into! I knew she'd come back to see us——"

"It is business which brings her now, Hallock, and grim business, too," Mr. Larkin interposed. "She wanted you and Henry here as her friends and witnesses, and there's apt to be a rather ugly scene."

"Do you mean she's coming right now, that she's here?" Ben Hallock touched his hip significantly. "I've come heeled for any kind of a little party that's liable to be sprung, but I little thought Billie'd be mixed up in it. What's the matter? Anybody been tryin' to stack the cards on her?"

"The dirtiest, crookedest game that was ever pulled!" Jim smote the bar a blow which made the glasses tinkle. "But she'll beat 'em to it yet, or she wouldn't be Gentleman Geoff's girl! She ain't here now, but we expect her any minute and when she comes the fun'll start."

As if in answer the hum and whirr of two high-powered motors chugging in unison stole upon the air and rapidly increased in volume. Ben craned his neck from the window and then turned disappointedly.

"It's only that Lost Souls crowd!" he grunted. "Jim, if anything in the line of a fracas starts here, you'll lose that passel of swell boarders of yours! Can you see them women when the shootin' commences?"

"They're in on it, too!" Jim grinned. "Not the women-folk, but the men, and more especially our fine young friend, Starr Wiley."

"Something to do with the Lost Souls——"

"Shut up, quick!" Jim advanced from behind the bar with an almost comic air of ceremony as the motor party trooped in at the door and headed for the stairs. Perry Larkin squared his pince-nez and recognized Mrs. Ripley Halstead and her daughter, Angelica, while behind them appeared seven men; Halstead himself, his son, Vernon, Starr Wiley, Harrington Chase, Mason North and his son, Winthrop, and a stranger whom a second glance revealed as Cranmore, the Mexican representative of the Chase-Wiley interests.

"Excuse me, ladies and gentlemen, but we've been waiting for you!" Jim Baggott began in the voice of a showman. "I'll have to ask you gentlemen to step this way, all of you. It's a real-pressing little matter of busi-ness you're all concerned in, and the ladies can come, too, if they feel like it. There'll be more ladies present shortly."

Wondering, the whole party crowded into the room, and, recognizing Perry Larkin, greeted him with varying degrees of cordiality. Jim bustled about, setting chairs for them, and in the general confusion none noted that a little group of men in uniform had issued from a door behind the bar and taken up their stations at the windows and entrance. The last comers were in two divisions; the ornate ones, stocky and swarthy for the most part, the soberly attired, taller and stalwart with the paler hue of the North.

Starr Wiley was the first to observe their presence, and he uttered a stifled oath.

"These are just extra witnesses," Jim explained blandly. "They're here to represent the United States Federal Government and also Mexico. You see, this-here little matter has what you might call an international aspect.—Did you speak, Mr. Wiley?"

"I should like to, when you've finished shooting off fireworks!" that gentleman blustered. "What's the meaning of this, anyway? What sort of trumped-up game are you——?"

"Steady, Starr." Ripley Halstead interposed quietly, and turned to the proprietor. "Will you state the nature of this meeting to which you have called us, Mr. Baggott? We are waiting to learn."

"I'm waiting, too!" confessed Jim. "I've got my orders—gosh almighty! Here she comes!"

Unheard, a single touring-car had slipped across the plaza and halted before the entrance. A slim, girlish, heavily-veiled figure alighted, and at sight of the men who accompanied her, Starr Wiley emitted a second oath.

They paused in the doorway and with a sudden movement the girl tore off her veil. There was a moment of electrified silence, broken by a little cry from Angie.

"It's Willa!—That impostor, I mean——"

"No!" Kearn Thode, the second of the newcomers, advanced to Mason North. "You were appointed the guardian of Willa Murdaugh, were you not, Mr. North? I have brought her back to you, with proof of her absolute identity."

"Bless my soul!" The rotund little man advanced with shining eyes, and seized the girl's hands. "I am overwhelmed, my dear girl, delighted! And you have proof, you say? What an amazingly fortunate turn of affairs!"

No one echoed him for a moment. The Halsteads sat stunned, and Harrington Chase, his face a greenish gray, had slumped in his chair. Only Starr Wiley, his eyes glittering and a sinister sneer curling his thin lips, looked on imperturbably. Winthrop North gasped. Then he hurried forward.

"Good work, Kearn! Oh, Willa!" His voice broke as he took her hands from his father's and wrung them hard. "Our trails have crossed again, and it has been 'good luck' indeed!"

Ripley Halstead had risen, and his wife made a tentative movement to follow his example. Vernon, too, recovered himself and advanced eagerly, but Willa waved them back and took her place before the bar.

"This is quite a reunion, isn't it?" She smiled, but there was a grim menace behind it. "I'm glad you're all here, for I've got a story to tell you that I shouldn't care to tell twice. It goes back to before a lot of you ever knew me, but you'll find it interesting enough, for it concerns you all as well as me; you, and the Pool of the Lost Souls."

She leaned back with one elbow resting upon the bar

and her other hand in the pocket of her traveling-coat and surveyed them one by one, her expression unchanging. No one stirred and after a moment she went on:

"I have asked my old friends, my real friends, to meet me here that they, too, may learn the truth. Most of you have heard the legend of the Lost Souls' Pool; Mr. Larkin heard it from Ben Hallock and sent Kearn Thode down here to find it, if he could. Mr. Chase also learned it, and his partner came on the same errand, but I had the story from the lineal descendant of the first Spanish owner, and the one person in the world who knew where it was located, Juana Reyes. In her youth she married a cousin of the same name, and her only relative living now is her crippled grandson, José. My foster father scoffed at the truth of the legend, but I had faith in Tia Juana's knowledge.

"When El Negrito, the butcher, came down from the hills on his murderous raid and killed Dad among the rest, I learned that his visit had been prearranged and paid for by a white man. He had been hired to burn and rape and slay in order to evoke United States intervention, by a man in this room!"

"By God——" Jim Baggott leaped to his feet, and Henry Bailey and Ben Hallock emitted a simultaneous roar of rage; but she silenced them.

"The government men are here as much to protect him as to see that he does not escape, and hard as it is we must let the law take its course." She spoke with frank regret, but her steady, significant smile never wavered. "In Dad's name I dedicated my life to getting that man. I had a witness to prove his conspiracy, but I wanted to play a lone hand. Nothing else mattered, nothing else has ever mattered!

"When the Blue Chip was sold and Jim Baggott handed over the money to me I knew it wouldn't be enough; if I was to beat the man at his own game I must be able to match finances as well as wits. I thought then of the Pool of the Lost Souls and the fabulous profits to be made from it.

"Three days before Mr. North came to Limasito I took Tia Juana away, and she guided me to the Pool. It had been passed over by the searchers for generations, but she possessed an old map of its true location. I bought the Pool with the money from the sale of the Blue Chip, recorded it in her name with the Notary at Victoria and gave her a half interest. All she cared about, anyway, was the home of her ancestors.

"Then Mr. North brought the news of my inheritance. I didn't want it at first, as he can tell you. The name and the money meant little to me until I realized that they would be useful to my plan. They mean less to me now that my purpose has been achieved, but since they are mine and have been wrested from me by fraud I claim them—if only to trample them under my feet, if I choose.

"I realized that the name would carry me into the very inner circle of the man I was after, the man who had murdered Dad, and the money would help when I could exercise unlimited control of it. That was the only reason I consented to go to New York, and my ultimate purpose never wavered.

"I had no detailed plan, but I meant to keep Tia Juana

and the fact that I possessed the Lost Souls' Pool under cover until I had come into my full inheritance, when I would return and fight the man to the finish. Mr. North never knew that Tia Juana and José accompanied us to New York, although he did complain of my frequent disappearances en route, I remember."

Mason North sputtered.

"So do I! But why did you not tell me all, my dear? I might have helped you——"

"And taken the whole thing out of my hands?" Willa shook her head, still smiling. "The man was *my meat*, Mr. North! Vengeance may be the Lord's, but it was sweet to me, too, and I meant to taste it to the last morsel!

"The man was one of those who were still searching for the Lost Souls' Pool. After our departure he possessed himself by violence of the map which Tia Juana had only partly destroyed, located the Pool, learned of its new owner and started out to find her. He knew that I was her one friend, and suspected that I was back of the purchase. Before following me to New York, therefore, he made a journey West, of which I'll tell you more later, or rather Mr. Thode will.

"When he did finally appear in New York, he tried by every means in his power to force me to a confession of my knowledge of Tia Juana's whereabouts; he spied upon me and I removed her to new quarters just in time. He flattered and cajoled me, and, when that failed, resorted to vague threats.

"Then Tia Juana disappeared. She vanished from the home I had found for her, leaving no trace, and I feared that the man had abducted her, to coerce her into making the Pool over to him, until I met him outside the house from which she had gone. He accused me of having spirited her away to keep her out of his reach and demanded that I produce her in three days, or he would strip me of my position and name and inheritance, seeing me driven forth as an impostor! That man is Starr Wiley, and you know how he carried out his threat!"

Wiley made a sudden convulsive leap for the window, but paused transfixed at her significant gesture. The government officials had closed in about him, but he saw only the girl before the bar and the pointed bulge in her cloak, beneath her hidden hand.

"Better not try it, Starr Wiley, although I almost wish you would!" Her voice rang out in the suddenly stayed tumult. "I've had you covered from the first, and I'll drop you with a shot through my pocket if you make another move! The rest of you know only what he has done to me, but you shall hear how he has served you, too!

"I left the Halstead house, and then by a miracle Tia Juana was restored to me. After her disappearance little José remembered her interest in a conversation between her landlady and a friend concerning some Spanish gypsies who had settled in squatters' cabins north of the city, and conceiving the idea that she had joined them, he slipped away to find her. He succeeded, although how she ever reached her destination we cannot know, for she was bewildered and lost her mind, temporarily enfeebled. José, as a vender of tomales, established himself near the garage where I kept my car, hoping to attract the attention of my chauffeur, Dan Morrissey here, who had helped me all through that trying time and whom José knew he could trust.

"Once he was frightened away, but the second time he succeeded and Dan brought him to me. I took Tia Juana away to another city, but she was ill for a long time. When I could leave her, I placed her and José in the care of Dan's sister whom I summoned from New York, and went West myself to disprove Starr Wiley's story if I could.

"I found a witness who can swear to my identity as the daughter of Ralph and Violet Murdaugh and prove it by a scar I bear from the fire which cost my mother her life, but Mr. Thode, unknown to me, had gone West also in my interest and his efforts were even more successful than mine.—Will you show them, please, what you obtained in Arizona?"

She turned to Kearn Thode, who drew forth a folded paper which he handed to Mason North.

"It is a confession, signed and witnessed, from the forger Starr Wiley employed to manufacture that false article of adoption," he announced. "The child who died in the trapper's cabin was his own daughter and it was Willa Murdaugh who went on with Gentleman Geoff. I did not know until this morning the whole story of the Lost Souls' Pool transaction, but I suspected it. Starr Wiley had a strong motive for getting Miss Murdaugh out of the way if she did not prove amenable to his schemes, and he provided himself with a strong weapon, but he overlooked one salient point. I happened to know Gentleman Geoff's last name, I learned it from his own lips as he lay dying, and it was not Abercrombie."

"After I left New York," Willa took up the story,

"Starr Wiley came down here, registered a deed of sale, signed by Tia Juana, giving him possession of the Lost Souls' Pool and proceeded with his partner to develop it and float it on the market. I believe Mr. Thode tried to warn Mr. North through his son not to go into it, but unfortunately for him, Mr. North would not heed, and he and Mr. Halstead invested heavily. I say 'unfortunately,' for the money is lost! Gentlemen, Juana Reyes and I still own that property. Starr Wiley—and in this his partner, Harrington Chase, is equally guilty with him —had induced a poor ignorant old Mexican woman, Rosa Mendez, to sign the name of Juana Reyes to the bill of sale, copying it from the original signature in the registry. He thought the trick which had served him so well in Arizona could be safely repeated, but I have Rosa Mendez upstairs at this moment, together with the real Juana Reyes and José. Shall I call them?"

"No, no!" shrieked Starr Wiley. "I will not face that old hag! What's the use? You've got the goods on me! It's all true, all of it except that I instigated El Negrito's raid! That I never——"

"It was Tia Juana herself who witnessed your secret negotiations with Juan de Soria, El Negrito's agent!" Willa interposed swiftly. "It's been a fair fight, Starr Wiley, for I warned you once, but you have played directly into my hands. I've paid my debt to Dad, but you have yet to meet the penalty. For your crime against me, and those you have victimized in the Lost Souls venture you will not live to make restitution; you know what awaits you for summoning El Negrito down from the hills!"

For an instant Wiley cowered, shuddering. Then with

a supreme effort he straightened and turned to his
guards.

"Take me out of this!" he demanded hoarsely, through
white lips. "I'm through! Take me away!"

With a scream Angie flung herself forward, but he
put her aside as if in a dream and marched out with his
guards on either side and his eyes fixed straight ahead
over the abyss of the future. Muttering and cursing,
Harrington Chase was led after him from the room, and
for a space there was silence.

Ripley Halstead sat as though turned to stone, his wife
had collapsed in her chair and Mason North's head was
buried in his hands. Winthrop with his arm across his
father's shoulders met Vernon's dazed eyes and with one
accord they turned to Willa.

Her quiet, set, terrible smile was unchanged, but her
face had blanched and with an effort she motioned to
Jim Baggott.

"Jim, do you remember what happened in Manzanillo
away over on the West Coast ten years ago when you
were pay clerk for the Colima-Zamora Company and a
man stuck you up in broad daylight?"

"I sure do!" Jim returned. "I shot him in the head!"

"Not *in* but across," observed Willa. "You left your
mark on him from brow to ear, only you didn't recognize
it while he was here under your own roof."

'What!" Jim's eyes were fairly starting from his
head. "That feller was a swindling promoter down on
his luck; he broke jail afterward, I heard. His name
was Harry Carter."

"It used to be, but now it is Harrington Chase."

The smile faded at last, and Willa swayed suddenly,

catching at the bar for support. Jim Baggott sprang for her, but Thode reached her side first, and for a moment she clung to him. Then she raised herself indomitably upright once more.

"It is not easy to hate, after all!" she murmured. "If it were not for the memory of Dad I could find it in my heart to forgive."

CHAPTER XXV

Into Her Own

SPRING was well advanced and the Casa de Limas was a veritable paradise of tender virginal green and delicate mystically perfumed blossoms, when Willa, a frail shadow of herself, ventured for the first time to the veranda, on Sallie Bailey's sturdy arm.

The protracted strain and final tragedy of her triumph had proved too much for even her robust vitality, and when the news came that Starr Wiley had killed himself in his garrison prison rather than face the firing squad, the inevitable collapse occurred.

For weeks she had lain helpless and inert with a low fever sapping her last ounce of strength and no incentive to take up her life again, until one day she had chanced to overhear a remark of Sallie Bailey's which brought a new light and glow to her world.

"I declare!" announced Sallie to her husband. "I don't know what to say to that young Thode every day when he comes ridin' in with his heart in his eyes to ask if she's better. I never see such devotion in my born days! He's worn to a shadder with the worry over her, and it hurts, I can tell you, to send him away lookin' like I'd hit him a blow when I tell him there's no change. Love's a pretty-fierce thing sometimes, ain't it?"

Love! Willa buried her face in the pillow and a little

creeping warmth stole through her veins. It was good
to be alive, after all.

But he was still ignorant of the truth about that letter!
At the thought Willa's heart contracted and the quick,
scalding tears of weakness came to her eyes. He still
believed that she had wantonly led him on and trampled
him beneath her feet in sheer joy of conquest. Oh, she
must become strong enough to tell him how sorry she
was, to make amends!

Now as she lay back in her chair, awaiting his coming
in the cool of the soft spring evening, the events of the
past few months seemed very far away and unreal,
almost as though they might have been a dream born of
her fever. She could scarcely believe that she had ever
left Limasito; the climacteric weeks in New York, the
trip to Topaz Gulch and the later scene in Jim Baggott's
hotel had alike faded into a vague, nebulous shadow
without substance or coherence, and she herself seemed
drifting. . . .

Again it was Sallie who brought her back to earth with
a matter-of-fact remark.

"I don't s'pose you know, or care either, that the Lost
Souls is producin' thousands of barrels a day since they
struck that gusher. You'll never miss the stock now that
you gave to Mr. North and them Halsteads to make up
for what they lost on their own hook in the fake company, though I did think you were a little fool at the
time, Billie. Served 'em good and right after the way
they treated you."

Willa shook her head wearily.

"They were pretty decent, Sallie, and both Ripley Halstead and Mr. North were always kind. I couldn't have

let them suffer for a mistake.—How is Tia Juana? You must let me see her the next time she comes."

Sallie chuckled.

"She's buildin' a chapel to the lost souls who was drowned in that pool, and she's bought a big, bright-yeller automobile! José's learning from Dan how to drive it for her, when Dan gets time enough off from his work with Mr. Thode. Since you gave him that stock in the new Murdaugh-Reyes Company you can't hardly pry Dan Morrissey loose from the oil business to eat.—Say, honey!" Her tone dropped persuasively. "There's something that's not quite clear in my mind yet. I've been bursting to ask you, but you were too sick. Where does young Mr. Thode come in on this and how did you find out that old Rosa Mendez was the one who signed Tia Juana's name to that false deed?"

"I didn't. It was Mr. Thode who found that out for me," Willa explained. "You see, when I met him out in Topaz Gulch I told him I was coming down here and he said he'd be here, too; his presence would have been necessary, anyway, to prove that I was really Willa Murdaugh. Dan's sister was taking care of Tia Juana and José for me in Philadelphia, where those who were fighting me wouldn't think of searching.

"When I settled up my affairs out West, I wired Dan, and he brought Tia Juana and José down to Victoria to meet me. There I found Mr. Thode again. He had suspected trickery and fraud in connection with the making over of the lease, and when the Notary Public described the woman who had appeared before him as Tia Juana with—with Starr Wiley——" Her voice sank at mention of the name which had cast such a shadow over her for many days. "Mr. Thode knew it was an impostor. He realized that Wiley would not have selected a woman from either Victoria or Limasito to play the part for she might have been recognized, so he scouted around in the neighborhood of the Lost Souls' Pool itself, and found that a poor, old, half-witted creature, who had lived all her days in a wretched hovel near the Trevino hacienda, had suddenly come into money from a mysterious source, and moved away. That was Rosa Mendez.

"When he talked to her closest associates in the poor quarter where she lived, Mr. Thode found that Rosa had had a fair education, but all the money she could earn or scrape together went for hootch."

"I remember her from the time we lived out that way," Sallie remarked. "I hired her to help in the cook-house when we had extra hands on for the pickin', and she stole all the pots she could carry off."

"Mr. Thode found out, too, that for the last few days before she went away she shut herself up in her hut and wouldn't let anybody in, but one of the neighbor women peeped in through a window, and saw her writing something over and over on scraps of paper and burning them carefully in the stove." Willa went on. "That must have been Tia Juana's signature. Then when he heard that she was seen talking to a man who answered to Wiley's description, he was sure. He traced her to Palmillas and when he confronted her she broke down and confessed without a show of fight. He brought her back to Victoria and was waiting for me when I came."

"He's a smart one!" Sallie vociferated admiringly. "You'd go far, Billie, to find a regular he-man in all that crowd you've been traveling with that could beat him!

But you might have let me in on that party over to Baggott's! He sent hot-foot for Hen, but little I thought you was in it or I'd have come, invite or no! How'd you fix that up?"

"I sent Tia Juana and José and Rosa Mendez on ahead to confront the others if necessary——"

"Yes, and they tried to kill each other all the way down——old Rosa and Tia Juana, I mean," interrupted the other. "Them Federal officers told Hen they'd rather have had charge o' two wild cats! Them and the other government fellers got there while that bunch o' robbers was out on a trip inspecting the oil well."

Willa nodded.

"I knew they'd return that morning, and I arranged the affair with Jim Baggott and the officials. It was a terrible business, Sallie, and I wanted to get it all over with at once."

"Well, you did it!" Sallie chuckled. "You took the wind out o' the sails o' them relatives o' your'n, too. They've been milling around these parts like nothin' was good enough for 'em, and it give 'em a pain to hear your name mentioned, but it was different after you showed up with your powder-blast, I can tell you! When they found you was goin' to let byegones be byegones, and give 'em a chance to get back the money they'd lost, it would have done you good to see the way they came around here, trying to do something for their dear young relation!"

Willa smiled faintly.

"I wish I might have seen my cousins before they went North."

Sallie endeavored to maintain a discreet silence, but the effort proved too much for her.

"Well, if you ask me, you're just as well off! The menfolks may be all right, but that Mrs. Halstead wouldn't have let you call your soul your own; wanted me to put ice-bags on you and all manner of outlandish things, and told me to my face that my house wasn't sanitary! I soon sent her about her business.—There! I declare if that good-for-nothin' Chevalita isn't callin' me again!"

She retired precipitately into the house, and her ruse was apparent; her quick ears had caught, not the voice of her criada, but the sound of a pinto's hoofs on the road, and she recognized its portent as did the girl in the shadows.

A pale young moon had risen, and in its light the drive lay like a curving white ribbon, the approaching figures of pony and man melting together, yet sharply distinct. Willa waited until the rider had dismounted, then bolstered herself upright and held out a thin little hand.

"Willa! It is really you, at last!"

He sank down on the steps beside her and somehow forgot to relinquish her hand.

"Yes, it is really I!" she smiled. "Mrs. Bailey told me of your never-failing calls and inquiries. You have been very kind——"

"Kind? Did you think that I could help myself, that I could have stayed away?" He broke off, his voice hoarse with pent-up feeling. "Forgive me! I did not mean to annoy you again, but the sight of you after so many days, lying here so white and frail and crushed——"

"I'm not!" She laughed nervously. "But you don't annoy me! I love to hear you say that you have wanted to see me, that you could not stay away!"

"Oh, don't, please!" He turned away with a gesture of pain. "Don't play with me again, Willa, girl! I can't quite bear it!"

"Kearn!" her voice thrilled, low and surpassingly sweet in his ears. "I never played with you, never! I told you in Topaz Gulch that I had much to explain and you much to forgive. I was deliberately misled, my mind poisoned against you, but the fault was mine, in being so easily influenced against the real truth. I knew it in my heart, but I was in such a maze of difficulties and cross-purposes that I did not know which way to turn, and I shut my ears to the dictates of my own belief. Do you remember that night in the conservatory?"

"I am not likely to forget it." His tones were shaking and he had turned his head away.

"Someone was listening, someone who hated us both, and acting under the impulse of a blind infatuation, had become a tool in stronger, more ruthless hands. When I reached home that night, a letter in your handwriting was put before me; a letter which seemed to prove that you—you had known before ever Mr. North came to Limasito who I was and that you had planned to marry me.—Oh, can't you understand?"

"A letter in my handwriting?" he repeated slowly. "It could not be——"

"But it was!" Willa laughed, but there was a little running sob through her words. "You told me the truth about it yourself, out in Topaz Gulch."

"I?" Thode turned to her, amazed.

"Yes. Don't you remember the letter you wrote to Mr. Larkin, telling him you had found Tia Juana, but nobody knew who she really was—her last name, I mean—and it wouldn't matter if they did? A page of that very letter with the top torn off was put in my hands and as you didn't mention Tia Juana by name I thought it referred to me. That was the inference I was supposed to gather from it, and like a credulous little fool I believed! The bottom of the page ended with: 'She is the undoubted owner of almost boundless wealth and when I have gone after her, and won her consent——' "

"Good heavens, of course!" Thode jumped to his feet. "I remember it all now. That was one of the letters that was stolen from Larkin's desk by a clerk we found to be in the secret employ of Chase and Wiley! They'd corrupted him in an effort to keep tabs on the progress we were making down here. We didn't prosecute him because of the notoriety, but we made him leave the East when we discovered his operations. It never occurred to me that any of the stolen letters could be put to such a use!"

"Or that I could be so ready to believe the worst of you?" she asked sadly.

"You! My poor little Willa!" He dropped on his knees beside her chair and gathered her hands again in his. "I thought you were heartless, intoxicated with admiration and trying your power wilfully on everyone who came within your reach. Half the men in your set were at your feet, and it drove me a little mad, I think! And all the time you were beset by enemies, making your brave fight alone, and even our friendship turned to something low and base! Oh, my dear, I have nothing to forgive, but there is much that I must teach you to forget."

"Unworthy things are soon forgotten!" She gazed with shining eyes into his. "Only the real, true, beautiful things remain, Kearn, and they—why, they are all before us!"

He looked away, straight ahead of him into the moonlit darkness.

"When I come back," he said. "Much has happened while you lay ill, dear. We've gone into the big fight at last, we're going to help set the world free from barbarism, and I must do my share. I ran up to New York long enough to get a commission again in my old regiment, and I'm listed to sail for France with the first army the government sends. I couldn't stay behind, Willa; I'm sure you wouldn't have me wait when the call has come."

"No," Willa responded quietly; "I wouldn't. Not for all the world must you miss your chance to help. It's a sacred privilege, Kearn. I shouldn't wonder if all of us, men and women, will have to put our shoulder to the wheel, but if we can only help to get the world out of this hideous rut of wholesale oppression and savagery it will be gloriously worth it all. No, I wouldn't keep you back if I could, but I'm glad, somehow, to feel that I couldn't, anyway."

"And you will be with my sister," he reminded her. "She's coming to-morrow, you know, to take you back with her as soon as you are able to travel. She liked you from the start, dear, and when I tell her what is going to be, some day, she will take you quite to her heart."

"I shall be so glad to see her again!" Willa sighed

happily. "It is dear of her to offer to take me into her home. The Ripley Halsteads suggested, of course, that I should go back to them, but I couldn't think of it! It would recall too much that I must try to forget, and poor Angie's face would give me no peace. I know that in her heart she must blame me still for the tragic end of her romance."

"Angie is no longer there," Kearn remarked. "She is taking a nursing-course in some hospital, preparatory for work in France, and Vernon writes me that she seems earnest and sincere for the first time in her life. Verne himself is off for Plattsburg, and Winthrop North is already across the water, driving an ambulance on the western front. My sister will put you to rolling bandages as soon as you can lift your hands. Life is getting pretty serious for all of us."

"And wonderful, too," Willa amended. "It is as if we were all just finding ourselves, isn't it? As if this supreme struggle were to bring out all our hidden strength, the deepest, most-enduring, best part of us!— And isn't it strange, too, that I should be going to make my home with your sister, after all? That was what you first suggested to me—do you remember?—when you thought me just Gentleman Geoff's Billie, before ever Mr. North came."

"Yes, dear." He pressed his lips to her hand. "Everything works out all right in time. And when I come back——"

"There is every indication that I'll be over myself before then, nursing or something. I'm not the kind to sit at home when there's work to be done. But, Kearn——?"

"What, Billie?"

"I don't mean to complain, for everyone has been wonderfully good to me since I was a wee bit of a thing, but do you suppose anyone was ever more buffeted about by Fate than I? Orphaned and thrown out upon the world at four, orphaned again last year, made an heiress, then an outcast, and finally reinstated again! I—I'm getting awfully tired of not really belonging to anyone!" She drew a deep breath. "Kearn, dear, do you suppose you could manage to marry me before you go to war?"

"You darling!" He hugged her close, pillows and all. "I didn't dare ask you that now, but, oh, I wanted to! If I could feel that you really did belong to me, dear, I'd go with a far-lighter heart and surer courage to meet whatever comes, and with ten times the strength, too, for I should go to fight for my own!—And then, you are such a changeling, you know! I love Willa Murdaugh, but I have always loved Gentleman Geoff's Billie since the day I met her coming from the Blue Chip, and I think that I love her best, after all! Gentleman Geoff's Billie, *my* Billie, will you be my wife, soon, *soon?*"

There was a pause, while a little breeze stirred the starry, perfume-laden branches about them, shimmering mistily in the moon's haze. Then, far away, a night bird called eagerly, tenderly to its mate, and Willa lifted tired, happy arms and placed them about the head bent above her, drawing it down.

"I thought you were never, in all the world, going to ask me!" she sighed.

THE END.